Curse of the Healer

ALSO BY ASHLEY YORK

The Warrior Kings series

Curse of the Healer

Eyes of the Seer

Daughter of the Overking

The Norman Conquest series

The Saxon Bride

The Gentle Knight

The Irish Warrior

The Seventh Son

The Order of The Scottish Thistle series

The Bruised Thistle

Curse of the Healer

Ashley York

DEDICATION

To my Lindsay Bells,
the blessing that
changed my life forever

AUTHOR'S NOTE

The ancient people of Ireland had a very sophisticated social structure. One historian described it as a "hierarchical but intimate" system because their noble kings lived among their subjects. The term "noble" designates a person, male or female, as coming from the line of previous kings.

To become a king, a man must be a great warrior, have his own war band supporting him, and be from the line of kings. The inauguration of a king or *ri* was a sacred ceremony that took place outside, often carried out in places that the druids from their pagan past had also used for such ceremonies. Though there was no crowning or enthronement, the procedure included anointing, ritual bathing, and the reading of an inaugural poem praising the king's abilities.

A glossary of the levels of kingship, explanation of certain words, and a pronunciation key for the names can be found at the back of this book.

My special thanks to Sheila Currie for her expertise, patience, and generous spirit. Her love of the Gaels is a never ending source of inspiration for me.

Chapter One

Clan Meic Lochlainn, Ireland

"Ugh, Lorccán, ye're ripe as a dung heap in full sun!" Aednat turned away from the boy to fill her lungs again before hunkering down and returning to her work. More long, spiky thorns protruded from his little leg than she'd ever seen in a person's flesh, but she had already removed most of them. "I do not know why ye stink so."

The small redheaded lad nodded, the path of his tears the only clean spot on his face. "I went after the eggs."

She stilled, piercing him with her look. "Eggs? Not from the nests along the cliffs."

Her tone was biting, and he looked away as he

nodded. The sheer cliffs along the coast were a dangerous spot for anyone, and only trained men were given the duty of retrieving the eggs from the puffins that nested there. And the path was well protected by blackthorns. It required steady feet to avoid the sharp plants and the huge amounts of slippery, slimy dung. Lorccán had not been so prepared.

"D'ye need to be getting into everything, even here?" Aednat flattened her lips into her most disapproving expression. They were only visitors here, and already he'd gotten himself into trouble. "Not a good thing for a wee lad to be taking on by himself."

"But Diarmuid the Despicable arrives any day. I had hoped to appease him with some of the precious eggs so he'd not eat us all up."

"Eat us all up? Who told ye such a thing?"

"Mary… and Sibéal. They said he is massive! His hunger and thirst are never satisfied. They say the clan leaders do not know, but he eats up all the children who cross his path… the redheaded ones first."

"They were teasing ye," she said.

His shaky breathing tugged at her heart. She sized up the rest of the remaining thorns. Probably best to be quick about it.

"Aldred agreed with them."

"Oh, did he?"

Ah, Aldred. The much older and supposedly wiser lad Lorccán had latched onto as soon as they'd arrived. In truth, he was just bigger, not very wise, and only two years older.

"He said that was how he'd lost his wee little

cousin. Diarmuid the Despicable ate him!"

Damn Aldred and his tiresome wish for the girls' approval. "He lied."

"'Tis true! His cousin *did* disappear!" Lorccán's voice cracked.

Latching onto to three more thorns, she said, "His cousin died winter last of a fever. No one ate him up."

Closing his eyes tightly, Lorccán gave a quick nod just as the last of the offending needles let loose. The punctures drained clean, adding to the blood that streamed down the little boy's leg.

"There. That's a brave lad." Lifting him into her arms, she turned about to set him before the small lough. "Now into the water. We do not need to scare yer mother when she sees ye covered with blood and stinking like ye rolled in something dead."

A flash of fear crossed Lorccán's face and he obeyed, whipping his knee-length *léine* over his head before walking out into the water.

"Rub yer face clean, too."

Several clans had arranged to meet in the nearby village. It was a beehive of activity as the visiting *rig túaithe* continued to arrive. It was Sean, Aednat's own overking and cousin, who had proposed this meeting of the northern and western clans and the only reason they'd traveled so far from home. The great Diarmuid's agreement to attend the meeting had increased the likelihood of all attending. The warrior had been making quite a name for himself, enough so to find his way into the children's tales. He was due to join them any day now.

Such a gathering offered many opportunities for an unwatched, curious lad to get into trouble. That was the reason she'd brought Lorccán out here with her, supposedly to collect herbs, rather than leaving him underfoot in the village. He was a good boy but always getting himself into scrapes.

She would have to keep an eye on him in the days to come. He was gullible enough to believe every tale he heard, and in a gathering of all these clans, there would be plenty of stories told about heroes both living and dead. Bigger than life stories. It was understood that not every detail was to be believed, except by gullible children likely to take every outrageous detail for fact. She needed to set poor Lorccán's fears to rest.

Aednat carefully returned her precious tweezers to the ring hanging from her girdle and then settled at the edge of the water to watch the boy splash around.

"Is ought amiss, Aednat?" A guard stood at the edge of the clearing.

She waved and smiled.

The men who had been forced to accompany her had quickly scattered. They knew better than to stay too close. Not only would they be in her way, trampling the very plants she sought, but she would not hesitate to set them to foraging for her herbs if they insisted on lingering. They didn't want that, and she didn't need them. She could fend for herself as she'd always done.

The sun, low in the sky, warmed her skin, and Lorccán's laugh did the same for her heart. She was hit with a sudden urge to join him, splashing about in the cool water, but there was no time for such idle pursuits. When his head broke the surface, he barked like the seals they'd seen earlier and she smiled.

"Lorccán," she said. "Diarmuid is only a man—"

Lorccán whipped his damp hair away from his face, revealing a stern expression. "Diarmuid the Despicable."

Oh dear!

"Do not be calling him that to his face!" That's all the lad needed. Offending such a powerful man was to be avoided at all costs. "Even if he is big, he is no threat to us. Yer father invited him to come here, and ye know Sean would never put us in harm's way."

"Here" being the land settled by Clan Meic Lochlainn, along the northernmost point of Ireland. Aednat had been exiled from this very clan as a young child by the old *ri túath*, her own grandfather. Born with a clubfoot, she'd been forced to live in the forest with others who were considered broken. After his death, she had moved south with her grandmother and cousin. Sean had fostered her within his own clan.

Returning here after so many years was surprisingly peaceful. Like coming home. She'd had a difficult life in this place, but she had been young. Now, after many years of being loved and accepted, the pain was all but forgotten. And these woods were more familiar than the houses that lay nestled along the cove, where her clan was now expected to stay for the duration of the meeting.

"Do not believe all that ye hear, Lorccán." She glanced back toward the trees that she knew like the back of her hand. The guards were no longer visible.

"Come! Let us take a look."

He held his arms close to his chest, dripping wet, and hustled up to stand in front of her.

"Is the water that cold?"

He nodded, his teeth starting to chatter. She yanked the *léine* back over his head, rubbing his arms with the coarse fabric. The cloth quickly absorbed the water.

Aednat sighed. "The bleeding has stopped. That is good."

Seeing the truth of her words, he burst into a smile and threw himself at her.

"Many thanks!" He squeezed her, saturating her own clothes, his voice muffled against her shoulder. His stench was horrendous still, but she squeezed him back, the little body quivering slightly with the rush of relief. "*Mamaídh* doesn't need to know."

"Yer *mamaídh* may not need to know… but she will."

Lorccán yanked away, his brows lowered and lips puckered. An intense look of betrayal.

Aednat lifted the soaked material away from her chest. "Ye can tell her or I can. Makes no difference to me."

When his mouth fell open to voice his protest, she held up her hand.

"No discussion! Thomasina will have my head if she finds out ye've been going after the wild eggs alone and her none the wiser."

"She doesn't need to know. I'll not do it again." Eyes all wide and innocent, he whined in his defense, stomping his little foot at the injustice of it all.

Arching a brow, she tipped her head. "Lorccán, how dare ye tell me a lie right to my face!"

His sweet face screwed up into a pout. She tipped his chin to look into his large, green eyes, glistening with unshed tears.

"D'ye promise to never go nigh to the cliffs again?"

He nodded with great enthusiasm, his lips returning to a more natural red hue.

Impulsively, she kissed his cheek. "We'll see. Now get ye back to the village straight away."

He reacted without hesitation. His long, curly hair splayed out behind him as he ran like the wind across the field. Going up on her knees, she stood and smoothed out her linen kirtle. Her foot ached, as it often did, and she shook it to lessen the pain before standing.

"If he'd fallen from the cliffs, he would be dead now."

Aednat started and jerked around to see a lone, fierce-looking warrior coming toward her from the forest. She caught herself before she lost her footing. "Ye startled me."

There were so many warriors in the village, she wasn't surprised that she didn't recognize this one, but there was no mistaking his look. His face was tight with fury. A suspicion that this man may have been watching and waiting until she was alone to show himself flashed through her mind. But she wasn't truly alone. The men who'd accompanied her were nearby. Somewhere.

Scanning the trees, she saw no sign of them. Mayhap she shouldn't have been so sharp with them, demanding they keep their distance.

"Ye should have taken a strap to him," he said.

Her breath caught at the very idea. Unheard of! Certainly he could not mean such a thing.

"He is like every other lad his age. Inquisitive."

The warrior's expression did not change.

She swallowed down her fear and used her most commanding tone. "Ye're on Meic Lochlainn land."

The man continued toward her, looming over her. "And well I know it."

"Mayhap ye need to seek the *ri túath*'s permission to be here."

"Mayhap I have the overking's permission."

The Meic Lochlainn had attained overking status, with several lesser kings under him. These men, the *rig túaithe,* were from the direct line of former kings, had proven themselves in battle, and had been properly anointed. This man could be one of the visiting *rig túaithe,* but Aednat sensed he was not.

She scoffed. "I do not believe ye."

He stopped close enough for her to see the tiny lines at the corners of his bright blue eyes and the quirk of his heavy brow before he asked, "And why would ye not believe what I say to ye?"

"I do not know ye." Arrogant! "And who are ye to say what the lad's punishment should be?"

He had long, dark hair. Taller than most, he was probably seldom overlooked, and she had a notion his will was rarely denied. His broad shoulders and warrior's stance were, no doubt, quite frightening… to some. Then he crossed his arms about his broad chest, tucking a hand under the intricately carved silver band clasping his bare upper arm. A wealthy man, then. Perhaps he was a *ri túaithe.*

"Mayhap ye do not recognize me, but ye should heed my warning."

Any king could order that a little boy be punished with a strip of leather, if he were cruel enough, but it was not an accepted practice. Her grandfather had been a cruel *ri.* She'd witnessed one lad, Will, barely older than Lorccán, having his fingers sliced right off his hand for stealing food. Aodh Meic Lochlainn had thought it better that the boy starve to death than steal. Will had become her friend—a fellow outcast in the woods.

The stranger's eyes narrowed and she nibbled her lower lip. She couldn't back down now. "Well, then, 'tis a good thing ye do not get to decide."

He closed the remaining distance between them in three strides, his face etched in angry lines. She instinctively backed away, half expecting him to grab her arm.

"Ye're a lousy mother… or nurse maid… or shepherdess… or whatever ye are, if ye think 'tis all well and good for a child to put himself in harm's way as long as he lives to tell the tale."

She recoiled at the insult. Although she was well past marrying age at two and twenty, she was no one's mother and never would be. With her limp, there would never be a husband or family. Too many fears of children with the same malady. Shepherdess? Did she still bear a resemblance to the folk who lived apart from the villagers? But he hadn't finished his tirade.

"He must be taught to heed the warnings he's been given if he's to survive and become a man."

The words stung, thrown at her like a venomous curse. She cared for Lorccán as if he were her own and would never do anything to hurt him. Squaring her shoulders, she refused to show her inner turmoil.

"The lad learned his lesson." She spat the words right back at him.

"Ye said yerself he'd be doing it again." Despite the even keel of his voice, his increasing anger was unmistakable. "Or am I so old and feeble that my hearing is failing me?"

Staring in the face of his obvious vitality and strength, she hesitated. A finer specimen of a well-honed man she'd not seen. "I do not really believe—"

"NO?" A sheer wall of exasperation now, he waited. His square jaw tensed beneath the shadow of dark stubble. "Mayhap the next time ye'll find his young body impaled on a rock at the bottom of the cliff."

The menacing declaration, delivered in a low, controlled manner, made her gasp. The image flashing through her mind caused it to reel. She slapped the man's face so hard, his beard burned the palm of her hand.

Aednat froze, horrified at her own reaction. Striking a man was no small offense, and if this man was a *ri*, the consequences would be serious. His eyes widened right before he caught her arm and yanked her close. Her breath caught, though his grip was not overly firm. They stood that way for a long moment—his head lowered to hers so they stood nose to nose, his broad chest brushing against her forearm in time with his heavy breathing.

His gaze dropped, to slowly follow up her length before settling again on her face.

That he continued to study her kept her fully watchful. His features relaxed, but she sensed mounting tension in him. The many possibilities of what he might be thinking flitted through her mind like little mice avoiding a hungry hawk. Outrage. Indignation. Superiority.

"I forego the fine I have every right to demand for yer action. Instead, I demand a kiss."

He delivered the words as a man in authority.

And he did not look away.

A kiss? Heat poured off him, but it was no longer anger riding him. She forced down the lump in her throat, holding his intense gaze as her thoughts raced. She had never been kissed by a man. Or kissed a man, but it was not a high price to pay to dismiss the entire incident.

Refusing would certainly result in a steeper demand, and the last thing she wanted to do was to cause any problems for her *ri túath* and cousin. Sean acted as her father, so any honor price demanded or paid could be half *his* worth. A king held no special power outside his own *túath*, but at a gathering this size, ruffling any fine feathers was to be avoided.

Aednat glanced at the warrior's lips. His eyes brightened, and she struggled to breath evenly as she held his gaze, anticipation making a mockery of her show of bravery. She wetted her lips, and his long nose flared ever so slightly.

"Aednat!" The sound of Sean's voice had her exhaling in relief. Her reprieve.

One dark brow quirked as if to question her thought.

"Here," she answered, irritated that she sounded desperate.

"A timely interruption." The warrior spoke in a quiet voice, his teeth white against the thick brown beard when he smiled. A satisfied smile. "But I'm a patient man."

She should have slapped him harder.

With Sean close, her bravery doubled. In truth since he took her in and fostered her, he was more like a father. *Datan.* And he would certainly protect her as she deserved. She shoved past the man before she lost her nerve, her jerky gait nearly causing her to bump into him. "I am here, Sean!"

She made it to the edge of the forest just as Sean burst through on his mount. His men, including those sent to protect her, were in close proximity as if they'd remained nearby all along.

"What d'ye here, little one?" Sean's intent gaze soothed her, reminding her she did have protection. "Aednat, ye're soaked right through."

Taking in her own soggy condition, she nibbled on her lower lip. She probably did look like a shepherdess. Heat rose in her face, but she kept her back to the stranger. "I—"

"Diarmuid!" Sean finally noticed the man behind her, but rather than come to her defense and question the brute's intentions, he burst into a huge grin and jumped from his horse in one leap.

Diarmuid? This was the *ri túaithe* who ate small children? She believed it!

"Sean!" Diarmuid said.

For the first time since she'd met this Diarmuid, his voice sounded… pleasant. When she turned around, she could not believe her eyes. The warrior's relaxed expression and wide smile mirrored her cousin's. His countenance was so transformed, he might even be considered handsome by lasses who favored the overbearing warrior type.

Sean and Diarmuid embraced, pounding each other on the back before separating.

"When did ye arrive?" Sean asked.

Aednat wished to be anywhere but here. She remained still, hoping not to call attention to herself.

"This day. Did ye not come across my men?" Diarmuid asked, looking beyond Sean.

He scanned the forest before his eyes came to rest on her.

Damn.

She refused to respond to his questioning glance. Diarmuid put two fingers to his mouth and whistled, a high piercing sound that made her jump. Sean turned toward the forest as well, an expectant expression on his face.

Ten mounted men appeared, well-armed with battle axes, shields and spears. Their horses were huge, covered with animal hides. A rider-less black destrier trotted past them, making a direct line to Diarmuid, who caught up the horse's reins and immediately raked his hand along its muzzle, whispering something unintelligible.

The lead man, a broad, black-haired warrior, called out, "*A thighearna*, is aught amiss?"

Diarmuid raised his head but continued to stroke his horse, his large hand moving down the length of the great beast, stopping to rub its flank. "All is well, Marcán."

The warriors in either group eyed the other with suspicion. They looked to be equally matched in both number and size.

"Were ye able to track them down?" Marcán asked.

"We were not," Diarmuid said. "No sign of them."

"Did ye have some trouble?" Sean's concern came through in his tone.

"On the way north, we came upon a small village that had been attacked by some thieving bastards," Diarmuid said. "We had hoped to track them down."

"Are *these* the men we've come to meet?" Marcán asked.

"The same, Marcán. Be easy." The horse lifted its

muzzle, its eyes closing in appreciation at its master's attentive caresses. Diarmuid turned back to Sean. "Did ye come across a young lad by any chance?"

Aednat's breath caught. Was he going to tell on her? Her face could not get any hotter.

"Lorccán?" Sean said. "He told me he'd tumbled in some spiny bushes."

Aednat had not expected the boy to confess his mischief to his own father.

"Blackthorns." Diarmuid scowled. "The boy had been on the cliffs. After the wild eggs."

Sean's nostrils flared, a sure sign of irritation. "My thanks for telling me. I wish I'd caught him myself."

"This lass *did* catch him."

Both sets of eyes suddenly on her, she found her breath trapped again.

"Did ye go to the cliffs, Aednat?"

Sean's accusing tone, delivered as if from a parent to a misbehaving child, riled her. She opened her mouth to answer, but Diarmuid interrupted.

"This is Aednat?"

Sean smiled at her. A smile full of pride and sheer joy that helped calm her racing heart and soothe her hurt feelings.

"*This* is Aednat," he said. "My cousin."

She couldn't stop her lips from turning up slightly. Now Diarmuid *the Despicable* knew the way of it.

"I'd not learned his name, *Cousin,* but we did exchange words." She stressed the familial association, rubbing it like salt into Diarmuid's wounds of embarrassment.

Sean glanced between them, his eyes narrowing.

"Did my friend rescue ye from the cliffs?" he asked, wrapping an arm around the warrior's broad shoulders, almost as if he were showing him off. They were of a similar height and build, but Sean had a few more years on the rougher man, and a much kinder disposition.

"*Rescue* me?" Aednat was safe with Sean; none would threaten her while he was present. That knowledge made her bold enough to use her most belittling tone. "No. He did not 'rescue' me and a good thing he did not try, for who would have come to *his* rescue?"

"Huh?" Sean's face screwed up. "Diarmuid has no need of rescuing. He's a highly skilled warrior of great strength."

She harrumphed.

Sean shook his head, his confusion apparent. "I ask again. Did ye go to the cliffs, Aednat?"

"I. Did. Not. Why ever would ye think such a thing?"

"So *ye've* been taught to obey?" Diarmuid's low voice vibrated through her, igniting her smoldering irritation. An innocent enough question except for the stiff jaw and that arrogant raised brow.

Irritation blazed into outrage. "I've a brain in my head. I know not to go nigh the cliffs."

She straightened to her full height, assured of her safety now and the rightness of how she had handled young Lorccán. When they both stared at her with identically bewildered expressions, she sealed her lips shut lest she say something else to shock them. They exchanged glances, but it was Diarmuid who finally spoke.

"And was it a father or uncle who walloped that pretty little arse of yers to teach ye to listen?"

She gasped and her wide eyes locked with his.

The memory of being held over someone's knee flashed through her mind. "How—"

She closed her mouth tight as a trap.

Diarmuid crossed his arms about his chest, his haughty smile assuring her he hadn't missed her near confession and that the heat rising in her cheeks did not go unnoticed. Sean dipped his head, and she'd swear he was hiding his own smirk. The warmth continued to spread down her neck.

"I'll see to Lorccán," Sean said, thankfully cutting short her embarrassment. "Glad I am that ye'd not lost yer senses." Without warning, her cousin tossed her onto his courser as if she weighed nothing at all, then handed her the reins. "Head back with my men. I'll be there anon."

It wasn't until Diarmuid signaled his men to leave with them that she finally turned away and faced front, her back stiff.

Without awaiting her consent, Sean slapped the horse's rump. She jerked as the horse trotted down the little path winding between the trees, followed by Diarmuid's group and the men who'd accompanied Sean. Her nose in the air, she struggled against the overwhelming feeling that she was being sent away so the adults could talk.

Chapter Two

Diarmuid had a bad feeling in his gut. The long journey had put him in a foul mood, heightened by the worry that his home had been left nearly unprotected, and the scene by the lough had made him only more ill at ease.

At first intrigued by the shapely, dark-haired woman, he had hoped to witness her bathing in the lough, joining the child. That she was indeed a beauty, he couldn't deny. With her straight, little nose and almond-shaped eyes that creased at the corners when she smiled.

Before dismounting and edging closer for a better look, he'd ordered his men to continue their search for the thieves without him. Ever since he'd accepted the title of *ri túaithe* and had the clan leadership thrust upon him for lack of another, he had missed many of the simple joys of life, such as leisurely enjoying the view of a naked woman. His long-unused member immediately stood to attention at the very thought.

His mood had changed the instant their voices drifted up to him. He had been horrified to hear what the lad had done and how near he'd come to death. Witnessing the forgiving kiss she'd bestowed on the lad had swept any amorous thoughts out of his head. Women coddling children was a curse—one he'd learned to loathe. As was often the case, his irritation had gotten the best of him. That her defiance had incited his lust spoke of his needs. It had nothing to do with her personally.

"Yer cousin needs to be taken to task."

"Aednat? To what purpose?"

Diarmuid rubbed his face where her handprint still burned. "I'm not convinced she'd have shared the lad's disobedience with ye. Such protection does not bode well for him. If ye do not know what mischief the boy is determined to get into, how can ye train him up properly? Ye need to take her in hand."

Sean scoffed. "No one takes Aednat in hand. She's a will of her own, and no man will bend her to his."

Many a disobedient woman was the ruination of an otherwise great leader. He did not suffer from the malady himself, unattached as he was, but his father had. "The Norman knights send their lads off to be schooled by another."

"I can teach him better than another whose only interest is in training him for warfare."

"Warfare is our life. Yer protectiveness may be his downfall."

Sean scowled. "Diarmuid, I'll not make the mistakes of yer father. I knew he was safe with Aednat, or I'd not have sent him with her."

Diarmuid sighed. The loss of his brother still weighed heavy on him, but he set it aside. That was not what had brought him so far north. "I've come as ye ordered."

It had been many years since they'd last met. Diarmuid had learned much from Sean. His own reputation had been made with the many battles he'd fought at the older man's side.

"Ordered? I gave no orders. I only asked ye to attend me."

"Then I have come as ye asked."

Sean smiled before averting his eyes. It was a bit disconcerting to see the otherwise commanding man shifting with uncertainty.

"Are yer reasons not sound?" Diarmuid's impudence was an attempt at humor, but Sean's fierce scowl brought home exactly how tense the man was. "I'd have been more pleased to come at a less troublesome time," he added.

"The troublesome times are exactly the reason for this meeting. We need to come to an understanding with all the clans."

"Understanding? I've no reason to forgive the transgressions done to me. The Meic Murchadha continues to poke at me, prodding me into action against him."

Sean's steely gaze reminded Diarmuid he spoke to one above him in rank. "Transgressions? Stealing a cow?"

"I beg ye do not make light of the act. Starving through winter does not sit well with any of us."

"And well I know it, but ye paid them back, have ye not? Was it sheep ye stole?"

As *ri túath,* or overking, of several clan lands including his own, few details got past Sean. Diarmuid grinned at his perceptiveness. "A ewe and the lambs she bore us. A fine flock we have now."

"Ye did not starve?"

"That ye're belittling me makes me wonder what yer concern is truly for?"

"There are bigger problems afoot. A single tribe violating our code of law causes trouble for all of us." Sean looked off into the forest, too dark now to see beyond the tree line. "And some will go to great lengths in search of power."

"Stealing land?"

"And worse."

"What could be worse?" Diarmuid scoffed.

"Rape? Abuse?" Sean's eyes were dark.

Diarmuid saw the earlier incident in a new light. "We were but a few hours behind the marauders. Close enough that I'd hoped to catch them."

"The women?"

"It appeared the men had their way with them and left. I went after them and did not hear the women's story." Diarmuid nodded. "With such treatment of the women, I did not consider it possible they might have a connection to one of our clans."

"And there have been similar incidents. Our laws must be respected! It may only be one band of outlaws now, but we need to make it known that we'll not turn a blind eye. If we join together against them, we can find them and bring them to justice."

Diarmuid asked, "So, we're to put away our differences?"

Sean nodded. "I fear we will regret it if we do not. There may be wolves hiding in the shadows. Watching us."

"Wolves?"

"The Normans, for one."

It was bad enough that the bastard Duke of Normandy had invaded and conquered all of England. Now his sons' knights could be found in every village across their small island. Sometimes making friends. Sometimes not. Always coming in the guise of trade.

"Their eyes are set on us. Controlling us. Commanding us. Subjugating us as they have the Saxons," Sean said.

"We are *not* Saxons. We are warriors. They'd be daft to try."

"When we cannot stop our own people from sneaking in and raping our women, we make it easy for the Normans." Sean nodded. "We need to meet and plan, present a unified front, see these miscreants stopped. That way, when the Normans attack—"

"*If* they attack. I do not believe they are that stupid."

"*If* they attack, we are not caught unawares."

"These Normans are not so different from the Norsemen, the *Vikings*." Diarmuid said.

"Who came by way of England. Ye see my concern?"

"I do."

"And ye see how that turned out for us."

"Have a care. I'm from the line myself, Sean, as well ye know."

Descended from a long line of islanders, the ocean's pull on Diarmuid was strong still. Even here, the sound of the waves in the distance, the smell of the salt—it called to him, beckoning him back to it. That feeling of home stirred deep inside him even though his own tribe was landlocked, the troublesome Meic Murchadha clan separating them from the sea.

"That there is no 'we' is the problem. Some of our own *rig túaithe* would sell their souls to the devil for more power. In their quest to become *árd rí,* a high king like Brian Boru, they would do the unthinkable and violate our laws. And even though we are followers of the true faith, there are still those who practice pagan rituals. Who look to the legends for answers. More often than not, 'tis they who ruthlessly seek power."

Diarmuid could not argue with that fact. It was as common for the men to say a blessing before a battle as it was for them to be careful not to rile the fairies with their praying. It occurred to him that Sean seemed to have a concern for one *ri* in particular, but he could wait until the overking was ready to share that information.

"If we do not unite to keep our own in line, the Normans are not so foolish as to miss that opportunity to divide us further."

"The in-fighting is not new, Sean. It keeps us able, gives us practice, so we do not grow fat and docile. Our warriors like to fight amongst themselves. Show the others who is the strongest."

Sean nodded dramatically. "Warriors fight, and there is an orderly way about it. Those who would seek power at any cost threaten our way of life."

"Our way of life?" Diarmuid smiled now. "Aye, the threat to our ability to fight only amongst ourselves."

Sean nodded in agreement, turning to give the horse a pat before sighing. He seemed tired, but the sudden smile he bestowed on Diarmuid wiped some of his weariness away. "And now ye have met our Aednat. What are yer thoughts?"

Sean had surprised him again. "A comely lass," Diarmuid said, choosing his words carefully.

"Indeed. Aednat is a healer. The best. She'd be a worthy healer for any clan."

"*Any* clan?" Diarmuid looked at him askance. "As in *my* clan?"

"Any clan. She's a treasure."

"A real joy."

A real joy, indeed. By Sean's expression, he'd not missed the sarcastic tone.

"Ye two seemed to be at each other's throats."

Diarmuid shook his head. The sight of the lad shivering as he recounted his near fall along the cliffs had set him off. It had ignited the memories of his brother, and that always caused him pain. Pain he would prefer not to relive.

Now, her standing up to him? Even despite her obvious trepidation? That had sparked something else entirely. Something more tender.

"It matters little now. Our unexpected meeting did not... go well. Headstrong, that one."

"Innocent, Diarmuid. 'Tis not the same."

"A handful."

"Any woman can be taught to obey."

Diarmuid halted. "I've a mother and a sister who prove ye wrong."

"The right enticement is all that's missing there." Sean chuckled. "How is yer sister?"

"Astrid is stubborn as ever. That one will never be out of my hair. Who would want her?"

A slow smile spread across Sean's face. "Ye and

she are very close and well ye know it. And what would ye do without her seeing to ye? If ye've no mind to take a wife, that is."

"I do not need another woman thinking she can tell me how to piss."

Sean guffawed. "What woman would dare to tell ye anything?"

"They all try." The memory of Aednat, a fist to her hip and her dampened kirtle revealing the generous swell of her tantalizing breasts, came to mind. More than a handful. "*All* of them."

He might have enjoyed spending time with a gentle woman. Who knows where a kiss might have led. It had been a long time, and abstinence did not suit him. But a *báirseach*, no matter how tempting, was of no interest to him. Well, of less interest.

"Come. I've spoken of ye to the others and they want to meet ye."

Mounting his horse, Diarmuid gave a hand to Sean, who came up behind him. "And where did ye get such a fine animal?"

"I did well at a battle south of the Lough Derg." Diarmuid shrugged, clucking the horse to motion. "Norman horses. Norman weapons. I've a Norman slave from the same area. Astrid says she speaks our language."

Silence followed as they made their way through the heavy growth of trees, each deep in his own thoughts. When they reached the longhouse that sat facing the cove, Sean jumped off the horse.

"Ye can stable yer horse there." Sean directed him to the left. The small, enclosed area was filled with horses, from coursers to destriers. "But unless ye've a woman to warm ye tonight, ye'd best stay inside."

"And how is yer own little Thomasina? Big with child again?"

Sean smiled. "Not at the present, try as I might, but she has her hands full with four. Lorccán is my youngest."

"Ah! I should have seen the resemblance. He is much like his father."

"Do not worry, Diarmuid, I will see to his training myself. Nothing bad will befall my children."

The pain was there again, but Diarmuid nodded. "Good. I'll be in anon."

Just inside the stable, Diarmuid wiped the mud from his hands before patting his horse's flank.

"Ye're set for the night, m'lady." A finer horse he'd never had. Whoever had trained the beast had done it well. Its answering whinny brought a smile.

"Diarmuid?" A familiar voice called to him from the yard.

"Here, Marcán!"

The shorter man, though tall by most standards, dressed in a long, wool *brait*, approached him. The cloak reached nearly to the ground.

"Checking that all is well?" Diarmuid wrapped up the skins that had protected his mount, tucking them into the bag with the rest of his belongings. "Good man."

"I've first watch tonight, the others are within. Have ye learned the reason for the summons?"

"A gathering. Clan unity. But I fear 'tis not all."

"And the bonny lass ye had the company of

earlier? Will she be meeting ye this night?"

"Ah, well *that* is Aednat."

Marcán's eyes widened. "The woman ye received the missive about? She's a comely lass."

"And a healer."

"A healer?" His tone spoke of surprise.

"Quite good from the sound of it."

Marcán nodded, a thoughtful expression on his face. "The men who attacked that village were searching for a healer."

"Was someone ill?"

"I do not believe so. The leader was Black Oengus. He told them that if they gave up their healer, he would leave the others untouched. They claimed not to have a healer."

"And did they lie?"

"Black Oengus believed they lied and his men acted accordingly."

"Raping all the women?"

With a shrug, Marcán said, "He did not stop the rest of his men from taking what they wanted once he'd found her."

"Strange. It puts me in mind of a story told to us by the warriors of Clan Meala. Do ye remember?" Diarmuid couldn't summon the details.

Marcán's nodding steadily increased. His bright eyes, one green and one blue, stood out all the more beneath his thatch of deep black hair. "Aye, and a grand tale 'tis. They spoke of a healer—a virgin healer—and if a warrior could be her first, the power she used to heal would flow into him, making a remarkable warrior. Mayhap even high king."

"By bedding the lass?" Diarmuid frowned. "What warrior could be fool enough to believe 'tis so simple to become *ard rí?*"

"I've heard of it afore." Marcán, a great storyteller, leaned closer, his eyes glowing with the pleasure of a tale. "It is called the Curse of the Healer, this strength a virgin healer wields. Able to heal or maim."

Marcán paused, glancing around before he continued. "That power can be stolen away, so she must always be on guard against any who would leave her powerless."

Diarmuid resisted the urge to shift nearer like a gossiping old woman—Marcán was a natural storyteller—and forced himself to speak at a normal level. "Leave her powerless? By bedding her?"

"By being her first. Her power comes on ye as sure as the blood on the bed sheets."

Diarmuid heaved a great sigh and shook his head. "And ye believe this story?"

"Like all legends, the details change with the storyteller." Marcán straightened, offering a wide smile. "I know many stories. This one? Just as true as the one about the man with two differently-colored eyes being a Seer!"

Diarmuid patted his back. "Ye're a fine warrior, my friend, but ye've never been much use to me as a Seer."

Although his friend had never shown such ability, the sight of Marcán often caused villagers to cross themselves, warriors and women alike. Diarmuid's own mother was usually one of the first.

"Then be sure to ready yerself for any attacks since ye won't know when they might happen." Diarmuid started toward the opening around the back of the building where the sun was casting its last rays.

"Stay watchful, Marcán. This is quite a gathering of our best fighters. It wouldn't do to have some lesser warriors sneak in and kill us after we've passed out drunk."

"And if I find a willing, bonny lass?"

"I've yet to see any bonny lass *not* willing once she sees ye, but no visitors this night. Tend to yer duties alone."

Marcán's scowl tweaked Diarmuid's sympathy.

"But if I find one for ye, I'll be sure she meets ye come morning."

Most warring clans had their female followers. A warrior's ability required focus, not distraction for need of a woman. That Marcán had not voiced any interest confirmed Diarmuid's suspicions that the man still had his sights on one woman in particular. Diarmuid's sister. Although a beauty, Astrid showed no sign of ever letting go of her childish ways. Or of having any interest in Marcán. She stayed close to their mother, believing everything she said. If Astrid turned out like Beibhinn, she'd be too much for any man to handle, and he wouldn't wish her on his closest friend. Or enemy, for that matter. Much like this Aednat.

Chapter Three

Aednat wiped her damp brow. The heat of the open fire burning behind the longhouse was unbearable. The group of women all pushing and shoving to get their work done made it even worse. Yet another elbow dug into her side, and Aednat decided she'd had enough. Between the wives, the children, and the clan followers, all working together to prepare the feast, her help was not really needed. She wiped her hands on a coarse towel, handed the bit of cloth to another woman, and went straight to the head table inside the longhouse.

This table of honor was for all the *rig túath* and their wives, which included Sean, Brian of Clan Meic Lochlainn, Tadhg of Clan MacNaughton, and two others she did not know. Sean had made certain Aednat would be seated with them before he went off with the other men.

Thomasina smiled when she sat beside her. "Welcome, Aednat."

By silent agreement, both of them glanced out across the many trestles overflowing with strangers. Aednat recognized a few from Clan Meic Lochlainn and the warriors who had traveled with them from her own clan, but there were many more she did not know. Some had so much rich cloth in their covering, she wondered at their great wealth and rank.

"Have ye seen the warriors from Clonascra?" Thomasina finally asked.

"I do not know. There are so many at this gathering."

A smile stole across Thomasina's face even as she rubbed her hands together.

"Ye would like me to meet these warriors from Clonascra?" Aednat asked.

"And why not?" Her friend's eyes twinkled. "Great warriors. Very handsome."

This must be where Thomasina's youngest son got his mischievous side. More than ten years separated the two women, but Aednat never felt the difference. Thomasina seemed younger than most women her age. She'd had Sean to protect her since she was six and ten, and her brother before that. It was the lasses without such steadfast protection who grew up faster. Aednat included herself in that group. Her struggles had made her wise.

Aednat narrowed her eyes. "What are ye about?"

Her friend's shrug flooded Aednat with apprehension. When Thomasina moved to stand, Aednat grabbed at her hand.

"Do not!" she hissed.

Thomasina's expression shifted to concern and she relented, settling back on the bench. "Aednat, ye're pale. What is amiss?"

"Why?" Aednat kept her voice quiet. "I can tell ye want me to meet a particular warrior, but why?"

Thomasina shrugged again, this time with a bit less enthusiasm. "Just to meet him."

"Is he ill?"

"I do not believe he is ill."

"Does he require my healing skills?"

Thomasina shook her head.

"I'm a healer. I heal. I have no other reason to meet a man."

Thomasina's expression softened and she smiled. "Ye're also a beautiful woman."

"Are ye trying to insist I wed?"

"Of course not." Thomasina patted her hands, now gripped in her lap. "Ye would never be used in that way. Ye have great value to us, married or not."

"Then why do I need to meet him?"

"Aednat, I sense ye are lonely. I do not wish that for ye."

"Ye are wrong!" Aednat shook her head. "I am not lonely."

"I have seen the way ye look at the girls yer age with children. Some have several. Our own Brighit will soon be marrying. D'ye not want the same? I know ye want yer own family." There was an earnest look in her eyes when she met Aednat's gaze.

The words stirred a sense of longing, but Aednat swallowed it down. "No, Thomasina, I care for *yer* children. I am of help to *ye*, am I not?"

"Certainly."

"I am happy for Brighit. I hope she finds happiness

with Darragh even if she worries over the match now."

"She worries over the match?"

"I should not have shared that with ye. She has concerns." Aednat looked askance. "As for me, I will go without children. I have a greater purpose than motherhood."

Thomasina scoffed, but Aednat pushed on.

"Healing is my gift, Thomasina. 'Tis what I was meant to do." She shifted closer, wanting to ensure her words were not ignored. "My gift is strong because I have remained untouched."

"What?" Thomasina's loud voice caught the attention of a couple nearby, but they quickly turned away. "Where did ye hear such a thing as that?"

"'Tis the legend."

"One of many. There is also the tale of how Brian Boru got his mighty strength from sleeping with the Great Healer. A virgin as well. His wife!"

Aednat shifted in her seat. "The greatest healers have set aside their own desires. They are stronger for not being double-minded. And I find such satisfaction from healing. I do not feel lonely, truly."

"The greatest healers? Ye think much of yerself. And what of Tisa of Drogheda?" Thomasina's stubborn side was showing; that tilt to her head and dead expression said it all.

Still, she did have a point. Tisa was indeed a great healer. And married to Tadhg. When Aednat was just a small child, Tisa had taught her much about healing.

"Her gift is not the same as mine."

"Because Tadhg has 'touched' her? I know ye're fearf—"

"—I am not fearful!"

The couple just opposite stopped their chatter to

glance at them. Thomasina offered them her most gracious smile before turning back.

"—to be with a man, but they can be gentle. It does not have to be cruel. If he is not a harsh man, ye may even have great pleasure. What ye know about healing will not vanish because ye are no longer a virgin." Without another word, she stood and motioned someone forward. "Come."

Aednat averted her eyes, turning away from the room. She did not want to meet this handsome warrior to whom Thomasina thought she should lose her virginity. Besides, he'd reject her when he saw her foot.

"Diarmuid!" Thomasina all but gushed the name.

Aednat clamped her mouth shut to stop her jaw from dropping. The huge warrior moved against the crowds still settling down at the tables, but he commanded their attention even as he passed. Taller than the other men, he appeared as a ship gliding along the horizon, and her stomach tightened despite herself.

"Meet our healer—Aednat." Thomasina's face expressed her fondness, resting a hand lightly on Aednat's shoulder.

Aednat didn't know exactly how to react, but Diarmuid saw to that.

"We are acquainted." His face hardened as he tipped his head in recognition, crossing his arms over his chest once again. His eyes narrowed almost imperceptibly, and he nodded as if he'd come to some great conclusion. "Not getting into more mischief, I hope?"

"Diarmuid." Aednat's tone was so sharp, the same couple opposite turned toward her with a wary expression. They'd brought their child to her just yesterday, trusting her to care for the rat bites, and she had. Mayhap they questioned their decision now. *This damn man.*

"The comfort of yer seat tells me ye've yet to be seen to for yer show of insolence. Did ye not confess yer transgression?" He quirked a brow at her, then turned his undivided attention and a beaming smile capable of melting the hardest of hearts, to Thomasina. "Ye look well, Tommy."

Aednat prayed thanks to God above for having locked her lips. So this was going to be the way of it? Him making reference to her having struck him? Certainly, she should not have done it, but implying she should have her bottom spanked? Enough to keep her from sitting comfortably? He had demanded a kiss, but his decision not to share the offense with Sean had seemed akin to a dismissal. *She* would not be telling anyone. Was he going to continue to taunt her? She was tempted to roll her eyes, but the couple was still watching her. Instead, she smiled. A tight smile.

Thomasina dropped back on the bench as if the air had been knocked right out of her. "Ah, my thanks, Diarmuid. I am in good health."

"I see that Sean is treating ye well, for ye're more beautiful than when last I saw ye. And how fares yer brother, Niall?"

She glanced at Aednat, her face a mask of confusion. "Niall is well. He sends his regards."

At the distant sound of Sean's laughter, Thomasina's expression shifted to pleasure, and she immediately sought him out.

"Thomasina!" Sean's delight at seeing his wife

was equally apparent. He hurried forward, the Meic Lochlainn *ri túath* beside him.

When Sean leaned in to kiss his wife's cheek, Aednat heard his private whisper, intended for Thomasina's ears alone, "*Mo mhíle stór*."

The quiet words tugged at Aednat's heart. Sean's adoration of his wife had never lessened even after these many years. She was not blind, though, and knew theirs was not a normal joining.

"Diarmuid!" Sean had finally noticed the arrogant warrior. Gesturing to the man at his side, he said, "I wish to make known to ye Brian of Clan Meic Lochlainn."

The man named Brian seemed familiar to Aednat, but not overly much. Her grandfather had been the overking back when she had lived here. She did, however, have the strong urge to stick her tongue out at that haughty Diarmuid when he finally returned his gaze to her. She was not prepared for the intensity of his blue eyes, the way he took in all of her with that one single glance, or the unexpected rush of excitement caused by his blatant appreciation. Then he was drawn into Sean's conversation and the men drifted away, deep in their talk. She took a shaky breath.

Thomasina leaned in close, her gaze direct. "I have no explanation for his behavior. *Transgression*?"

"'Twas nothing."

"He is a most pleasant man."

Aednat nearly choked upon hearing those words. "'Tis not my experience of him. I did not know where he was from at first, only that he thought much of himself."

Thomasina's frown deepened. "How so?"

"He cared not for my treatment of Lorccán."

"Lorccán?" Thomasina gasped, her eyes going to the bench against the far wall where the younglings sat, their heads close together as they talked. It certainly looked like more stories were being spread. Lorccán, the youngest of the group, sat between Mary and Sibéal. Aldred held their attention now, his mouth flapping. Wide-eyed, Lorccán soaked in every detail. The girls appeared much less impressed.

Irritation washed over Aednat anew. She resented having to retell the story now, but she'd prefer Thomasina hear it from her than from Diarmuid. "Lorccán had been along the cliffs and I scolded him."

"As well ye should!" Thomasina huffed. "I need to take a strap to that one."

Bold words aside, Thomasina would never take a strap to anyone. Aednat knew that.

At that moment, all four young heads turned toward Diarmuid who had stopped, Sean and Brian beside him, to talk to some warriors at a nearby table. With lips pressed together, the children watched him intently. When the big man glanced their way, Lorccán's mouth fell open and his eyes widened even more.

"But 'tis not my place to see to his punishment, and the arrogant man took exception to that," Aednat replied, but her attention had shifted to Diarmuid and his darkening expression.

No doubt he knew of the children's rumors and did not appreciate them. He was quite large and frightening. So when he shifted toward them in a mock attack, gnashing his teeth as if enjoying a particularly scrumptious meal, she couldn't hold back a smile. All the children shrank back in fear, even

Aldred, the master storyteller himself.

"Arrogant? Diarmuid?" Thomasina asked.

A sudden rush of men scrambled in through the open door, demanding everyone's attention. They dragged something heavy between them. An unconscious man.

"Is that Michael?" Brian asked. Both he and Sean stepped up to take the body from the exhausted men.

"He was in the cove, Bri. We got him here as quickly as possible." The stocky man handed off his heavy burden, wheezing from exhaustion with every word.

"Is he dead?" A woman voiced the question they all had in their minds.

"He is," Brian answered.

Aednat came out from behind the head table, assessing the drowned man. His face was slightly blue, but she had seen a man brought back to life when she was very young. The old healer of Clan Meic Lochlainn, a strange little woman with wild, haunting eyes, had told her and Tisa that it was the water in his chest that had stopped his breathing. Getting the water out would make the air come in.

"Let the healer attend to him," one person called out.

"No!" another cried out. "If God deems this man should die, only the devil would want him alive."

"Give her a chance."

"The devil's work!" another person shouted.

"She does not look like the devil to me."

A few people laughed at that. Aednat stayed silent despite all the comments and stares directed at her. There were a lot of stories told and retold of the work great healers had done. Whether they were true stories or not didn't matter, they were believed, and some sounded like miracles. In the end, some trusted her and some did not.

She found herself glancing back at Diarmuid, whose narrowed eyes watched her intently as those around her both cursed and blessed her with their comments. Aednat's stomach roiled.

"We'll let her try." It was Brian who spoke, and a blanket of anticipation fell over the room.

The crowd parted and the small, drenched man was carried closer to Aednat. Many here did not know her, but they all knew *of* her. She had been responsible for enough unusual healings that her fame was as well known as any warrior's.

Once the men placed her patient on the ground, they stepped away and she moved in close. Kneeling beside the man, she sniffed at his mouth before dragging her hand along his chest. There was no breath in him. No heart beating in his chest. But his body was still warm—a good sign considering how cold the water was.

Finding no other injuries, she moved quickly. There was one chance to save him. It required getting the water out of his lungs. She bent his legs at the knees, supporting them with her own body until she was able to anchor his foot into the cup of her joined hands. She shoved his knee up toward his chest. And repeated. A slow process. Too slow. Although a small man, he was waterlogged and his limbs heavy. Her labored breathing was the only sound in the room.

The water had to be sent back out his mouth. Aednat knew she was doing the one thing that could bring him back, but she was quickly tiring. She focused on the job at hand, her eyes on his mouth, willing him to spit the water out. There was always the chance that the crowd would turn against her, one and all, if she failed. Sean could protect her from them if they were home, but there were so many strangers in this hall, all gathered around, all watching. She hoped since Brian was the one who'd called on her, he would not allow them to attack her.

So intent on her work, she was startled when someone settled beside her. Diarmuid. He nudged her away and took both of the man's feet in the same hold. Much stronger than her, he was able to mimic the motion she'd done, only much more quickly. Settling back on her heels, she struggled to catch her breath and slow the heaving of her shoulders.

The gurgling sound came first and then the water gushed from the man's mouth. She grabbed at the man's *léine*, Diarmuid assisting, and flopped him onto his side so the liquid flowed more easily.

When the man groaned, the crowd cheered and the room erupted with spontaneous chatter. A few stepped back, their eyes wide from fear, but she tried to block them out. Her smile could not be contained. This was helping someone—a heady feeling indeed. A kind of drunkenness.

Diarmuid stood and offered a hand to her. The light-headed feeling persisted and she stumbled. His large hands were suddenly gripping her hips, steadying her stance while bringing her more fully in front of him. Intense heat radiated through her core. The warrior's eyes flashed before he released her, and she had the distinct impression he'd wanted to pull her against him.

Aednat gave him a shy smile before ducking her head and returning to her spot beside Thomasina.

"Very well done," her friend said, leaning in to hug her. "Ye amaze everyone with yer ability to heal."

"Not everyone." Aednat kept her gaze focused on Thomasina, her expression of pride a boon.

"The doomsayers! Of little importance." Thomasina gestured toward the revived man surrounded by well-wishers. "Look what ye've done! Ye brought the man back to life."

Aednat gasped. "I am not God."

Thomasina scoffed. "I know that."

Aednat could not help but glance at the small group gathered at the back of the room. A dark-robed priest stood with them, and his expression made her chest tighten in fear.

"Oh, dear Aednat. Forgive me." Thomasina cupped her cheek. "Pay them no mind. *We* all know ye are a good Christian woman. Do not vex yerself."

Their dark stares were unrelenting, and Aednat felt a powerful need to escape them. "I need to remove myself," she whispered.

"But ye have not eaten."

"I need to rest."

"I will have food set aside for ye."

Aednat kissed Thomasina's cheek. Everyone in the hall fell quiet as she passed the formerly drowned man on her way out—subjecting herself, unintentionally, to their renewed scrutiny. Even the grateful ones had been struck speechless, almost as if they were in awe. She understood that they didn't know what to say to her, and she could read their unspoken appreciation. But their reaction, coupled with the open hatred of those who considered her evil, made her the outcast again. Just like her crippled foot. She tried to summon a smile and hurried through the open doorway.

Blowing a heavy breath, she paused outside, attempting to settle her disquiet. She glanced over her shoulder to ensure the priest hadn't followed her and then released a sigh of relief when she realized he had not.

She needed time to herself, time to reflect and restore. The gloaming was just beginning. It was a lovely summer night and she wanted to enjoy it.

She had enjoyed many a beautiful display in this sky in her younger years. A calm settled over her despite the voices that carried from the hall behind her, where she was, no doubt, the topic of conversation.

A light twinkled on the horizon, and she could again hear her grandmother's voice.

"That's the one now, lassie. Quick. Make yer wish."

Aednat closed her eyes with no idea of what she would wish for. The handsome face of Diarmuid floated into her mind, startling her, and her eyes flew open.

"Aednat? Is that ye?"

She twirled around, almost expecting Diarmuid to have materialized behind her. Instead, she came face to face with the man who'd played a role in her childhood nightmares. Gerrit. Her grandfather's cruel lackey. Gerrit was the man he'd ordered to keep the outcasts away from the village by any means necessary. Sitting atop his huge, black horse, he had seemed like the devil himself.

Many years had passed since then, and he looked different than she remembered. Smaller. Older. He had lost most of his hair and what remained had gone white. Bent over at the shoulders, he neither scowled nor smiled.

"Ye've grown into a beautiful woman." His voice was far gentler than she remembered it.

Her heart sped up, throbbing in her ears so loud even the ocean was drowned out.

"How dare ye speak to me!" What had been intended as a yell came out as a gasp. She stepped back, struggling against the overwhelming panic that threatened to swamp her. Swamp her and send her running from him as if her very life depended on escaping him. "Ye vile, vile man!"

Turning, she refused to register his hurt expression at her outburst. Mayhap he was wizened now, but the man had been brutal to the outcasts. He'd run her down in the forest when she was but a small child and she'd fallen, breaking her wrist. Tisa had lived in the village then and set it to mend, but it still pained her whenever it rained.

As Aednat hobbled away on shaky feet, the ground shifted from packed mud, hard beneath her feet, to a soft cushion covered with pine needles. She stopped, suddenly hit with the reality that she'd sought refuge not by returning to the throng of people, but to the forest. Her eyes adjusted easily to the dim light. A glance over her shoulder assured her that no one had followed, and she struggled to find her inner peace.

Things were different now. She was no longer a little girl at someone else's mercy. She was a woman full grown. Capable. Strong. Sean had seen to all that. He'd taught her to use a bow and a sword, to control a horse with her legs alone, and, most importantly, to trust her own judgment.

Aednat had no trouble finding the cave even though the entrance was overgrown with dark, green foliage dotted with large white and red flowers. She closed her eyes and breathed in their sweet scent. Calmness covered her like a heavy fur on a bitter cold night.

Inside the darkness of the cave, memories rushed over her. This had been their refuge. Aednat and the other outcasts. The boys she'd called friends, Will and Cad. Her grandmother, tall and beautiful, whose husband had set her aside when he became overking, marrying another. She'd stayed in the caves to care for Aednat.

The old man who had loved to tell them stories. His expressive, low voice echoing back from the cavernous walls. They'd lain on their pallets listening, all of them shivering in the total darkness, too afeared to keep the fire going lest they be discovered. It should have been a fright-filled life, but she'd found solace here. As she did now.

The sharp pain of loss took hold. Her grandmother had been more like a mother to her, teaching her to be a gentle woman despite the world she lived in. With her grandmother's loving ways, it had been an easy lesson—until she had been struck down by an attack from a neighboring clan. Sean had received just compensation, but not Aednat. It had felt like losing her own mother all over again, and being here now brought back all that grief.

Suddenly overwhelmed by sadness, Aednat couldn't leave fast enough. Back outside the cave, she settled against a tree and focused on the familiar sounds of the forest, its inhabitants preparing for night. In her mind, she saw each bird when she heard its call, and she saw the owls and bats too as they prepared for their night of feasting.

She could hear Will's voice again in her mind.

"'Tis the mayvis's evening song."

Will had known each bird's call and the name of every creature in the forest. She had loved learning about the animals from him. He was not from the area and had strange names for even the most common beasts. And he would always hold her hand, helping her along the barely discernible path just as the light was fading. The time to return to the cave. Always patient. Always kind. When she'd left this place, she'd left behind that family, and she couldn't help but wonder what had happened to them all.

Diarmuid sat squeezed between two fat warriors at one of several trestle tables filling the hall. Sean had introduced them. They were from somewhere east, but Diarmuid had forgotten their names. His focus, instead, was on the view through the open door. The ocean. The sun slipping beneath the horizon. A red sky. Tomorrow would be a good day to head back down to the *Sionainn* and home.

He sighed. He knew it was not to be.

"Are ye going to eat that?" The man on his right spoke. Ian? He had a double chin and a thick line of grease running down both.

Diarmuid shook his head and the last of the pheasant was gone. After refilling his horn from the clay pitcher, he stood. Sean sat at the table of honor, facing the room. They locked eyes. Sean gave an imperceptible nod, and Diarmuid continued out the door. He settled himself on the rough-hewn bench halfway between the building and the shore. Within a few minutes, Sean joined him.

"Still not much for mingling?" Sean asked.

"As I remember, yer mingling was always more about finding a willing lass."

"A terrible teacher I made for ye."

"Ah, no. *Yer* lessons were the most enjoyable."

"Well, now we've new lessons. We must find a common ground with the other clans, some way to form an understanding of mutual respect."

Diarmuid snorted and took a swallow of the sweet drink. "*Ye're* hoping to find that."

Sean's eyes pierced him, his face stern. "I need ye with me on this."

"Is Tadhg not coming?"

Sean was still close to the clan in Drogheda where he'd lived for many years. Tadhg, their overking, was like his own brother.

"He has his hands full as *ri túath,* working with the eastern clans, building support against any one leader's desire to be all powerful, a high king. We're struggling to convince them of our wisdom."

"Ye're descended from the King of Connacht, and ye cannot make them listen?"

Sean settled beside him and shrugged. "I do not know if they recognize the name of Eachna. The people and lessons of the past matter little to some except to incite their own desires to become as great, but they all seek the easy way. They turn to myths and superstition only out of the hope they'll find a power beyond their own ability."

"With no *árd rí* uniting us, many of the kings continue to strive for more power and hope to become that high king."

"At any cost." Sean murmured the words as if

speaking to himself.

"The village that was attacked? Marcán told me they knew the attacker. 'Twas Black Oengus and he wanted their healer."

"That miscreant!" Sean rubbed his face, his weariness apparent.

"Ye need to spend some quiet time with Thomasina."

Sean's wife was a special lass. She had a way of restoring Sean's strength. Diarmuid would never admit it, but he envied their closeness.

"She has much to handle now," Sean said. "That is why I sent Lorccán with Aednat this morn."

Diarmuid's thoughts again turned to the long-haired maiden's honey-coating of the lad's disobedience, making him soft when he would need to be tough. It reminded him he had a bone to pick. "So why the mysterious message about wanting me to meet Aednat? Are ye offering her to me?"

"I've invited ye to come to me many times."

"To what purpose? Battle takes me away enough. And each time I'm away, I come back to more strife I must settle. Ye know Beibhinn."

"She is certainly baleful. Vicious." Sean glanced toward Diarmuid. "Forgive me for speaking ill of the woman who bore ye."

"No forgiveness needed. I know her for what she is."

Sean's thoughtful expression arrowed through him. It had been a mistake to mention Aednat's name. If Sean offered her now, how could Diarmuid avoid taking her to wife? Excitement he couldn't explain set his heart to racing.

"I wanted ye to be happy with a woman, Diarmuid.

Someone to warm yer bed when ye've returned from battle. Is that so bad? I thought she could be the one."

Clearly Sean had a great blind spot where Aednat was concerned. A wife like her would never give him peace. Admittedly, Diarmuid had been impressed by her ability, her passionate desire to save the drowned man. The intensity of her expression had sparked an undeniable urge in him to aid her. To help her make her desire a reality. To make these naysayers regret they ever doubted her.

Sean offered an understanding smile. "No matter. Yer silence says enough."

Diarmuid was surprised to feel a pang of regret, but surely it was better this way. "Mayhap I am not the man ye believe me to be."

The dark brows rising nearly to Sean's hairline filled Diarmuid with a sudden urge to laugh.

"Ye know damn well I know ye fine. Since ye were a lad at yer mother's breast. I do not wish ye to spend yer years old and alone."

"I am in my prime! I have but one use for a woman, and it does not require taking her to wife."

"And if ye had daughters of yer own, ye'd see the error in that." Sean leveled him with a serious look.

"Error? Are ye not a fine one to talk!"

"I never gave a lass what she didn't want."

"No matter how long ye had to sweet-talk her into the wanting of it?"

Sean shook his head. "Ye've made yer thoughts clear. No matter. Pleased I am to have Aednat in our clan."

"I have never seen a healer like her." Diarmuid's thoughts turned to the memory of her working alone, hefting the man's legs up to bend and straighten them.

No one else, not even those nearest her, had thought to offer a hand. Could they not see the difficulty she'd had with the task? How hard she'd labored? Her petite body exhausted after only a few attempts? Something stirred inside him, much though he'd like to deny it.

Taking a deep breath, he closed his eyes for a moment, regaining mastery, before he spoke again. "Is there another ye could wed her to?"

His friend's expression darkened. "Ye're not hearing me. I do not want to marry her off. She's a part of my clan that I do not need to marry off. Did ye see her bring the man back to life? She is more than a healer. I will not willingly lose her."

More than a healer? And more confusing words! Diarmuid was done trying to decipher his meaning.

Diarmuid did not want to say something he'd regret in his irritation, so he stopped the conversation by getting to his feet. "I need some time to myself."

Sean tipped his head and returned inside.

The waves in the distance and their promise of refreshing coolness called to Diarmuid. The ocean would help to calm his ire, but not here. The lough would be a better place. He veered toward the forest.

Chapter Four

As a child, Aednat had first learned about the healing arts from Tisa, before she had married Tadhg of Drogheda. Then after Aednat had fostered with Sean, Tisa and Tadhg would come for visits. But it was always *here* that Aednat had wanted to return to seek out the precious plants she needed for her supplies. Their healing strength was increased by the north winds and longer winters. She wished to make even better tinctures than most healers—tinctures that could speed healing and save lives.

Aednat took a deep breath, clearing her mind, and hunkered down to the earth. She had a childhood memory of huge flowers that bloomed through the night, only to fade at dawn's first light. Could they be real, or had they been mists of smoke, fancies of her young mind? She searched in the dimming light for the first signs of the dark blooms. A sprout of mushrooms lay beneath the shiny leaf she plucked up. Instinctively, she pulled away.

These were the rarest and most valuable of all, but Tisa had taught her well that touching the mushrooms was to be avoided. Their powers were that strong. The bell-shaped caps had been scarce these past four years, and with all the recent fighting, her supply was depleted. A godsend indeed to find such a bountiful supply. The spores were already darkening with age, so she could not wait to collect them.

With no protection from the caps' slippery coating, she used the ever-present knife at her waist and cut at the roots, barely touching the mushrooms with her fingertips. A few would be better than none. Letting them drop on the ground beside her, she swiped her hand along her skirt. She hoped the sooner she removed the oils, the less they would affect her.

The paltry amount barely seemed worth the effort. These would be used up before winter. The sight of the caps spurred her on. If there were more to be found, she would find them. She crawled on her hands and knees, low along the damp, black earth, to follow the quickly fading row of the conical-shaped fungus, repeating the process, including wiping away any traces left on her hands.

Her loose-fitting kirtle, now black with the mushrooms' oil, blurred as the oil's strong inebriating effects took hold of her. The elbow she'd been leaning on slipped, and her chin smacked the ground. Sitting back on her haunches, she huffed in and out before filling her lungs and holding the air in an attempt to clear her mind. The line of mushrooms, lying like felled trees, grew fuzzy. She searched the area for still more as she fought to orient herself. It was a struggle, for the trees were extremely tall and the rustling of the leaves was louder than she'd ever heard it. The wind caressed her skin like an open palm, and she shivered at the pleasing sensation. Her tongue stuck to the roof of her mouth, making it hard for her to swallow.

These mushrooms were more potent than she'd imagined. No wonder the men she administered them to simply smiled, their eyes narrowed and unfocused, as she saw to the cleaning and sewing of their bone-deep gashes.

"What have we here?"

The loud voice behind her should have startled her, as should have the fact that she was now alone in the woods with a man, but it did not. The man's voice, deep and resonating, actually soothed her. She was in no condition to be in anyone's company, with her thoughts scattering like mice and her heightened awareness of everything around her. But her mouth relaxed into a big smile that swept across her face.

She turned over to plop into a sitting position, her knife still gripped in her hand. The tall stranger was no more than a shadow as he came closer. The traditional *léine* he wore, tucked into his belt at the sides, did little to hide his well-honed legs, and she was impressed by the length of the fur *brait* that covered his shoulders to drape behind him. The shiny brooch that secured it was mounted with a bright, red gem. She'd swear each muscle flexed as he made his approach. Hanging from his belt was a two-handed axe on one side and a nasty looking sword on the other. The garb of a warrior.

Her breath caught at the intense pleasure worming

through her innards as she perused his long, muscled length. A handsome warrior indeed. Mesmerized, she admired his slow, cat-like grace as he moved closer still. A memory pricked at the edges of her consciousness, but try as she might, she could not quite grasp it, and it did not seem to matter overmuch.

"Who are ye?" she asked. Her words sounded breathy, and her heart beat faster when he peered closer. The deep blue of his eyes seemed to twinkle. She shook her head. Darkness was fast approaching. Surely she could see no twinkle. But he kept his eyes on her, almost as if he could see into her very soul.

"Ye do not know me?" he asked.

Aednat tipped her head, searching the cobwebbed edges of her memory, but soaking in the sight of him was much more pleasurable. He seemed so much bigger than other men and much better built. Her smile widened and she lifted her shoulders. "I do not know."

The slight crease between his brows disappeared. She crossed her legs beneath her skirt and attempted to sit up straighter. When she moved to smooth her hair, the knife dropped onto the ground beside her, the blade twinkling like his eyes had. It seemed a fine idea to leave it there.

He closed the distance between them, pushing the dark animal skin behind him, and his eyes darted to her row of mushrooms. "Suffice it to say we have met."

She cleared her throat, fighting the disorientation that seemed to be intensifying rather than lessening. Somewhere in her brain she knew her reaction to this man should be different. But any other reaction would be wrong. *This* was what her reaction should be! She wanted to know this man. *Longed* to know this man. "I am called Aednat."

"Little fire." The man nodded, a slow thought-filled gesture. "As I said, we have met."

It surprised her to realize that aside from feeling intrigued, she also felt… safe. Some inner voice told her this man was not a threat. And he was so very handsome. With a long, straight nose and a strong chin. She did not wish to leave before she knew everything there was to know about him. Such an interesting warrior.

She couldn't stop herself from smiling anew and said, "I am at a loss."

"I can see that."

And how much more could he see? Such an intense gaze. An unaccustomed fluttering took hold of her belly. A foreign feeling, she was certain. She nibbled at her lip.

"Aednat. A lovely name. For a lovely lass."

Flattered, she shifted her shoulders back, trying to appear aloof like the other lasses did when complimented. But then his eyes slid down her length, and all such thoughts flew from her mind. Her breath escaped in a slow, steady stream through her parted lips. He smiled then. A smile of appreciation. A smile of interest. The white of his teeth stark against his tanned skin.

He found her appealing? But she was sitting, and he didn't know about her foot…

She closed her eyes, still struggling to string her thoughts into some kind of coherence, but his scent drifted to her. Surrounded her. So manly. And he was even more exciting to look upon, with those broad shoulders that begged for her touch. She was not unfamiliar with the feel of a man's body beneath her fingers, but it had never before been for the sheer pleasure of it. She wanted that pleasure now. Desperately.

His gaze was powerful. "Have ye been collecting mushrooms, Aednat?"

She liked the way he said her name. "I have. Are ye familiar with them?"

"A bit." He handed her his water skin. "To quench yer thirst."

"Oh!" Exactly what she needed! Appreciation welled inside her. Unchecked, she gushed. "Thank ye."

Never had water tasted this cold and clean, and she closed her eyes to more fully enjoy its taste. In her mind she saw the brook, heard the birds in the trees overhead, and her skin tingled in response to the imaginary warm breeze. Something stirred low in her gut, and it was hard to catch her breath.

She wiped her mouth with the back of her hand and leveled her gaze at him. "My gallant hero. I thank ye."

A slight smile tipped up his lips as he nodded to her. "Whatever ye need."

The man settled himself beside her. She sighed and heard the sound come back to her as if from someone else.

Bending his knee up to his chest, he rested his arm on it, his other foot lay just short of touching her. A glance down showed him modestly covered. Keen disappointment rushed over her. When he smiled as if he'd read the direction of her thoughts, her face heated.

"And what are ye after out here, Aednat? Just

finding mushrooms?"

She looked about her, trying to remember. "I'm… gathering herbs."

The scents around her were overwhelming and she closed her eyes again, breathing it all in. The dampness of the soil. The honeysuckles behind her. The leather of the belt wrapped around the man's middle.

When she opened her eyes, he was watching her. Intently. She swallowed more of the refreshing liquid.

"Gathering herbs so late at night?" He glanced around them before turning back to meet her gaze. "That cannot be a simple job. 'Tis quite dark out here."

"Mmm. Dark." Heat pooled in her belly.

The slightest flick of his brow and the trace of a smile as he dragged his thumb along his lower lip. A speculative gesture. His gaze traveled lower.

She glanced down at herself, expecting to see a mark from where his gaze had caressed her so intimately. Seeing none, she struggled to remember what he had said.

"I was gathering them earlier, then…"

The touch of his calloused hand gliding up her arm set her skin aflame, and she took a deep breath, holding it in.

"Ye were interrupted," he said.

His voice was so close, and his touch, excruciatingly gentle. And pleasant. So very pleasant. She brought her gaze back to his handsome face. Tightness spread across her bosom. An uncomfortable tightness she wanted him to ease.

"And now it must be done by the light of the moon?"

"Aye, it must."

His head moved toward her and she closed her eyes, anticipating with great eagerness her first kiss.

"Yer skin is soft as silk, Aednat. And what of yer lips?"

He did not disappoint, brushing his full lips lightly over hers. Did he find them soft? That was her greatest desire at the moment. That and the easing of the constriction in her chest. As he worked his hand beneath her hair, goose bumps raced along her neck. He brought her face closer to his.

She arched her back, needing closer contact, and pressed her parted lips against his. His tongue delved inside her mouth, stroking its sudden dampness into full bloom. An exquisite sensation indeed.

He broke the kiss, his eyes hooded and his breath, smelling of ale, brushed her cheek. A sly smile. "And what of yer neck, sweet fire. Shall I find it as alluring?"

A kiss and a prolonged sweep of his tongue. Her eyes closed again to more fully appreciate the sensation. Little waves of pleasure cascaded over her like water lapping against the shore.

"I do." His voice, no more than a whisper.

A tentative caress to her breast and her nipples tightened, painfully. His open palm running across that sensitive area increased the heat beneath her skirt. She squirmed under his ministrations as he cupped one breast and then the other. Grasping and releasing. The tension bloomed into pleasure and she exhaled.

"A lovely night." He moved back to her ear, his warm breath making her heart beat faster. "And we are of the same mind."

She nodded, pressing her breasts against the eager

hands that stroked her, blessedly soothing.

"I've a great need for ye, Aednat." His husky whisper intensified her longing.

A hand caressing her backside urged her closer. She molded herself to him, allowing her breasts to be more fully grasped in his hands, the heat becoming nearly unbearable. His persistent mouth suckling at the crook of her neck sent waves of delight through her body, settling between her legs.

"Mmm, my fiery one, is yer need as great?"

She heard the guttural sound as if from someone else. A gnawing alarm grew somewhere in the back of her brain. She pulled away, immediately missing the heated contact, and resisted the nearly overwhelming urge to return.

She couldn't speak, and he remained where he was, watching her, ready to resume as soon as she returned. A mere hair's breadth away. She need only move in closer, and she would again know his touch. He could ease the tension now centered much lower, she was certain of that. Taking a shaky breath, she struggled to remember why she had pulled away from his tempting seduction.

His intense gaze never wavered from her. She imagined what he must see. Surely he must think her a peasant with her blackened skirt, her hair tumbling about her unkempt. He was being… too familiar. Too enticingly familiar, and she relished it.

"I'm no peasant." Her words were again breathy.

"Ah, dear Aednat. I see only a woman desiring a man's touch. I am most willing to oblige."

His low voice sent a wash of goose bumps across her skin. She glanced at his lips and wetted her own. That kiss had been exceptionally pleasant. With the slightest adjustment, she could know his kiss again. Her entire body called for it, but still she hesitated.

"I am a healer." Her voice sounded far away now, like her ears were stuffed full of straw. A memory of him calling her… something.

"A great healer." The man's attention never wavered. He did not touch her again with his hands, but he caressed her with his voice. "And a beautiful woman I find most desirable."

The warning bells were louder now, her head clearing. He seemed to care about only one thing, but her own desire for the same thing was vanishing like smoke. She glanced around. "Where are my men?"

"*Yer* men? So ye are not a lass alone in the woods?" He sounded disappointed.

"I am not alone."

He followed her gaze, looking around the area. His thick, expressive brows raised high. "And yet I see no one else."

In a sudden panic, she moved to stand—and immediately stumbled. Damn mushrooms were making her body feel limp. The man reached out a hand to steady her. His touch was hot. A strong grip like he didn't want to let her go. Then he stood alongside her, close enough that she felt the heat pouring off him. A soothing heat she longed to know, to become lost in.

He tipped her chin up with a single finger at her jaw, and she looked into his face. He glanced at her lips, his longing evident, but still made no moves toward her. His scent enveloped her. She swayed toward him, wanting what he offered. Realization hit her and she jerked away.

"Unhand me."

"I have not 'handed' ye." His tone remained playful, but he did not release her. "Ye've come willingly into *my* arms, Aednat."

"I do not…" She rubbed at her head. An incessant pounding started at her temples. "Forgive me…"

"Ye have done nothing requiring forgiveness." He brushed a strand of hair from her face and ran a gentle finger along her cheek. "Now if ye'd struck me? That would require my forgiveness and… so much more."

Diarmuid.

Embarrassment washed over her, and she tried to right herself. She winced at the pain shooting through her head.

"I—I need to return." She would have stumbled if he'd released her, but instead he swept her up into his strong arms, settling her against his solid chest as though she weighed nothing at all.

"I would prefer ye stay here. With me." His husky voice vibrated throughout her body. "But if that is what *ye* prefer, I will see ye returned."

She wanted to insist he put her down, wanted to get as far away from this man as she could, but her body refused to respond. Exhaustion washed over her and she dropped her head against his solid shoulder, her eyes drifting shut. Her last thought was of how safe she felt in his arms.

Chapter Five

"Did ye sleep well?"

Despite Diarmuid's foul mood, Thomasina's kind smile tamped down the irritation sitting in his gut like bad lampreys.

"I did." It was a lie.

Diarmuid placed the leather sack on the table in the longhouse, accepting the mug of mead she offered him. He glanced around at the warriors passing by, the servants still setting the room back to rights after the food had been cleared away.

"Have I missed yer husband?" he asked.

"Sean has gone to meet with Tadhg's men. Do ye remember Tadhg of Drogheda?"

Diarmuid resisted the urge to snort at the ridiculous question. He and Tadhg had fought side by side on several occasions. There was no forgetting a warrior like that.

"I do. Sean tells me he will not be coming?"

Thomasina shook her head before sipping from her own silver cup. "He will not, but he has sent a message that has Sean beside himse—Aednat!"

Diarmuid tensed. He was in no mood to be seeing the cause for his sleepless night. If he'd just accepted her blatant offer last night, he'd be satiated now. Any fool could have seen she wasn't in her right mind, and he had decided to wait until he could take his time and savor her. He'd chosen to be chivalrous, and he'd paid the price—tossing and turning all night on his hard pallet.

"Thomasina."

Aednat's voice sounded as it had on their first meeting. In control. Stubborn. It held none of the seductive, husky qualities from the night before. That *other* voice had filled his dreams, begging for his touch as she eagerly saw to the needs she'd sparked in him with her own unquenchable desire.

"Ye remember Diarmuid?" The seemingly innocent prompt reminded him of how rude he'd been to Aednat in front of Thomasina. Thomasina raised her brows slightly, as if challenging him to behave better. He smirked and turned.

"Aednat." The single word came out just before his jaw dropped.

All coherent thoughts escaped him at the sight of her. Her silky locks had been swept away from her face, cascading behind her slender neck, leaving it exposed but for a few wayward wisps. A dark blue gown hugged every curve the kirtle had hidden the day before. And generous curves they were. Curves he'd enjoyed the feel of and wanted to know again.

Diarmuid took her hand to his mouth. Their eyes met, and the memory of their kisses came back in full force, along with his body's reaction to her. The taste of her was not something easily forgotten. Had he actually thought it would have been enough to lie with her once? Only if he'd had at her the entire night would he have been sated. No, maybe not even then.

Aednat's eyes narrowed just before she yanked her hand away.

"Diarmuid." She moved closer to Thomasina, giving him her back. "Thomasina, did the man I cared for last night come to break his fast?"

Not the reaction he'd wanted. Diarmuid was decidedly unrepentant, and the pleasurable view of her luscious backside was a boon. The curls of her long, dark hair teasing each firm mound. He'd not had nearly enough time to explore her many treasures, and his palms itched to know the feel of her.

"He was here," Thomasina said.

"I had hoped to check on him. D'ye know where I might find him?"

"I can bring ye to him," Diarmuid said, sounding a little too much like an eager-to-please pup. He wanted Aednat alone. He tore his eyes from her tempting bottom just before she turned to face him. "Come."

He refused to acknowledge Thomasina's surprised reaction. Instead he retrieved his sack and walked to the door before Aednat could object, hoping she'd have no other choice but to follow.

Within a few strides, she walked abreast of him.

"His name is Michael," Diarmuid said.

She nodded but kept her eyes averted.

He struggled to watch where he was going; his

gaze kept darting toward her. All of her. Her parted lips. Her swaying bosom. Her tiny feet poking out from beneath her gown with each step, one slightly faster than the other.

Aednat, on the other hand, didn't look at him at all. If not for the way she'd looked at him last night, he'd believe she found him unappealing. Even dislikeable. Not so last night. She'd stared at him. Long and hard. As if she couldn't get enough of him. She had wanted him. He wanted her still. Certainly he could remind her of those feelings if they could just be alone together.

"What will ye do once ye see him?"

Aednat halted, put her hand to her hip, and turned to face him. "And this interests ye for what reason?"

"We need to… talk." He struggled for a calm demeanor even in the face of her own irritation. The sight of her cheeks, flushed in exasperation, was not quenching his overpowering urge to take her in his arms. He'd enjoy finding other ways to keep that blush on her face.

"So speak." She motioned to him. An impatient gesture.

Her cheekiness knew no bounds this day. He tightened his lips to keep from smiling at her impertinence. His eyes darted around with dramatic flair.

"People are everywhere." He closed the distance between them and dropped his voice. "I wish us to be somewhere… more private."

She glanced around in an expression of complete confusion. "Why not here? If ye wish to chastise me again, this works as well as any other place."

That knocked the wind out of him. "Chastise ye?"

Her eyes pierced him.

He realized she referred to her treatment of Lorccán.

"I said my piece about the lad."

"Then whatever would we have to talk about?" Her doe eyes widened, but each word dripped with annoyance.

"Talking would not truly be necessary, would it, Aednat?"

Her brows slashed lower, but she remained silent.

"We could finish what we started? Last night?"

"Last night?" Her lovely features contorted with irritation. "Last night I slept like the dead."

Diarmuid paused. She wasn't being impertinent? He searched her face for an answer, and it was written across her features. She didn't remember their kisses, let alone how she had clearly wanted more. Wanted him. Not exactly what he had been hoping for. No wonder her attitude was back!

Diarmuid's jaw clenched.

"Michael is beside the boat," he said.

Aednat wrinkled her nose and shaded her eyes to scan the direction in which he pointed. Diarmuid waited until she spotted the man busily coiling rope. When she turned to him, he tossed the sack at her, which she easily caught.

"Enjoy yer mushrooms," he said.

Then he strode away without a backward glance.

"How is Michael?"

Aednat was returning from the small *curragh*

when Sean's voice carried to her. She waited for him to join her.

"He is well," she said and resumed walking toward the longhouse. "Though he has little enough to say to *me*."

Sean draped an arm around her shoulders, giving her a quick squeeze. "I know ye do not understand why the people keep their distance. I wish it would not bother ye so."

"I am an outcast still."

Sean's eyes rounded, and she regretted her thoughtless words. He was a good man, and the debt she owed him could never be repaid. While her own grandfather had treated her as less than human for her deformity, Sean had not hesitated to give her a place of honor in his clan.

"I am sorry, *Datan*. I know 'tis not the same."

"'Tis not! Ye are an important part of our clan. Never an outcast."

Sean was a solid leader, demanding absolute obedience. And his protection of her was unwavering. All of his people saw that. They would never dare speak ill of her in his presence.

"Aednat?"

She started at his tone. "Forgive me, *Datan*."

"Ye were far off in yer thoughts. Does yer solitude bother ye so much?"

"They fear me unless they need my help." She forced a smile, hoping to relieve his concerns. "I am melancholy today is all. Think no more on it. I need to go collect Lorccán so yer poor wife can get some work done."

"No need. I am taking him with me today."

Aednat tightened her smile and nodded, fighting

back the disappointment that threatened to swamp her. "As ye wish, Sean. I've many things to see to myself."

"Do not wander far. There are many warriors about that do not know ye."

"I will not. Good day."

She stumbled slightly in her haste to get away. The lad's companionship had been taken from her because that damn man had convinced Sean that Lorccán was not being properly seen to by her. Diarmuid had only been here for a single day, yet he was already upending her life, drastically changing her daily duties. The leather sack that had hung forgotten from her wrist slapped against her leg. Mushrooms? She had little patience or interest in puzzling out his meaning.

She halted her steps to yank open the sack, only to be assaulted by the pungent fumes. A coughing fit started that she struggled to stop. She cinched the leather and dropped to the ground between two of the round buildings and out of sight of others.

Leaning against the house, a flood of memories assailed her as the light-headedness returned.

The touch of his lips. His hands. His caresses.

Strange dreams had haunted her sleep, dreams she could barely remember in the morn, though the feelings they had stirred lingered even after sunrise. Darkness. Heat. Longing. It could not have really happened—and yet here was the proof.

Leaving the leather sack behind, she hobbled up the hill to the round building she'd been invited to use for her healing work. She closed the rough door and leaned back against it. Diarmuid's expectant expression floated into her consciousness.

Never would she willingly lie with a man, even if she had been intoxicated. And men like him did not force themselves on women. They had no need. Women dropped at their feet.

She fought down her panic and searched through her foggy memories. He had kissed her. She remembered the sensation of his supple lips on hers, exploring. Warm. Firm. Insistent. It had been pleasant— She shook her head. She must not think that.

Sliding down to the floor, she covered her eyes with her hand. Yet nothing could block out the memories now that she had unloosed them.

The sensation of his fingers slipping up her arm. The touch of his hand on her breasts, cupping them.

"I have a great need for ye, Aednat."

And *she* had felt that same great need.

"It cannot be!" Aednat stood with so much force, she staggered into the middle of the room, grabbing the hard, wooden table to keep from tumbling. She lowered herself to the small bench.

His kisses *had* been pleasant, inviting even. There was no denying it. His persistent tongue had set her aflame, and when he'd touched her? She fisted her hands and stood. At least it had ended there. She was made of stronger stuff than to be tossed around by overwhelming passion.

We need to... talk.

What would he have said to her? Would he have called her out? Threatened to tell of her shameless behavior? So be it! Had it not been for the mushrooms, she'd never have allowed him to kiss her. She'd certainly never have wanted more.

Aednat wavered.

But she *had* wanted more, and worst of all, he knew it. Had he come to secrete her away? Mayhap to even have his way with her? She groaned out loud. A desperate sound indeed. The thought had sparked a deep, smoldering need inside her—something she hadn't realized she was capable of feeling. Surely if she kept her distance, the need would subside.

Aednat nibbled at her bottom lip.

While she didn't know exactly why he'd wanted to talk, he'd certainly not try to get her alone again. He'd returned the mushrooms, reminded her of her indiscretion, and now he would no doubt stay away. Any number of women would be more than willing to see to his needs.

And that would be fine with her.

Chapter Six

The sharp sounds of the warning bell pierced the quiet of Aednat's roundhouse workshop, nestled a short distance from the others. She dropped the spindle she'd been working with, the long fibers leaving a trail behind as it rolled away. All had seemed well when she'd gone to retrieve the mushrooms. They were far too valuable to leave behind. She'd found them untouched and the bag now sat beside the small wooden door, unopened.

So why the bell? When she opened the door, people were already hurrying past her, answering the summons, and she followed them down the hill at a slightly slower pace.

When Aednat cleared the trees, she watched with horror as the horde of people surrounding the longhouse shifted into battle. The ringing sound of metal on metal was undeniable, and even from this distance, she could see the pools of blood and hobbled bodies. Women and children were fleeing the scene by way of the woods to the west and along the beaches. The considerable number of warriors chasing them down, despite all the men still attacking the longhouse and the open beach, indicated the sheer size of the assault. But it was the single-sailed vessel in the bay that caused her mouth to go dry. Norsemen? A longboat was beaching along the shore, dispersing more men, but they wore the *léines* of Irish warriors. The bell was finally silenced, only for the racket to be replaced by screams of sheer terror. The sound pierced her heart and forced her feet to move more quickly toward the fleeing victims.

"Aednat! Wait."

Aednat had to scan the area to her left twice before spotting Thomasina hidden by the trees, a frightened Lorccán clutched in her arms. No one else was about, and Aednat ducked in beside them.

"What is amiss?"

Thomasina's face, awash with tears, spoke of her fear. She set her son down beside her, the lad's wide eyes mirroring his mother's. "The clan north of Tadhg. They lied to him, Aednat! He sent word this morning. He said they've come to cause trouble and take whatever they want."

"Can we not win the day? With all these warriors encamped?"

Thomasina's face tightened into angry lines. "They planned their attack well, and us none the wiser. Some of the men here last night were spies, and they brought back the news their whoreson leader wanted."

"And did they not tell them the number of warriors? Surely that would dispel any intention to attack."

Thomasina's expression of defeat made Aednat's heart sink. She wished she hadn't asked and now didn't want to hear the answer.

"No. They know that *ye* are *here*."

"Me?" Aednat winced. "No! What do they want with me?"

Thomasina shook her head. "We must go to the cave. Ye know the one?"

"I do. Come." She took little Lorccán's hand and led them through the forest and away from the longhouse. They followed the dry riverbed to a fallow field before coming to a stop at the edge. Aednat dropped low and snuck a peek. Seeing no one, they made a dash for a copse of trees.

"D'ye know this place, Aednat?" Lorccán asked, his small voice full of amazement.

"I do, Lorccán. Like the back of my own hand."

After checking that the path was clear, they ran across to the forest where the cave lay hidden, its pink and white flowers a bright beacon against the darkness of the undergrowth. Aednat pushed the vines aside and led the way deep into the back of the cave, following a narrow gap into a much wider and taller cavern. The tall man standing in the shadows gave her a start.

"Be easy." Diarmuid shifted until he stood beneath a small opening overhead that allowed some light. His touch was warm on her arm, and he watched her with narrowed eyes before shifting his attention to Thomasina.

"Does she know?" His no-nonsense tone was less than reassuring.

"I know they've come for me, but I do not know why," she said. "Is someone hurt?"

"Many will be hurt, Aednat."

Aednat shook her head. "Because they have come to fight? To kill our warriors?"

"Only if we do not give them what they want."

Regret and fear slammed into her gut like a hard punch. They wanted *her*.

Diarmuid watched Lorccán, who couldn't stop looking around the cave, enthralled by the hidden room. He dropped down in front of the lad.

"Have ye ever seen such a place as this?"

Lorccán's eyes widened at first, but then he tipped his head and glanced around again. "I have not," he said quietly. "Have ye?"

"A few here and there."

"What did ye do there?" The lad looked at Aednat. "And what did *ye* do here? Is this where ye played?"

She shook her head, too overwrought to speak, but Diarmuid intervened. "Once I hid in a cave such as this."

"Ye hid?" Lorccán's eyes widened. "How long did ye hide for?"

"Seemed like a very long time, but no more than a few days."

Thomasina put a hand on the lad's shoulder. "Do not bother Diarmuid now."

Lorccán backed away, his mouth dropping open and his lips moving soundlessly. Diarmuid's expression registered shock at the sudden change from the boy.

Aednat's spirits lifted, and she hid her smile with her hand. Unlike Diarmuid, she'd had no problem reading the lad's lips.

Diarmuid the Despicable.

Apparently, the boy had not recognized Diarmuid from the longhouse. He'd had no idea this was the man who'd pretended to lunge at his table, the man who supposedly ate redheaded children, until he'd heard the name. After a shake of his head, Diarmuid stood to his full height and crossed his arms.

"Thomasina, why do ye not take this young lad to watch by the entrance?"

"I wi—" Aednat smiled and reached for Lorccán.

Diarmuid halted her arm, a small gesture that ended with her hand held in his loose grip. When she turned to him, his eyes were dark and intense. Her heart sped up.

"Ye must stay," Diarmuid said. "Sean has sent me to ye."

Aednat wanted to demand answers with Thomasina present, but her friend merely gave them a quiet nod and turned to leave. Aednat remained silent as she watched mother and child slip through the narrow passage in the cave.

Diarmuid's intense gaze bore into Aednat, making panic flutter up through her chest, demanding release—release in whatever form it might take. Still, she refused to look at him. Though they were alone now, he did not speak. Of all the people she could be hidden with in these memory-laden walls...

Finally, Aednat swallowed down the panic, forcing herself to breath in slow, measured breaths.

"Ye're very beautiful."

Wide-eyed, she turned to him. His words were unexpected, and she did not know how to respond. He held her hand more tightly, moving closer.

"If ye remembered last night, ye'd not look so surprised." Closer still, his voice husky now.

The fluttering moved lower, and she was struck by the familiarity of it. She wanted to feel his lips, but he didn't move to kiss her.

"I wanted to take ye then, hold ye in my arms and take ye. 'Twas what ye wanted as well."

When she started to shake her head in denial, he placed a finger to her lips.

"It does not matter now. I did not know ye were untouched. Ye seemed… to know what ye wanted." He released her hand and took a step back from her. "Those men attacking? They've come to take ye. They believe ye are a virgin with a power they can take from ye… if they lie with ye."

Each word sounded like a death knell. He must have seen it on her face because his features softened— he smiled and reached for her again, stopping short of actually touching her. Instead, he folded his arms about his chest. "I will not let them have ye. Rest assured. Ye've been entrusted to me, and I care for what is mine."

She opened her mouth to protest, but he shook his head.

"I'll see ye safe until ye can be returned, if that is what ye want."

She breathed easier. Easier except for the fluttering.

"We need to get away now," he said.

"What—" Her throat constricted. "What will happen? Do they not need ye in the battle? Ye would do more good there than here."

"Trying to be rid of me so soon? I am where I'm needed. Reinforcements will be here anon if they have not yet arrived. There will be a halt to the fighting. When they learn ye are no longer here, they will listen to reason."

Aednat looked back toward the passage.

"Thomasina has gone to assure Sean ye are safely with me so he will not worry for ye."

Sean certainly had great faith in this man, but she struggled with the idea. Being alone with him did not seem like the best idea for her. She found him far too appealing for her own good.

"We need to go." Diarmuid wrapped his large hands around her hips and lifted her up toward the top of the cave.

She gasped. "What are ye about?"

Air blew across her scalp from an opening in the ceiling where light shined through.

"Reach up now!" was Diarmuid's only answer. Two large hands lowered through the gap above.

"Yer hands!" An unfamiliar voice called down to her. She did as she was told, peering up as she lifted her arms, and her wrists were immediately grasped and pulled. Once her head cleared the opening, she saw it was Diarmuid's man who was helping her out of the cave. He wrapped an arm around her waist to pull her the rest of the way out.

Aednat stood and brushed the dirt from her bottom, looking about as the black-haired man assisted Diarmuid. The area around them was a small clearing in the forest, the ocean barely visible through the trees. Two saddled horses waited a few feet away, chomping on the grass. Oblivious.

"If ye'd explained, I could have been more helpful." She couldn't resist making excuses for the awkwardness of the situation.

They both turned toward her.

"Ye did fine, lass," the black-haired man said, a reassuring smile on his handsome face. As if remembering his manners, he bowed and then kissed the back of her hand with great gallantry. "My name is Marcán. I am at yer service."

"Marcán. My thanks for yer assistance." She glanced back through the small opening into the cave below. "I'd often wondered if an escape was possible that way."

"Ye know this place?" Marcán's shock was not well hidden.

"'Twas my home when I was a child."

Diarmuid's expression darkened. He held her gaze for a moment—a moment that sent a strange tingling down her back—before he began checking his horse, the same warhorse he'd ridden earlier. "Did ye get the supplies?"

Marcán turned his attention to his *ri túaithe*, showing him the supplies in the saddle bags. Food. Blankets. Water. Fodder.

"Good. Then get back and see that we're not followed."

"Ye're not coming with us?" Aednat's sense of calm quickly evaporated. She preferred to not be alone with Diarmuid.

"He is not!"

The words were sharp, and the flash of a frown on Marcán's face confirmed he'd heard it, too.

Diarmuid's next words were more controlled. "If we hope to travel in secret, 'tis best if we do so unaccompanied." The words were delivered with a pointed stare at his friend.

Marcán hesitated, sighed, and mounted his horse.

"Very nice to meet ye, Marcán," Aednat said. There was a sinking feeling in her stomach, and she couldn't help but feel her protection was riding away.

She trusted Diarmuid to protect her from any physical threats, of course, but there were other temptations to consider...

The dark-haired man offered a shy smile and a wink before directing his horse back toward the village. Diarmuid's voice was barely above a whisper, but he was talking to his horse, and his hand slid gently along the beast's stomach as he adjusted the saddle.

"How far must we go?" When his eyes fell on her, it seemed she had interrupted a private conversation. She couldn't stop the heat that flooded her face. "Well, there's only the one horse, so we are riding together..."

"As far as we need to go. They're chasing after ye."

He turned his attention back to the horse, leaving her with the definite impression he was through talking... to her. After a few more minutes of attendance to the horse, he paused to glove both his hands, eyeing her as he did so. She stiffened. There was no sign of the tenderness he'd shown her in the cave. His brows were slanted as if he found her most irritating—an inconvenience. No doubt seeing her to safety was not his choice, preferring battle to protecting her. But running away was not what she would have chosen either.

Diarmuid lifted her onto the horse and mounted behind her in a quick leap. Before she could adjust herself away from him, he wrapped one arm around her and pulled her flush against his body. His warmth made her gasp, and then they were racing across the hill at breakneck speed, their bodies rising as one with each movement.

Eventually Diarmuid slowed their pace, and Aednat was at last able to get her bearings. They traveled west. It was a side of the island she had never seen. She had heard stories of the people here, how they were not all of the faith, despite St. Pádraig himself having spent time here. The clan rivalry, however, was as intense as it was everywhere else. That alone was a good enough reason to stay away.

Diarmuid did not stop to eat, and her stomach reminded her repeatedly of its yearning for sustenance as the day progressed. Her escort didn't seem to notice, but his hold on her was unrelenting. Each time she tried to straighten and get some space between them, he'd pull her back as if determined to hold her, one hand clasping her waist and the other gripping the reins. His size alone made it impossible not to feel surrounded by his hard body. Like the twisted rocks that ran down to the sea, surrounding the relentless waves. So when he abruptly stopped his horse and leapt off its back, pulling Aednat down with him, the sudden change caught her completely off guard. She'd have stumbled if he'd not supported her.

Grabbing the horse's lead, he plowed through the tall brush that grew along their route. The sedate horse showed no sign of distress at having large branches poking its side, merely blinking as if this were an everyday occurrence. Diarmuid stopped beside a tree and backed Aednat flush against him, one arm slanting across her chest to hold her shoulder and the other wrapped just below her waist.

When he put his lips to her ear to whisper, his beard touched her lobe, sending a shiver across her skin. "Dare not even breathe."

He rested against the solid trunk and Aednat stayed as she was, arched back against him. His lips lingered by her ear. Each warm breath caressed her, and the rise of his chest against her back somehow both calmed and excited her. His hand slipped lower to adjust her stance, fitting her good foot between his, flattening her to him even more. Just as she gathered enough nerve to protest the unnecessarily intimate position, the heavy panting of horses met her ears.

There were two of them, and neither horse nor rider was familiar. They stopped just beyond the brush, in full view. Diarmuid must have felt her gasp because he slipped his hand up her neck to gently cover her mouth.

"Shhh, now." His words, quieter than a whisper, were hot against her neck.

"We've lost them," the big man on a brown sorrel said. "They must have seen us and thought to get her away."

Aednat broke out into a cold sweat. Somehow the nightmare had only just become real for her. They truly were hunting her down.

The other man, mounted on a gray steed, sat tall and nodded. His quiver of arrows and the bow strapped to his back were plainly visible. "They hope to hide her from us, but there is no place we will not find her."

When he turned, she couldn't make out his face, but there was no mistaking the blood-stained gloves gripping his saddle. "Rest assured. We will get her yet."

Her breath quickened with the need to escape, but Diarmuid tightened his grip. When he shifted behind her, she jumped and would have cried out but for his hand still settled over her mouth. Neither man showed any sign of having heard her.

"Stay still now."

She wasn't sure whether Diarmuid had said the actual words or merely moved his lips, but the command forced her to focus and listen. The horses on the road tossed their heads while their riders exchanged a skin. The one with the stained gloves stopped the container, and then the two turned their horses about and went back the way they'd come.

Her body slumped against Diarmuid's, air *whooshing* out of her. If not for the strong support of his arms, she'd have collapsed on the ground. He appeared unaffected and rested his shoulders against the trunk, widening his stance, as if settling in for a long stay.

Aednat could barely contain herself, so great was her need to escape this place. She wanted to slap him into action, or mayhap grab his horse and take off on it. Why weren't they moving?

Instead, she clenched her teeth to remain silent. All she had was him. If she couldn't trust him, she had no protection at all.

More time slipped by. Aednat began to shiver, and Diarmuid wrapped both arms around her chest and pulled her tighter still.

"Listen!" he whispered urgently. "They're returning."

Her entire body tensed. There it was, the sound of approaching horses. The two men were now three, and they raced by, low in their saddles, without a glance to either side.

Awed into silence, Aednat took a breath, willing her body to relax.

Sean had chosen the correct guardian for her. She had to believe she would be safe in his hands until she could return to her clan.

"Be brave now, little one. I take ye to safety where

ye need no longer hide in fear." Sean's words to her the day she'd left the cave. She had been so small and frightened. He had seemed a force larger than life, surrounding her, cradling her in his arms, offering to protect her as no man had in her memory. A grandfather who had cast her out. Her parents both dead.

Taking a deep breath, she let her body relax against Diarmuid. Surrounded by this huge warrior, she felt as small now as she had then. Once relaxed, however, she could feel so much more of him. His chest was rock hard beneath her head. His shoulders hunching forward so that his lips met her ear. Their touch, light as a feather. Faintly disturbing. Or was it exciting? Setting off waves of warmth beneath her gown until she was on fire. Did he feel the heat as well?

"They're gone." Diarmuid's voice sounded strained.

One arm slipped lower to tighten like a band across her hips, flattening her buttocks against him. His arousal pressed into her. She closed her eyes, willing herself to breathe more slowly and ignore the pleasurable sensations spreading up her core. He coughed and loosened the hold.

"They are using the most well-traveled route in search of ye. We will need to take the slower way." He sounded more himself the longer he spoke. "If we can avoid them all together, that would be best."

She nodded, not sure if she could find her voice right now.

"Ye're breathing heavy." Diarmuid's sharp words came at the same instant he released his hold of her altogether.

Aghast, she tried to push off him but fumbled. With a hand on each hip, he held her apart until she was sure on her feet. Neither spoke. He stepped away, mounted his horse, and reached down to pull her in front of him.

As night fell, he slowed the horse and veered off toward a narrow path heading due east. A small stone building came into view, and the arrow slits fashioned into crosses at either side of the opening designated this as a place of worship. Its simple design no doubt dated back to St. Pádraig himself. The wooden door hung open as if in anticipation of their arrival. Diarmuid halted the horse in the shadows and helped her down, his eyes on the chapel. Watchful.

"Stay here a moment."

"Wha—"

His finger to her lips silenced her.

He left her hidden by the horse. She was unable to watch his approach or see if he was greeted at the open door, but soon voices carried to her. The voices were not ones she recognized. Not even Diarmuid's. It sounded like arguing.

She bit her lower lip, unsure how she should proceed. The horse shifted as if aware of her sudden tension, its large dark eyes glancing back at her. Smiling, she rubbed its velvety flank. Surely the horse would know if something was amiss. Without warning, it waved its head. Irritated. Was she not doing it right? Aednat stuck her tongue out at the spoiled beast.

"Aednat!" That was a voice she'd recognize anywhere.

Thomasina.

Her spirits lifting in an instant, Aednat came out from behind the horse to fall into her friend's arms.

"Oh dear! Ye are a fright," Thomasina said. "Ye're trembling!"

Tears of relief welled, but Aednat fought them down and smiled. They would not see her complete terror. She wouldn't worry them if she could help it.

Sean's silhouette appeared in the dim light of the doorway and he hurried out of it, moving toward her.

He held her in a close embrace, smelling of fresh air and leather. Warm and solid. She sighed in relief.

"Why are ye trembling, Aednat?"

She smiled at him, shaking her head. "It is over, *Datan*?"

"It is not."

She covered her mouth, swallowing the bile rising in her throat. When would this nightmare end?

He lowered his gaze to look her into her eyes. "But I will never allow any harm to come to ye."

A tear slipped down her cheek. She wiped at it, nodding her head.

Taking her hand, Sean led the way inside the building with Thomasina following behind. An altar to her right was adorned with a single burning candle, a bunch of wildflowers beside it. Lilacs. The small space was crowded with people, some of whom she didn't recognize. Two men with fierce expressions and wide stances stood straight ahead. Warriors. One crossed his arms as if to intimidate. The small man to her left, balding and gray haired, was dressed as a peasant.

Diarmuid secured the door after they had all entered, then moved to peer through the arrow slits. She wanted to ask why he seemed so angry, but he crossed his arms and leaned a shoulder against the hard stone wall, a serious expression on his face.

"Sit, Aednat." Sean directed her to the lone bench opposite the candle.

"May I return now?" she asked as soon as she was seated.

Sean faced her, propping a foot on the bench beside her. "No, ye may not return. The men who came for ye will not relent."

Aednat worried her hands in her lap. The men she didn't know, the warriors, were moving closer. Sean signaled them away with no attempt at hiding his annoyance.

"Aednat, I love ye as my own." Sean spoke in a low tone. "Ye know that?"

Her gut tightened. This was not good. "I do, *Datan.*"

"Their *ri* demanded we hand ye over. He insisted he would either take ye as his wife or just take ye. Our choice."

The candlelight flickered, and the room dimmed around her. This could not be happening.

"We told him we'd not give ye up, and that… that ye were wed to another. That surprised him."

Her weight lifted. "And he believed ye?"

The men beside them grumbled despite Sean's glare.

"I thought they had. They called a halt to the fighting and came in to discuss terms. They would only speak to me as yer overking, so I agreed to meet with them. But their leader had played us false and sent others to search for ye."

"That son of a whore Black Oengus." It was a husky redheaded man who spoke, his hand flexing on the grip of the *miodóg* at his side. "He's a conniving bastard, getting the help of other clans to attack us."

"Alroy, will ye shut yer mouth!" Sean said. "Ye're scaring her."

"I am not scared," Aednat managed to say, though even she knew her voice did not match her words.

Alroy continued, painting a vivid picture indeed. "He's a pup, but he has the strength of twenty men."

Sean kept his eyes on her. She struggled to keep the dread from her face.

"Black Oengus has been an ongoing problem," Sean admitted. "He is always searching for more power. The easier it is to attain, the better he likes it. Nothing we cannot handle."

Alroy snorted.

"We won't let them have ye." Sean never looked away from her. "But they found yer belongings and no sign of a husband." He held her gaze. "It may not be possible for ye to avoid this."

"This?" Her fear made everything he said sound so much worse. Or mayhap this was simply what her life had become, a living nightmare. "Are ye telling me I must marry him?"

"I would prefer a different course, but—I do not want this man for ye, Aednat. He's cruel. He's…" That Sean struggled with his words made the lump in her stomach double in size. "If not him… now… another will come. The stories of yer talent are too widespread."

She gripped her hands to stop their trembling.

"I would have ye marry another. A man of my own choosing."

"We can escape them." She stood and looked toward Diarmuid to back her up. He had evaded her pursuers before, surely he could do it again. His expression was dark and far from reassuring. Her legs threatened to buckle beneath her.

"Sweet Aednat, ye cannot escape." Sean took her hand. "If this man believes he can still possess ye, he'll not stop until he finds ye. He means to make himself high king by any means. Taking ye will be his way to get there."

Aednat's mind scrambled for an escape.

Sean planted his foot on the ground, a determined expression on his face. "I will have ye wed Diarmuid. He'll take ye away from here, and I'll know ye're safe."

Her jaw dropped and she looked at the handsome man Sean would have her marry. The memory of his heated embrace and strong arms surrounding her quickened her breath. The arguing she'd heard must have been Diarmuid objecting to the union. She'd swear his already dark expression had turned into an even fiercer scowl.

"Ye would have me marry a man who does not want me? One who will spank me like a child? Belittle me? I will not marry him!" That Diarmuid was not quite as bad as she had first assumed seemed unimportant. She needed to convince them not to force her into this marriage. He would not want to remain married to her once he saw her foot. He'd be repelled by it. That would be a rejection she could never get past.

Sean and Thomasina exchanged confused looks before they both turned accusatory eyes on Diarmuid.

"What have ye done to make her believe these things?" Sean asked.

It gave Aednat pleasure to hear Sean rise to her defense, until she noticed Thomasina was watching her with a disquieting expression and flattened lips.

"I told ye she needed to be taken in hand." Diarmuid stood away from the wall, defensive. "And that is all!"

When Sean opened his mouth to respond, Thomasina lifted a hand to halt him.

"Tell me, Aednat," Thomasina began. Her tone was the one she used with Lorccán when he continued to profess his innocence after being caught in the thick of things.

Aednat's stomach roiled.

"Why would ye believe this kind warrior would be anything but gentle with ye?"

She shook her head, her lips quivering, her chest constricted. She could only manage little intakes of air. She fought to take a deep breath, but panic was setting in. Thomasina would never understand—she'd always been treated with the greatest care. Aednat knew not every woman received such tender care. She'd heard many tales.

"I told ye men can be gentle, did I not?" Thomasina pushed her point. "Diarmuid is kind."

Aednat continued to struggle for air. If she said one word, she would break down.

Thomasina moved closer, her eyes rounding with sympathy as her cool palm reached out to touch Aednat's heated cheek. "Easy now, blow out the air. Now take a breath."

Aednat did as she was told and her lungs filled.

"He *will be* gentle." The words, barely a whisper, were for her ears alone.

Sean's expression hardened. "Mayhap ye are just being strong-headed, as Diarmuid has said."

Aednat glanced sharply back at Sean, her eyes wide. "Ye've discussed me with him?"

Sean had the decency to redden at the accusation, but Thomasina took her husband's hand. Aednat missed neither the slight nod of her friend's head nor the deep sigh Sean heaved before he moved in front of her, filling her view.

"Do not do this, *Datan*." Her whispered words were for him alone, her eyes pleading.

He kissed her forehead, the gentlest of kisses. She knew then that she would have no chance to refuse. Her overking had decided, and it would be done as he had proclaimed it.

"I will have ye safe, Aednat. Diarmuid must take ye to wife."

Diarmuid came forward, his face unreadable.

Her throat tightened with unshed tears.

"Aednat, hear me." Thomasina gripped her hands, her eyes wide. "Ye're cold as ice! Calm yerself. What does the healer prescribe for such an ailment?"

Aednat struggled to make words while all her thoughts jammed up in her head. "Cham— chamomile?"

The peasant pressed past Sean and moved closer. Aednat noticed for the first time the crude wooden cross that hung around his neck. He was a priest!

"Just nerves the lass has. I've the cure!" Alroy produced a skin near to bursting. "My contribution. For the nuptials."

The wine skin was passed around, and when Aednat started to decline, Thomasina pressed it into her hand. "'Twill help ye relax."

She took a small sip and tried to hand it back to Thomasina, who shook her head, waiting for her to have more. When it came to Diarmuid, he refused it entirely.

"Relax now. 'Twill be fine," Thomasina whispered into her ear. "Allow him to show ye his gentle ways, and we'll give ye a proper ceremony with God's blessing."

The little priest flashed a bland smile. Aednat was going to be sick. She'd never thought to marry, and she'd certainly never thought to marry like *this*.

She wanted to resist the firm hand that pulled her to stand at the table opposite the priest. Diarmuid came alongside her, and when he looked down at her, those narrowed eyes and tight lips spoke of his own unhappiness. He was being forced into this, too.

Aednat turned imploring eyes toward Thomasina, but her friend placed a gentle finger to her lips and spoke to the priest. "Father, yer blessing please, and they need God's protection as well."

The little man nodded, his gaze resting on Aednat. "God calls each woman to cleave unto one man, and Diarmuid shall be this man for ye, sweet Aednat. D'ye consent to taking him as yer husband?"

Shooting a glance up at Diarmuid, whose eyes bore into her, she finally nodded. "I consent."

The priest's face remained expressionless. "He'll guard ye as his own person, and ye'll respect his words. And d'ye consent to take her to wife?"

Diarmuid dipped his head. "I consent."

"We ask God's blessing on this union and protection over ye both. In the name of the Father, and of the Son, and of the Holy Ghost. Amen."

"Amen." The response came in unison. All mirrored the priest in making the sign of the cross.

"A kiss as a symbol of unity." Despite the priest's tolerant smile, the order was unmistakable as anything else.

Diarmuid's stoic expression never wavered. Wrapping a strong arm around her waist, he leaned down to kiss her. He looked to be aiming past her lips and she turned slightly, offering her left cheek, but his warm lips surprised her by landing on her own.

He gripped her more tightly, deepening the kiss, gathering her against his length. As his tongue sparred with hers, he became her total focus. Little fires sparked low in her belly. She remembered this sensation. This desire. She kissed him back. When he finally broke the kiss, she'd have stumbled but for his firm hold of her. His face was tipped toward hers, and his eyes looked bright… and almost pleased. She pulled away from him, bewildered, and brought her hand to her mouth. Someone coughed, and she quickly averted her eyes, refusing to acknowledge the onlookers.

"Well, that's done." Sean's pleased tone was a sure sign he'd not missed their spark of passion. "Well, almost done. Ah, Diarmuid…"

"I know what to do, Sean." Diarmuid quirked a brow and took her small hand in his own, pulling her through the door and into the quiet night. Quiet except for the night insects serenading them.

"Wait!" Thomasina followed after them. "What of yer wedding night? The priest has a room."

And with the priest's own room being offered for their marriage bed, Aednat wished she'd accepted more of the wine.

Diarmuid winced at the thought of their first time together being in the priest's hard bed while the rest of them waited outside, ears pressed to the door. The fear he'd witnessed in Aednat's eyes was disturbing. She was petrified.

When he'd moved to kiss her, he'd had every intent to offer a symbolic peck on the cheek, priest be damned. It was the sight of those rosy lips, glistening and ready, that had changed his mind. They'd taunted him, reminding him of how she'd tasted, how she'd responded, and how she'd wanted him. All else around them had faded away, and it had become exceedingly imperative that he know that response again. That he satisfy himself with the proof that she *did* have some desire for him, despite her harsh words.

Diarmuid hadn't been prepared for her response, though. Her passion had ignited in his arms, setting him on fire. That had pleased him and gone a long way toward making this whole thing more bearable. It was only by an act of sheer will that he had released her.

He couldn't remember ever wanting a woman the way he wanted his wife. But it would not be at blade point with the sole purpose of ridding her of her precious maidenhead. It would be for enjoyment. His *and* hers. To hell with anyone else who sought to be her first. He'd slit their throats wide open before they could lay a hand on her.

Diarmuid positioned his tiny wife sideways onto the horse. He wanted to ease her fear, assure her their joining would progress naturally. Pleasantly. That he'd not force himself on her.

"Diarmuid?" Sean's voice, lifted in warning, was like a biting fly circling his head.

"I know what to do!" Diarmuid repeated the words—more like a growl—as he leapt up behind his motionless bride.

The others halted at his words, their expectant

faces staring up at them as if questioning the truth of his words. *That* he could handle. He *did* know what he was doing. But it did not sit well that Aednat had been forced to marry him, especially when he thought back to what she'd said this morning. The cave had been her home? What kind of life had she lived before Sean had found her?

"Aednat?" He cleared his throat. No need to sound so pathetically desirous of her. "Are ye going willingly with me or would ye prefer another?"

He held his breath, praying she'd choose him, though he had no idea why. He desired her well enough, but he'd never thought to marry, let alone to a woman who could hardly be called a biddable bride. He had only agreed to do so because Sean had asked it of him. Or so he had thought. After they'd settled the bride price, it had occurred to him—with no small amount of shock—that he'd have paid a much higher *coibche* to have her.

She'd not been given a choice.

"Another?"

"Is there another ye would wed? Speak now."

"I do not wish to be wed."

Why a beautiful woman with such obvious passion preferred to remain unmarried was beyond his understanding. "That choice has been taken out of yer hands."

"Then why d'ye ask?"

Diarmuid bit back a retort. "If there is another ye *would* willingly consent to marry, I will take ye to him."

She stiffened. "Ye will?"

Not what he wanted to hear. The tension in his gut had become unbearable. "I will. Ye need only direct me to him."

Silence followed, and he found himself gripped by the horror that she might have someone else in mind. If so, he would now be required to bring her to this man she preferred over him. He ground his teeth, fighting against the fact that *he'd* prefer to just run the other man through. It had been foolish of him to give her this out. He could wait no longer to hear the man's name…

"Aednat?"

A loud sigh. "There is no one I wish to marry."

Diarmuid let out the breath he'd been holding. Not exactly the reassurance he'd hoped to hear, but at least there was no one else.

Her shoulders back, she took a deep, cleansing breath. Diarmuid did the same—and was tormented by the scent of wildflowers and rainwater that wafted from her hair. He fought against the desire to dip closer to her neck. To touch the pulse there with his lips. Would it be racing as fast as his own?

He put a heel to his horse, and they were off, traveling toward the ocean, leaving the others behind. And with her small body pressed up against him, so soft and warm, it was going to be a very long night.

Chapter Seven

"I know what to do."

Diarmuid's words lingered in Aednat's thoughts as they road along the coast. Each time she remembered them, a shiver raced up her spine, but was it a shiver of fear or anticipation? He held her closer. The ride along the coast was exhilarating. The horse raced across the waterline, sending a spray up into Aednat's face, and the moon hovered over their shoulders.

Diarmuid tightened his hold around her waist, his huge hand stretching from just below her breasts to past her hips.

She glanced up and spoke to his chin. "I'm not cold."

"I did not believe ye were."

Soreness had started to set in, but when she shifted

her bottom, he held her tighter, his thighs tense beneath hers. His insistence that she be pressed against him at all times was getting tiresome.

"I'm not trying to move," she huffed.

His chin bumped her head when he looked down at her. His eyes were big and his lips held just the hint of a smile. "And yet ye are."

It took a moment for her to realize what he meant.

She scowled. He enjoyed holding her still, and that knowledge irritated her more than anything else. Refusing to give him any more entertainment, Aednat closed her eyes and vowed to remain motionless. Besides, she was beyond exhausted, and sleep would be a boon.

But she noticed so much more with her eyes closed. The crashing waves. The puffins in the distance. His strong heartbeat, steady against her back. And his scent, forest and musk, surrounding her in a cloud. These thoughts filled her with excitement and guilt, so she opened her eyes to dispel them. There was no change in his hold. After a time, she allowed her eyes to drift closed again. Sleep would surely come. Eventually.

His chest was solid. Immovable. His long hair tickled her ear where it hung down, barely reaching her. His legs were strong, her bottom dipping into the valley where they straddled the animal. Suddenly aware of *all* of him, she knew his need.

He pulled her tighter, and her breath caught. The motion took on an entirely different meaning. He was not doing it to control her but to stop her from rubbing against him. She was torturing him!

She yanked to a sitting position and smacked into his head. They both grunted in unison.

"What are ye about, lass?" He yanked the horse to a halt and dropped down beside it. "Ye bloodied my lip with that thick head of yers."

He wiped at the red liquid with his hand. Aednat rubbed her head, heat washing over her. "I'm sorry—I did not mean to—forgive me."

He reached up to help her down, his expression stoic. "See to yer needs then. We can rest here for a wee bit. Do not travel far."

Beyond embarrassed, she made a quick exit between some bushes. When she returned, he was rummaging through his sack. The cut on his lip had stopped bleeding, but his expression hadn't lightened. He retrieved a handful of dark, crusty bread. Her stomach growled loudly, but he made no mention of it, just handed her the bread. He took none for himself.

"My thanks," she said. The bread was heavy and filling.

Diarmuid withdrew a skin and took a long draw off it. He stopped, glanced at her, then repeated the motion, even tipping his head back to speed the liquid up. Aednat wiped at the crumbs on her mouth. At last he handed her the skin, a slight smirk on his face.

"What are ye laughing about?" she asked just before taking the vessel to her lips. Expecting water or the wine from Alroy, she coughed loudly when the warm liquid worked its way down her throat. "What is this?"

"It's made from barley, an old technique." Diarmuid quirked a brow. "I think ye'll like it more than yer mushrooms."

"I did not eat the mushrooms! I was cutting them and—oh, never mind."

"So now ye remember?"

The heat of embarrassment spread up her face again. Diarmuid closed the distance, stopping just short of touching her. She stood only as tall as his chest, but she seemed even smaller standing this close to him.

"I asked ye a question." His eyes were bright even in the moonlight. He pushed her hair back from her face with a gentle sweep of his calloused palm. "*D'ye* remember now?"

"I remember! I was collecting the mushrooms for my supplies."

Diarmuid moved the skin she still gripped in her hand to her mouth. "Slower now. Take a wee sip."

Acquiescing, she allowed him to maneuver the skin. Forewarned now, she drank some of the liquid. It went down smoother this time. The meaning of his words suddenly registered, and she yanked the skin away from her mouth. "What say ye? I'll like it more than the mushrooms?"

His dimple flashed. "And so ye will."

He took another healthy swallow and then stopped the skin up. He looked at her askance, his eyes trailing the full length of her before finally settling on her face. "Refreshed?"

Her body was relaxing, no doubt thanks to his drink. And she still thirsted for more. "D'ye not have any water?"

"There'll be water enough shortly. We will go deeper into the forest now to take the less-traveled road. There's a lough. We'll stay there for the night."

Crossing to the horse, Aednat's limp was even more apparent. It always was when she became overtired. He scooped her into his arms, holding her close against him.

"I do not mind giving my wife a hand."

The use of the title seemed like a slap to the face. She'd actually forgotten their new situation, and the total control he had over her now. And yet… his expression had softened considerably now that they were alone together, and the rest of his words were very sweet. She was tired of fighting, and exhaustion swept over her. She melted against him.

"Ready to have another go at it?"

Aednat bolted up, her foggy mind unsure of what he meant. Diarmuid had passed on the room offered by the priest. She had assumed he was in no hurry for the bedding, but his condition on the horse? He was more than ready. When he only tossed her onto the horse, she tried to ignore the slight pang of disappointment. Or the second one, because he didn't even notice she was disappointed.

"I'll see to nature's call." Diarmuid walked away with sure footing, disappearing into the undergrowth.

Aednat took a shaky breath and vowed to sit still for the rest of the ride, regardless of which body part was falling asleep.

When he returned, they veered away from the ocean and back into the darkened trees. She must have finally dozed off, because when she next became aware of her surroundings, the crescent moon was overhead, and they'd arrived at the lough. They paused just within the edge of the trees. The reflection of the moon on the water created a shimmering, glowing effect, but it gave no indication of the depth. Diarmuid jumped off the horse and helped her down. The tranquil scene elicited a long, slow breath that helped to calm her. Diarmuid moved about, seeing to the horse.

Sticky and smelly, Aednat longed for an opportunity to wash herself. The water looked to be a heavenly reprieve. Diarmuid walked his mount to the lough's edge and dropped down to his knees to drink some for himself. She licked her lips and followed, dropping to her knees beside him.

Dipping a skin into the water, he turned enough to smile at her. "Most refreshing."

She scooped the chilly water into her hands. It was delicious and she drank her fill before wiping it over her face and reaching beneath her hair to rub her neck. "Mmmm."

When she opened her eyes, she was startled to find him watching her. Contemplating her.

"Does yer lip still hurt?" she asked, unsure what else to say.

He flashed a smile, sat up, and started unlacing his shoes. "Not much. How is yer head?"

Aednat settled onto her bottom and rubbed a hand across her crown. "A bit sore. Ye've a hard head as well."

"'Tis a good night for a dip. The water will be warm."

She glanced again at the inviting lough. "I have nothing to change into if my clothing gets wet."

"Why would ye not just take it off?"

His eyes locked with hers, and she found she could not respond. She couldn't move either. He held her there with his gaze like a hunter spotting his game.

When he reached beneath her skirts, she became instantly alert.

His hand hot on her ankle, he pulled her foot out from beneath her skirts. It was her bad foot that he took in his hand first, unlacing her footwear, but then he did the same to the other as if he'd noticed nothing unusual. She gulped and forced herself to continue breathing. When he returned to the first, her breath caught again. Taking her misshapen heel in the palm of his hand, he began to rub it.

His face revealed nothing. Before the vows had been exchanged, no words had been spoken about her malady, no one had voiced the concern that any children might bear the same burden. Had no one warned him?

"Does yer foot give ye much pain?" He didn't sound surprised, just curious.

"On occasion. If I walk too much or if it's raining."

He nodded, his eyes never leaving her face. She could discern no disgust as he rubbed into her arch with a firm stroke, the sensation so pleasant, she closed her eyes. Now she knew why his horse was so dedicated to him—his touch was pure bliss. She could not remember anyone ever willingly touching her foot before.

"Does this lessen the pain?"

Unable to speak, she merely nodded. It did lessen the pain, but her grandmother had always insisted just the opposite was true. Will and Cad would steal glimpses of it when they were all playing in the loughs, but no one ever spoke of it.

Her grandmother's instructions had been very clear. She had told her to always keep it covered so it would not worsen. Now that Aednat was older, she knew the truth. Her grandmother had wanted it covered because it was ugly.

Aednat's eyes flew open, and she yanked back her foot. Diarmuid's concerned expression left her feeling guilty.

"Did I hurt ye?" he asked.

"No, but ye do not need to touch it."

"It? Ye mean yer foot?"

Aednat nodded but remained silent, afraid of the sudden tightness in her face and the tears that might follow.

He paused, searched her face, then took her foot back in his hand. "Allow me to lessen yer pain."

Between the heat of his hand and the small circles he rubbed into her arches, the ever-present ache in her foot began to lessen. She was amazed. When he took up her other foot, she opened her eyes to watch as he applied the same ministrations.

"Mayhap ye are a healer as well." Her voice was quiet.

His little dimple flashed at her when he smiled. "Mayhap I am."

Diarmuid was quite a handsome man. He could have married any woman of his choosing but had never done so before. So why would he marry her? Why now?

She pushed away the uncomfortable question.

"Best beware of the men who would wish to take yer power," she teased.

He smiled. "Beware of the women, did ye mean to say?"

"Only a man would think to steal something so precious."

His expression clouded, and he searched her face as if for an explanation. She had none to offer. With the graceful motions she remembered from that first night, he rose onto his knees, leaning toward her with his hands still at her ankles. He stopped just short of kissing her.

"Hear this, sweet Aednat! No man will steal anything from ye. Ye have my word."

The heat was there again. Mayhap it was always there when he was this close, but his words struck a chord. Something deep inside she couldn't name. With his gentle declaration, he had offered her a different sort of protection. One she could not receive from Sean. For a moment, she saw Diarmuid in a new light. This was a man who understood a woman's weakness and did not need to use it for his own gain.

"A kiss from my lovely wife?" His voice was low and it vibrated through her chest. She had the urge to stroke his cheek and pull him in closer. But she merely nodded her consent.

He edged even closer, rubbing her lips lightly against his own before kissing her. She responded to his tender assault, parting her lips for him. As his mouth continued to move over hers, his hands glided gently along her calves and back up over her feet, creating little waves of warmth that rushed up her thighs and settled at the apex of her legs.

When he pulled back, she whimpered in protest, and her eyes flew open with embarrassment. His face, a breath away, revealed hooded eyes and a quiet smile. A passionate man desiring her. Not something she had ever hoped to have.

"I will take only what ye give me." His breath hastened and he swallowed.

She sat up straighter and nodded. He closed his eyes, moving closer again. With his lips to her ear, he slid his warm fingertips along her calves.

"Yer skin is as soft as a silken cloth," he said.

The touch created a deep longing for something more. She remembered this sensation, this longing from last night, and it occurred to her that it wasn't the mushrooms that had sparked her desire. It had been this man. Her husband. The mushrooms had merely given her permission to act on that desire. Making her brave. Keeping her from considering possible rejection. She had wanted him then, and she wanted him now. Her heart raced in anticipation of what was about to happen.

"Well, well, what have we here?"

Aednat strangled out a sound at the intrusion of the unfamiliar voice. Diarmuid pulled his hands away, and she tucked her legs back under her gown. Blood rushed in her ears.

The men swaggering toward them looked ready for trouble. Fear spiked into her. Diarmuid would have to face these men alone with no one to back him up. The tools of her trade were also useful as weapons, but she'd left them behind this morning so that she could wear this dress. This revealing dress that she'd never worn before because it displayed her womanly virtues and left so little to the imagination. She'd wanted to be viewed not as the healer but as a woman. A confident, desirable woman, like the one she had been in her dreams. The kind of woman who took the man she wanted, accepting his intimacy. Even while knowing he would make her feel things she'd never experienced before.

With a start, she realized she'd worn this gown for Diarmuid.

Diarmuid was a trained warrior and not a fool. Never that. Keeping his weapon at hand was second nature. Even when seducing his wife. He gripped the hilt of his sword as he stood to face the impending trouble. The four men paused when they caught sight of his weapon. Varying in age from six and ten to two score, their telling eyes darted from his blade to his face and back, as if to measure his ability. They had no horses he could see and no weapon bigger than a dagger. Despite their numbers, they were poorly matched against him.

"Having a bit of sport, are ye?" A scruffy bearded man spoke first, but Diarmuid sensed no authority from him. Although he had stepped up, leaving the rest a few feet behind, this man was not the leader.

"Time with my wife, *gentlemen*."

The little man toward the back was the only one who showed a reaction to his tone and the sarcastic use of the title. Diarmuid smiled to himself. He had found the man in charge.

"Oh, now." The rest held back, but Scruffy circled them, his attention fixed on Aednat. "A bonny lass ye have."

Diarmuid did not want Aednat to be afraid, so he reached a hand out to her, never taking his eyes from the men. She stood and he pulled her close behind him, shielding her from their view.

"Indeed, she is." He kept his balance to the back, ready to press forward when needed, but took care to remain expressionless.

The men waited, watchful but unsure.

"So if there's nothing ye require, I would like to get back to my wife."

The smaller man finally edged forward, coming much closer than the others, as if to show he had no fear. Stupid man.

"*New* wife, is she?" he asked.

Groans of appreciation rumbled through the group.

They were looking for a virgin, but were they looking for Aednat? Had these men been set out to find her by the *ri* who had attacked Sean? She trembled beside him, but he remained focused.

"Not new. Just one I have been separated from"—turning to look in her face, he flexed his sword arm—"for too long."

As if on cue, the small man hurled himself at Diarmuid, earning a slice from his readied sword. Blood from the torso wound soaked the man's threadbare tunic. He dropped to the ground, writhing in pain, and a taller man, the youngest of the group, lunged toward Diarmuid with his dagger at the ready. Diarmuid easily dispensed with the pathetic weapon, knocking his hilt against the pup's extended wrist.

The remaining two moved forward, circling on opposite sides. Diarmuid kept backing up to keep them from coming at Aednat from behind. The lough loomed precariously close.

"Ye do not need to keep her to yerself," Scruffy said, producing a war axe that must have been tucked at the back of his belt. He swung it in an arc, stepping over his fallen comrades. "We'd only like a little piece of her."

"Afraid not." Diarmuid retreated again. "She's only for me, ye see."

Charging at the men, Diarmuid caught them off guard and easily within striking range of his sword. First he moved to the right, pummeling the hilt of the weapon into Scruffy's gut. The axe, deflected by his forearm, fell harmlessly to the ground. The man on the other side stepped up in time to receive the thrust of Diarmuid's blade as he drove it forward, piercing the man's flesh. He dropped to his knees, howling in pain.

Aednat gasped, but Diarmuid could not allow her to see to the wounded man, as her healer's heart no doubt strained to do, so he blocked her view. He was ready for her to try and break free. He eyed her with a stern expression, giving the slightest shake of his head, as she glanced at the foliage. No doubt to see if she could find whatever herbs would be needed to tend the men's wounds.

Diarmuid surveyed the group, blade still at the ready. "Does anyone wish to come back for more?"

They mumbled, averting their eyes, and shook their heads. The young one's wrist was no doubt broken, but he got up first and moved in close enough to grip the leader's arm and help him up. Scruffy helped the other come to standing, and the four hobbled off into the woods without a backward glance or another comment.

Still holding Aednat tight, he turned to her and spoke in a gentle voice. "How fare ye?"

"I am unhurt."

There were tears in her eyes now, her breath catching with sobs, but she wiped at them angrily.

"The excitement… it makes some cry," Diarmuid said.

"I do not cry." With a clenched jaw, she turned to him, barely able to squeeze out her words. "I. Do. Not. Cry."

"No?"

When he reached over to wipe her damp cheek, she smacked his hand away and pressed her lips together in a stubborn line.

"*Silly* women cry. *I* do not."

Quite a sight to behold. This wife of his. Proud and unbending. Denying a fear that would have assaulted even a seasoned warrior. "I am mistaken."

Her throat constricted and her nostrils flared, but she managed a curt nod. But when Diarmuid opened his arms to her, there was only a moment's hesitation before she moved into his embrace. Still, even in his arms, she refused to crumble. Even when he stroked her head, she would not press it against his shoulder. Even when he spoke words of comfort, she held herself apart.

"I know ye to be a strong woman, Aednat. There is no weakness in feeling relieved when danger has passed."

The muffled sob came just before she collapsed in his arms. Her shoulders trembled, either from tears or fear, but if she preferred to believe she did not cry, he was not going to argue the point.

He was a complete fool to leave her untouched like this. Sean had not wanted her to be treated cruelly, which was why Diarmuid had agreed to take her to wife. His desire for her was not in question, and with her softness pressing into him, her breasts crushed against him, he had difficulty reasoning out why he'd waited.

"They'll be back."

She tensed and pulled away, her eyes wide. Despite her brave show, she was afraid, and that alone was reason enough to wait.

"How d'ye know that?" she asked.

"Not tonight. Tonight they will tend to their wounds, return to their lair. We are safe, but they were sent after ye."

She searched his face. "They did not say that."

"They did not need to."

"No! Why?"

Diarmuid released her, giving himself space. "Sean explained the situation to ye."

Aednat shook her head in denial. "We've traveled all day. Certainly they would not come this far."

"These men seek power above all else, Aednat." Diarmuid waited to allow the words to sink in. "There are no lengths they will not go to."

She gasped. "Is that why they wanted to know if we were just married?"

"That is what I believe. And why I told them I'd only been away from ye. No one must know I have not yet dispensed of yer precious maidenhead."

Aednat blushed at the mention of her virginal status but only for the shortest moment.

"Those impudent dogs!"

Aednat's irritation was rising. He'd venture she was as irritated now as she'd been with him for reprimanding her about Lorccán. She was getting mouthy, and that pleased him greatly. He did not care to see her cowering. A passionate woman indeed, and she was sending off sparks he'd more than enjoy redirecting.

She snorted and put her fisted hands to her hips. "Well, I do not think 'tis right to be chasing after me like this. If lying with ye would make them go away, I would do it this very instant." Aednat had spoken in haste and quickly realized it. "I do not mean now, whenev—"

He stepped in closer, gripped her chin in a gentle hold, and leveled his gaze at her. "Ye will get only pleasure from joining with me."

Like a demon demanding obedience, his lust pushed him to forestall no longer. To ignore her innocence. Certainly he could convince her if he tried.

To ignore her desire to remain untouched. And to ignore all that she had gone through this day alone, never mind her childhood spent living in a cave. He would give her pleasure she'd never imagined.

Diarmuid shoved the urges away. She would not be taken in such a manner. He had seen her passion. Even if she believed she did not want a husband, she had wanted him. And she would want him again. That knowledge gave him patience. He would treat her like the treasure she was, and she would willingly give herself to him.

"Now go on and wash as best ye can. I will keep watch." He turned his back and settled on the cold, hard ground. "Just do not take all night."

That last part was added for his own sanity. His mind might be willing to wait, but his body had other ideas. As stiff as he was, he couldn't expect not to receive some sort of release even if it was at his own hand. It was going to be a very long night indeed.

Chapter Eight

The scratchy, coarse blanket on the ground beneath them kept Diarmuid awake the entire night. Not to mention the lumpy roots jabbing into his side. Or his wife lying an arm's length away with her backside to him. He'd not been able to rest. While she'd washed, his over-active imagination had experienced no problem seeing what he could only hear. Or imagining the water gliding betwixt her breasts and along her thighs, moved along not by her hand but by *his*. Even though she did not tarry, it had been an excruciating few minutes.

It was only out of consideration for her exhausting day that he'd kept himself away from her despite his raging need. If he'd touched her again, he'd not have settled for less than making her his in truth.

A hard life she'd had, but Sean had assured him she was strong-willed. A fighter even. That knowledge cast a different glow on her behavior. Her cheekiness wasn't necessarily out of defiance, and as his friend had said, she could be taught. Diarmuid found himself counting on that fact.

A rustling in the trees caught his attention. A mother owl come home to feed her younglings. The dawn was fast approaching, and its light was just peeking above the hills. If she was to be his wife in truth, and she'd said there was no one else she would prefer, he'd need her to trust him. His body wanted release. Was it too soon to push the point? His cock stood at attention, assuring him it was not.

Diarmuid moved in closer, placing his palm gently on her waist.

When he leaned in close to her ear, her female scent enticed him. "Aednat?"

She groaned, cleared her throat, and arched her shoulders back.

He fisted his hand to keep himself from caressing her nicely raised arse moving provocatively toward him. "Ye slept well?"

She rolled onto her back, her side rubbing against him as she did, and nodded. "I slept fine. And what of ye?"

He gave her his most tolerant smile. "Sleep is for when another stands watch."

"My thanks, but ye need yer rest as well."

"I need a great many things."

Her eyes held his, a questioning quirk of her brow. "And what can I do to alleviate this need?"

Aednat was an innocent but knew what she was

offering. Before he could reach for her, the cry of a golden eagle reached his ears. And then again. Marcán announcing his approach. Diarmuid stopped just short of groaning his objection. "Hmm, a question I am unable to answer as I would like. Marcán is coming."

Rubbing the sleep from her eyes, she sat up. "Marcán? How did he know where to find us?"

Diarmuid stood and gazed toward the lough. "He knows this place."

The horse approached from the far side of the lough. Marcán waved and dismounted, leading his destrier to the water. Diarmuid met him halfway.

"I hear congratulations are in order." Marcán asked, smiling and raising his hand in greeting to Aednat. "Any problems?"

"We did have visitors late yesterday, but I believe I sent them off our track or at least back to wherever they're camped to return with more men."

"And how was the bedding?"

She was too far away to hear, so Diarmuid answered truthfully. "We've yet to see to that."

"Ye cannot wait!"

Aednat approached, no doubt alarmed by the change in the damn man's expression.

"Wait? Will we be staying here?" she asked.

"And how are ye this morning, Aednat?" Marcán took her hand in his to bestow a light kiss. His carefree tone grated against Diarmuid's own irritation.

"I am well. And ye?"

"He's ridden the entire night to get here, Aednat. He will say he is well, but he is exhausted."

Her face tightened, not even attempting to hide her displeasure at his words. To his astonishment, Aednat gave him her back, head held high, and returned to the blanket. Irritation but no tears? Not even to get her own way? Mayhap she truly believed only weak women cried.

"A spirited lass, that one, and she'll take no shite from ye," Marcán said. He laughed, but Diarmuid could not take his eyes off her. "Ye seem smitten by her."

Diarmuid whipped back to glare at his friend. "And ye do not know what ye speak off."

"Ye're all but drooling at the sight of her lovely arse."

"Do not comment on my bride's arse."

"She's a comely lass. So what are ye waiting for?" Marcán blocked Diarmuid's view of her. "She's being stalked even now by men fighting to be her first, and here ye are, hesitating to take what is yer husbandly right."

"And ye overstep yer bounds."

Marcán tipped his head and raised his hands in submission. Not that Diarmuid believed this show of acquiescence. They were closer than brothers, and it was the norm for his friend to speak, even though Diarmuid did not always appreciate the interference.

"Did ye not hear her say she'd lived in the cave? A cave!" Diarmuid had turned that declaration over and over in his mind, trying to piece together how that could have happened. "Sean spoke of accepting his cousin and her grandmother into his clan when she was still young. Even that he'd only found out about her while visiting Clan Meic Lochlainn. He said nothing about her living out in the woods."

Marcán's expression remained unchanged.

"So she was forced to live in the woods like an

animal, and I should take her here as well? Not even a soft pallet beneath her?" Diarmuid's irritation was growing by the minute. He could not forget that he'd been intent on doing just that before Marcán's arrival. Or last night, before those fools had interrupted them. "A tumble with a lass I'll not see again is one thing. I do not want a woman I must continue to live with to have any reason to question how I will treat her. I will expect her obedience, but I will give her due consideration in return. Can ye seriously say ye would be so callous?"

"Mayhap not, but ye forget the pleasure she will receive in return."

Diarmuid frowned, looking over Marcán's shoulder to glance at Aednat. "Since her own plans for herself did not include taking a man to her bed, I am not certain it would be pleasurable in her eyes."

Even as he spoke the words, he knew them for a lie. He again saw her eyes closing in passion while he'd explored her alluring curves.

"'Twould not sit well for ye if ye cannot change her mind. Pleasurable or not, it must be done and quickly."

"I know what to do, Marcán. Ye're the last one I'd expect to question me on this."

"Forgive me, Diarmuid. Ye are correct. I am exhausted." He turned toward Aednat. "As ye both must be."

"And yet she looks fresh as a morning breeze." Diarmuid was speaking more to himself, but Marcán's surprised expression assured him the man hadn't missed the comment.

"And as I said, ye are smitten with her."

Aednat approached, giving Diarmuid a reprieve

from making up more excuses.

"I can no longer wait on ye." Aednat spoke with that know-it-all tone. "How far may I safely venture?"

Before Diarmuid could respond, Marcán crossed to her, a smile on his lips. The smile he used when he was about to make a move on an unsuspecting lass. Diarmuid's body tensed.

"Certainly. *I* will keep guard for ye. And then mayhap ye would like a refreshing dip?" Marcán asked. "The warmth of the lough this early in the day will chase yer concerns from ye."

"Concerns like men waiting in line to force themselves betwixt my legs?"

"Unfortunately that is true, but the legend says 'twill only be the first who can take yer power. We can pray they kill each other fighting over that honor."

"Dear Marcán, the legends ye know make me wonder what cabbage field yer mother found ye in," Diarmuid said.

Marcán laughed and Aednat's lips curled, her eyes twinkling in amusement. "As I mentioned to Diarmuid, I have nothing else to wear."

"Then bathe with nothing on. I've done so myself, as has yer husband." Marcán glanced toward him. "'Tis simple enough for us to keep watch. This lough is difficult to approach without forewarning."

"And mayhap she should wait until we arrive home." Diarmuid knew he scowled—the expressions on their faces confirmed it—but he couldn't seem to stop himself. Marcán's charm was renowned, though he seldom needed it, since lasses were drawn to him. Did the man think it was necessary to woo his bride for him? Get her to bare herself... and then what?

"We will be there by nightfall next, Aednat."

She nodded in agreement. Marcán quickly scouted the area before directing her to some nearby bushes to see to her business. Then he returned to stand alongside Diarmuid again, and they both watched her retreating back.

"And just what are ye about?" Diarmuid's question sounded more like a growl.

Marcán's innocent tone matched his wide eyes. "Of what d'ye speak? Kindness? A smile? She is no doubt overcome with the strain of her escape. 'Twas quite a change in her circumstances, and now to be married to ye?"

"What say ye? Her being married to me will be no hardship on her. I'll not be a bad husband."

Marcán raised his eyebrows but remained quiet. Aednat's reappearance brought the uncomfortable tension to an end.

"Come." Diarmuid intercepted Marcán, who had stepped forward to greet her. "Ye need something to break yer fast."

Thankfully, Marcán took the hint, remaining where he stood. Diarmuid offered her the best of the crusty bread that remained. "We should be at home by nightfall next, and then we can see to yer nourishment properly. And a bath if that would please ye."

Her speculative glance traveled from him to Marcán and back again. It stoked his irritation into full-blown ire. "Marcán was just leaving."

His friend's jaw dropped. "D'ye not need the added protection?"

"We need nothing from ye… but distance. 'Tis our honeymoon after all."

Marcán laughed. "And where is yer mead?"

Aednat blushed prettily. The cloistering away of a newly married couple for a month, supplied with a steady flow of the sweet drink to ensure pregnancy, was a long-honored tradition.

"We'll see to that soon enough." Diarmuid realized he wasn't certain she would abide by the tradition. That he could insist as her husband was fine for some, but how happy would a bride be if her very first duty as wife was something forced on her? Like marrying him to begin with. He'd prefer she come willingly to him. "If it pleases ye."

Wide-eyed shock met him from both sides.

"What?" He turned his irritation on his friend, who raised his hands yet again before mounting his horse.

"I'll wait for ye at the big rock."

Aednat worried her hands, her eyes averted. Compassion for her swelled and Diarmuid tipped her chin up. "Do not be concerned with any of this. I will see ye are well cared for. Ye will want for nothing."

"Nothing? My clan? My work?"

"Ye'll have a new clan. My mother and my sister will... welcome ye in." Diarmuid wasn't totally convinced that would be the way of it, but he'd tolerate no discord from those two. "Ye may continue as a healer. We have only an old woman seeing to our ailments, and her abilities are not as great as yers."

The smile she bestowed on him was like the sun bursting through the clouds. His breath caught. She was so lovely, and he paused to appreciate her happy countenance. Was it the mere mention of her ability as a healer that had brought her such pleasure? Her ability meant much to her, and this glowing side of her was something he hoped to see often.

He lowered his lips to hers. Their softness a boon to his own uncertainty and her eager response now, even more so. He pulled her against him where she fit perfectly in his arms. Her softness just the right amount against his own hardness.

When he broke the kiss, he once again struggled to remember why the consummation could not be seen to here. "I've a great need for ye."

"I seem to remember hearing those words afore."

Her light-hearted teasing surprised him. Mayhap she was relieved to hear that he knew healing was important to her, and she would be the clan's primary healer. She did not know him enough to predict what he would say or do. And he did not know those things about her either. They would have to come to know each other in the first few weeks of their marriage. He tipped his head, his eyes narrowing in mock annoyance. "D'ye remember all of that night now?"

"Bits and pieces."

Searching her face, he saw no repulsion. Far from it. Her gaze was intense, searing him all the way to his leather-encased toes, and her arms were wrapped around his middle as if to ensure his closeness. He wished he'd sent Marcán a bit farther away, but surely the man would be respectful after his going on about the importance of the consummation.

"Bits and pieces? Such as?"

"Yer kisses."

The glance at his lips was the only encouragement he needed. His hand at the back of her neck, he drew her lips to his. Sweet. Yielding.

"Yer hand caressing my arm…"

Diarmuid put light fingers to her cheek and dropped them to her arm, sliding his hand along the underside of her wrist.

Aednat's eyes spoke volumes, but she said no more. Still, he remembered what had come next—he'd thought of little else. He dipped to the crook of her neck and tasted her again, his hand sliding up her ribs to cup a breast. "And this?"

Her eyes closed, she nodded, pressing herself more fully into his hand.

"Our joining will not be unpleasant for ye," he whispered in her ear.

Through hooded eyes she gazed at him.

His relief could not be contained, and he kissed her again. Sliding his hands down her back to cup her buttocks, he held her against his stiffened rod.

His tongue sparred with hers while his large hands moved along her body in excruciatingly long strokes, exploring every bit of her. The dip at her back, leading to her well-rounded buttocks, quickly became his favorite route. He couldn't seem to get his fill, that was until he once again grasped one firm globe.

"Ye'll be having me begging if I must wait much longer." His breathless words were met by a smile and her own shaky breath.

If he had her now, it would make the rest of the trip go so much more quickly. Mayhap he was making too much of the when and where. Especially if she was so very willing.

"If taking ye to my bed will rid me of my pursuers, let it be sooner rather than later. And we'll have no need to run away."

The sight of her nipples tightening into little nubs had his mouth watering, hungry for the taste of her. Then her words hit home, and he stilled. He pulled back to search her face, not sure how to respond. She would take him to her bed so they wouldn't have to run away? And then what would she wish to do? Return?

He had given her the option to be brought back to her clan. Was that what she hoped for? For their hasty *urnaidm* to be undone? Diarmuid's agreement with Sean could be easily set aside. A woman had that right.

"Ye have my protection." He released her. "There is no price ye must pay for that."

Moving to his mount, he tucked away the feedbag and went about seeing to the preparations for their ride. He stroked the beast's flank, murmuring quietly. "Easy now. 'Twill be an easier ride today."

Diarmuid refused to acknowledge Aednat's perplexed expression or how forlorn she looked standing there. Her body had heated to his touch, but her calculated response had left him cold. That he had been so easily swayed by her while she had kept a clear focus on *her* intended goal irked him more than it should.

She was correct. The men chasing after her were the only reason they had wed in such haste. And after all the promises he'd made to himself about staying away from marriage, he had been fool enough to think it could be a pleasant joining. Like most women, she was using him. She hadn't used tears to get her way, but manipulation was something she seemed quite adept at. He needn't have worried. She would get along fine with his mother and sister.

<h1 style="text-align:center;font-style:italic">Chapter Nine</h1>

Aednat and Diarmuid had left the ocean behind when they'd crossed the tall, majestic hills of Mayo. Here, the forest was dark and foreboding, and the round tower in the clearing, the only indication of its otherwise hidden inhabitants.

When they reunited with Marcán, he had been joined by a younger man, Faolán, who stumbled over his words every time he spoke to Aednat. She wasn't certain whether his affliction always troubled him, or only when speaking with a woman, but his awkwardness charmed her. She enjoyed his company despite Diarmuid's growl every time she asked him about himself.

As they approached the stone tower, several wattle and daub outbuildings and one larger, cone-topped dwelling came into view.

"Beibhinn!" Diarmuid dismounted and helped her down, keeping his eyes focused on the large roundhouse before them.

"His mother," Marcán explained in response to Aednat's questioning glance.

"Where are they?" Diarmuid grumbled and took off his riding gloves.

"They, being his mother and his sister, Astrid."

She nodded, a smile playing over her lips.

Marcán gestured around the well-maintained gardens and freshly piled peat. "They have been busy whilst we were gone."

"They or someone else," Diarmuid said.

"Astrid alone oversees her garden and well ye know it!"

Diarmuid turned his attention to Aednat. She resisted the urge to pull back at his fierce expression.

"Ye stay here." The words were delivered in a low growl just before he stalked off toward the roundhouse. A small, gray-haired woman stepped out of his way, allowing him entrance, before following him inside.

His irritation had seemed to increase, souring like bad grapes, as the day progressed. She'd been determined to enjoy herself, so she'd talked to Faolán whenever the road widened and they traveled at a slower pace. The young man was quite the storyteller, despite his stuttering, and had given her much information about the different members of the clan, including Maeve, the old healer.

Nigh on sixty summers, Maeve spent most of her time napping. When battles occurred, the warriors often saw to their own wounds rather than awaken her.

At least Diarmuid had not been exaggerating about their clan's need for a healer.

Aednat waited patiently, looking around her. Several cows and goats roamed the area. The large number of animals and outbuildings said much about the clan's wealth, and she couldn't help but be impressed. She received a few curious glances from some of the mothers tending to their duties, their children close at hand.

Marcán began to pace beside her, restless and deep in thought. Stopping finally, he turned his worried gaze on Faolán, who had also dismounted.

"Think ye Diarmuid ordered the cutting of all this peat? After our battles at Comeragh? I do not know how he had time to even consider it."

Faolán smiled, his brown eyes twinkling. "Well, Marcán, mayhap A-A-Astrid has a suitor who sought to w-woo her."

Marcán blushed despite his fierce look. "I think not!"

Faolán remained unaffected. "Why not? A-Astrid is a lovely lass. Quite… desirable."

Aednat took Marcán's darkening scowl as confirmation that Faolán teased him. It was clear Marcán had an interest in Diarmuid's sister.

"Marcán! They're not about, and no one has seen them!" Diarmuid's booming voice carried to them before he even reached the open doorway. "They've been taken."

The trepidation Aednat had been trying so hard to keep at bay came crashing back down on her. Was nowhere safe?

Diarmuid had been on high alert ever since the

roundhouse came into view. His mother would normally have rushed out to greet him, ready to deliver her many complaints while he still sat astride his horse. She was nowhere to be seen.

With no hesitation, Faolán mounted his courser, and Marcán trotted toward the outbuildings.

"I'll check the fields," Faolán said.

Joan, one of the servants, stood in the doorway, the ever-present cloth at her waist. "I heard nothing untoward, but I was busy at my work."

"Rest easy." Diarmuid attempted reassurance despite the increased pounding of his own heart. He scanned the horizon, stepping to the top of the bank enclosing the wide field.

"The sheep are gone." Diarmuid called to Marcán and then ran back into the house for his horn. He emerged with it a moment later and took a long breath and blew into it. And again.

"The Meic Murchadha consider my sheep their sheep." He explained matter-of-factly. "But the women are not."

A gray-speckled horse ridden by two of his servants came into view. "Diarmuid! What is amiss?"

He shook his head until the men dismounted. "My mother and my sister are missing, and so are the sheep."

The freckle-faced man scratched at his head. "I saw the sheep last night but cannot remember if I heard 'em today."

"I'm going to the Meic Murchadha to kick some arses about. They've no right to the women. Get me a fresh mount," Diarmuid said.

The two headed to the stable, and Diarmuid turned to Aednat with a concerned look. It would be too dangerous to bring her, and yet...

"I've no mind to leave ye here unprotected," he said.

"I will not be unprotected. I can defend myself."

Diarmuid scoffed. "And yer weapon?"

Grabbing the bottom edge of her gown, she yanked it to above her knees. There was a wicked-looking dagger tied to her thigh. She gave him a good look at it and then let the material fall back in place. "There."

His face tightened and blood rushed to his manhood at the sight of her shapely legs. Quite naked. Admittedly, it was those lovely thighs that held the most interest, thickening his prick in an instant from the thought of them wrapped around him while he took his pleasure. And yet her expression indicated no such intent. Pride in the weapon and not seduction on her mind. He cleared his throat. "Then ye're well and able to take care of yerself. I wonder why Sean believed ye needed me."

Aednat pressed her lips tightly together. Why was it whenever she demonstrated her willfulness, he found her even more appealing? He'd always told himself he favored docile women.

"Ye think much of yer abilities."

"As well I should. Ye know nothing of what I can do."

The truth of those words stabbed him, deep in his gut. She was a stranger to him. This *wife*. In all ways. Mayhap he was wrong to have waited this long to take her.

"I'll not argue with that. At every turn ye've demonstrated ye're made of stronger stuff than other lasses. Tell me what exactly could ye offer? Can ye set off with me to retrieve our lost flock? Match the men trying to stop us blow for blow?"

One delicate brow raised ever so slightly. "I never claimed I needed special treatment, Diarmuid. However ye have need of me, I am here."

Those words stiffened his cock so fast, it was painful. He closed the distance between them in three strides, pulling her flush against him and claiming her mouth. With his demanding kisses, he went about setting her pulse to racing and scattering her senses. He ground his hips against her, showing her exactly what he needed of her. But when it became apparent that he was muddling his own senses, he released her. He wiped his mouth with the back of his hand, his labored breathing loud in his ears.

"Any questions about my needs?"

Aednat struggled to get her breathing under control. That she was as affected by the kisses as Diarmuid was gave him great satisfaction. Though lying with her would be a worthwhile release for the tension building in his body, there was no time to see to her as he would like. But later. Later he would take her to wife in truth.

When Marcán came around the corner, Aednat turned away and Diarmuid shielded her, giving her a moment to settle herself. But when she turned about and their eyes locked, he gave her a lustful look intended to assure her that he would wait no longer to claim her. Their time had come.

Diarmuid turned to Marcán. That the man was disheveled gave him only a moment's concern. Not so Aednat.

"Ye're a mess!"

"I've checked the hideaway." Marcán spoke to Diarmuid, ignoring Aednat. "They are not within."

The hideaway was a dank hole in the ground at the back of the stable, covered by twigs and hay, which explained the straw sticking from the man's hair.

"How long?" Marcán asked.

As one, the two turned toward the remaining animals. No sheep bleating to be milked or fed.

"It must have been this day. Mayhap very recently," Diarmuid said.

"Then we've no time to waste." Marcán paused, as if just remembering Aednat. "What of yer wife?"

"She assures me she can be of help."

The look she gave him spoke of her pleasure at his words. He sensed her mounting excitement, but he would have to disappoint her. Tough though she may be, he would not put her in danger's way.

"So she will stay behind with Faolán and keep watch," he added, looking at her as he said the words. He stiffened his resolve against her crestfallen expression. "I have no doubt she will be of use here. When the others arrive, have the men remain armed and at the ready."

Once Faolán and Aednat were safely inside the roundhouse, the door barred behind them, Diarmuid headed west with Marcán at his side. They raced across the open field, and Marcán was far enough ahead that Diarmuid had time to think. This abduction could not have come at a worse time. And Meic Murchadha was his mother's own clan, though many of her kin had now passed on. They had undoubtedly been after the sheep, so why take the women as well?

Leaving Aednat behind had grated against his last nerve. She needed him and he had promised to be there for her, so why was he being dragged away?

Because of the leadership he'd never wanted. He had little doubt that both his sister and mother would be unharmed, and the Meic Murchadha would start to wish they'd never taken them.

Pressing forward, Diarmuid came abreast of Marcán just as they broke through the trees again.

"We must be quick about this."

Marcán gave a sharp nod.

"I cannot leave Aednat unprotected."

With nostrils flaring and jaw clenched, his friend finally turned to look at him.

"This might even be some sort of ploy to get me to leave Aednat unprotected," Diarmuid said.

Marcán yanked back the reins with a sudden, forceful jerk. Working to control the confused animal that danced about, he said, "Then *I* will rescue them without ye. *Ye* can go back to yer wife."

Diarmuid stiffened at the angry retort. It was not like Marcán to speak to him in such a disrespectful tone. But he did not even have a chance to reply before Marcán turned the horse around and, with a sharp snap of the reins, lurched ahead.

Diarmuid took a moment to digest the man's behavior. It seemed to affirm his suspicions about his friend's regard for his sister, though Marcán had certainly never shared any such interest with him. Astrid could be whiny and demanding and all the things a warrior should avoid—behaviors she'd learned from their mother, who was never satisfied, critical of everything and everyone.

But Astrid could also be kind and giving. Is that what Marcán saw in her? Did he have the steadfast determination to turn her from the years of training she'd had at Beibhinn's side? Help her become the woman she was meant to be?

Forewarned, he would be prepared for the man when he expressed his interest in Astrid. A better man she would never encounter. Still, Diarmuid would need to see to Marcán's lack of respect. He dug his heels in, paying no heed to the left or the right.

"Diarmuid! Halt!"

Astrid's high-pitched voice carried to him—but Marcán was too far ahead to hear. Diarmuid forced his mount to slow and then retraced his steps. His blond sister lay partially hidden beneath a Rowan tree, her foot at an awkward angle.

"What d'ye here? Have they taken yer mother?" Diarmuid dismounted, shaking his head.

"*Our* mother! That damn feud of yers!" Astrid's normally bright blue eyes were dark as a stormy ocean as she reached up to him. "Give me a hand, will ye? I've broken a bone."

Astrid was accident prone and had been since she was very small, which only made their mother more overbearing in the guise of protection. After their little brother had died, even more so. Diarmuid wrapped an arm about her and dragged her out from beneath the overgrown branches to better see the injury.

"Ye've not answered my question." Irritation made his tone sharp, but he had a gentle touch, squeezing along her calf in search of any hard bulges.

"It may be broken." She sounded convinced of it, but she always thought the worst.

"It may only be twisted," Diarmuid said. Still awaiting her answer, he pierced her with a sharp look.

"Mother has not been taken. She has gone to the brook for some water."

"And who else is with ye?" He glanced around the

area. No horse. No men. "Why did they not go for the water? Or bring ye back home when ye fell? We thought the worst when we came home to no sign of ye."

No answer.

"Ye came alone? The two of ye? Even sharing a mount?"

"Mother does not share well." She blew a breath. "Damn ye, Diarmuid. We're as close to home as we are to the Meic Murchadha!" She averted his eyes. "I'd come to retrieve the sheep they stole in the night."

Diarmuid waited for her to continue. He raised his brows in expectation when she finally turned to him.

"I wanted there to be no reason for ye to take up arms again once ye returned, especially against the Meic Murchadha. I do not want to see our mother more upset." She slapped an irritated hand at her ankle. "Instead, I am nigh unto breaking my neck."

"Our mother is in a constant state of upset."

That was the way she controlled them, making them do her bidding to ease her mind. It was the worst kind of ploy.

"Ye're telling me the two of ye were going to retrieve the sheep?" he pressed. "Alone?"

Her pursed lips and stormy blue eyes were warning enough of the forthcoming tirade. He held up his hand to halt it.

"Glad I am that ye are safe." He glanced toward the path Marcán had disappeared down but saw no sign of him. "And how were ye to retrieve the sheep, just the two of ye?"

"*Ye* took most of the warriors. The others were in the field, Diarmuid. I could not bother them with this, and I was beside myself that they had thought to sneak in and take the beasts when ye were not even here." She dropped her gaze. "Mayhap I thought the Meic Murchadha would see reason."

"Ye thought to charm his son and convince him to go against his father's wishes?"

The slightest shrug was her only answer. She continued to look anywhere but at him.

"Astrid!" He gripped her shoulders, forcing her gaze back to him. "*I* stole the sheep from *them*! Why would they just hand them back to ye?"

"One!" She held up a single finger to emphasize her point, her eyes widening. "Ye stole one sheep from them. *We* delivered the ewes. *We* saw them through the cold nights of spring. They're our sheep now."

"And when I am ready, *I* will retrieve them. Ye should have awaited my return."

"I did not know when ye would return and—"

Diarmuid knew there was more to this than his sister was letting on, but he had not the time nor the inclination to think on that now.

"That is of no matter, Astrid. *Ye* are not *ri túaithe. I* decide how to handle this." Her ankle was indeed bruised and turning black. "I need to get ye back home and out of harm's way first."

"Marcán has gone off on his own!" She raised her voice at him. "Ye cannot just return home and let him see to *yer* business."

"Enough! I do not need ye ordering me about." He stood, towering over her, but despite his anger he managed to keep an even tone. "Glad I am to hear ye understand who should be seeing to this."

Astrid's color darkened. "Ye are right, Diarmuid." She lowered her voice. "But ye must go on ahead. Marcán will only make it worse. He does not get on well with the Meic Murchadha."

He snorted, glancing toward the trail Marcán had taken. "And why would that be?"

Her confused look was almost laughable. Astrid had no idea of her own worth to a man; she was too busy complaining, arguing, and manipulating.

Rather than respond to his question, she said, "Diarmuid, I can see to myself. Mother will be back anon. Catch up to Marcán."

"Again ye think to order me about." He scooped her up into his arms and carried her to his mount. "We will find Marcán—hopefully before he makes it to the Meic Murchadha and stirs up a hornet's nest. It appeared to us as if ye and Beibhinn had been taken along with the sheep."

Astrid gasped, covering her mouth.

"It comes to no good when ye take matters into yer own hands." Her sudden pallor caused his sympathy to rise. "Ye are a good woman, sister, but yer impulsiveness may be the death of me."

As was normally the case, any show of sympathy received the same reaction, her quivering lips.

Chapter Ten

Smoke drifted through the opened door when Diarmuid approached the roundhouse well after moonset. Meeting Marcán on his return from the Meic Murchadha, the sheep in tow, had been quite a surprise. Apparently his friend had demanded the return of the women and the sheep so fiercely, the Meic Murchadha had been too afeared not to give up the animals. And since they'd known nothing about Astrid or Beibhinn's whereabouts and had not wanted anything else laid at their feet, they'd offered the assistance of several men, including the young Meic Murchadha, Pádraig, to contribute to the search effort.

Astrid's injury had ensured a flurry of attention was directed her way. That had delighted their mother to no end since she, too, basked in the attention of the young men jumping to do her daughter's bidding. When the Meic Murchadha had invited them to come to their home and discuss the sheep, Marcán and Pádraig had nearly come to blows over who would assist Astrid. Both had vied for the opportunity to take her on their own mount for the short ride back to the Meic Murchadha's home. It had been almost laughable. Laughable until Diarmuid had realized it would be up to him as her king to see to any match. This would have been a most opportune time to observe the men and consider their worthiness as possible husbands. He'd want to make a good match for her, but he'd bowed out.

He needed to return to Aednat. He expected none of them back until the day next.

After seeing to his horse at the stable, Diarmuid realized he was dead on his feet. The few men he passed along the way to the roundhouse were sent off to their beds. He assured them he could see to his own needs this night. It was what he preferred.

Despite the late hour, exuberant laughter carried to him from the roundhouse, putting him in a foul mood. Faolán and Aednat's laughter. None of the men he'd seen had mentioned his new bride or his newly married condition. Had Aednat and Faolán neglected to explain the situation to anyone? And he had not shared it with Beibhinn or Astrid. Keeping his bride to himself for a while suited him fine.

Diarmuid entered unnoticed and dipped his hands into the waiting basin by the door. They spoke in hushed tones now, mayhap out of consideration for the others abed along the walls. His bride was being entertained by young Faolán's stories. The hint of a smile tipped up those full lips as she worked on kneading a lump of dark bread dough, her bright eyes darting from the dough to the lad's expressive face, enraptured by his storytelling. As she leaned into the dough with the heel of her hand, her shoulder pushed forward, rewarding Diarmuid with the slightest glimpse of cleavage betwixt her luscious breasts. That Faolán looked to be noticing the same irritated him even more.

"'Twas not all his doing."

They both laughed very hard. Faolán doubled over where he sat on the bench an arm's length from Aednat.

"Faolán?"

Faolán nearly toppled the bench when he stood, his face a dark red. "Diarmuid! I—I did not hear ye come in."

Diarmuid took a menacing step closer. "So I gathered. And who would this 'his' be?"

"Have y-ye found yer mother so soon?"

"I have. Marcán is seeing to them now. No need for alarm." Diarmuid dried his hands on a cloth and walked leisurely into the warm room. "And this man ye are telling tales about?"

"I-I-I was telling A-A-Aednat about w-winter last when ye fell on yer arse a-as ye were r-reprimanding me."

Diarmuid pursed his lips in consideration. It was that or throttle the man. "I remember it well. The ice. Was it not? The reason I fell on my arse?"

Faolán nodded and backed toward the door, far out of Diarmuid's reach. "That is the w-w-way it-it was. The i-i-ice. Ye slipped."

"And whose duty was it to rid us of that ice?" Diarmuid scrunched up his face as if trying to remember.

Faolán averted his gaze. "Mine."

"And yet ye find humor in the incident? Would it be so humorous had it been my mother or Maeve who'd fallen?"

"Never would I wish for such a thing as that." Faolán stood at the door. "Beg pardon. I-I-I will see to the ani-animals."

Diarmuid watched him go and considered following him out for the sound thrashing he deserved. He'd given the lad an important task, the most important task, and he'd used it as an opportunity to belittle his leader and get an eyeful of his new wife. He blew out a breath and when he turned to face her, he was met by narrowed eyes.

"Did ye need to chase him off?"

He crossed his arms. "I did."

"He wished to ease my nervousness with ye."

"And how did he know of yer nervousness? Did ye share that with him?"

Aednat looked away. "I did not. I might have mentioned yer size—"

"Ye spoke to Faolán about my size?"

Continuing with her kneading, she snorted. "Ye are quite big."

Diarmuid's lip curled, but he remained quiet.

"I wondered if all the men here were so large and..."

"And?" He quirked a brow.

"He said ye are the only man of such a great size." Her tone was exceedingly irritated. "He did not want me to be frightened by ye, no doubt."

"No doubt." Diarmuid nodded, a somber expression. "And yet I remember ye slapping me across the face the very first time we met. Not exactly afeared of me."

She finally looked at him.

"And I did not share that with him." She whacked the dough again.

He tipped his head. "Wise of ye."

The patting continued and he stepped closer for a better view. More than a handful, those lovely breasts. He would take his time with them, paying each the homage it deserved.

"He had no way of knowing I am not."

"No. Ye are not." He held her gaze, wanting to reach out and touch her, wanting to feel the heavy weight of those breasts in his hands. As if realizing that, she turned away. Reluctantly, Diarmuid settled into the vacated spot.

"*A thighearna?*" A woman wrapped tightly in bedclothes approached, wiping sleep from her eyes. "Is there ought ye need?"

Diarmuid gave the woman a cursory glance and said, "Return to sleep, Eibhlín. I have all I need."

The table was covered with the remains from chopped vegetables, an opened sack of ground wheat, and a cup of water.

"Have ye done all of this? Put all of this together?" he asked.

Aednat nodded.

"And Faolán did not tell ye that I do not stay here? That I have my own hearth?"

She froze, her eyes shooting daggers. "He did not!"

"D'ye see now why I took offense? Faolán is not the kind, innocent man he pretends to be."

Aednat glared at the door. If Diarmuid believed in the evil eye, he'd expect young Faolán to have a mishap at any moment.

Diarmuid picked up a wayward piece of a turnip end and nibbled on it. "If ye believe he needs encouragement to get his mouth into trouble, ye are mistaken. His stuttering is barely noticed by us, but he does like to start trouble anywhere he can."

"I… I did not realize."

"And did ye not realize the wife of a king does not bake bread?"

"I have always helped, and I wanted to get ye something hot to eat for when ye returned." She ladled out a serving of warm stew from an iron pot beside the fire.

"My thanks," he said, taking it form her.

The tasty broth settled nicely in his empty stomach, and her soft expression kindled the warmth seeping through his tired limbs. She slapped the bread into a round pan and placed it beside the fire.

"But ye are the wife of their king. As such, ye may use any hearth ye choose. And what ye make may go anywhere ye choose. Even yer own house."

"My own house?" Her eyes twinkled in the firelight.

"Much smaller than this. In truth, much more private. One ye share with me." An unexpected shiver of excitement traveled to his groin. Setting the empty wooden bowl on the table, he extended a hand. "Come."

Before she took it, she wiped her own hand on the cloth at her waist, which she then left on the table.

He led her through the doors, hand in hand, his tiredness forgotten and excitement racing through his body.

Aednat remained a step behind, whether from fear or fatigue, he wasn't sure. He stopped to scoop her up into his arms, and she clung to his neck. "Are ye destined to carry me everywhere?"

"I wish to be alone with ye, wife." He kissed her tenderly. She shivered. "We've things to see to."

Following the path that looped around the roundhouse, he bore left and away from the other buildings, making his way onto a less-worn path that dipped between the trees. The sudden darkness increased his anticipation. He hoped it would be the same for her and nuzzled beneath her ear. His steps quickened. The small longhouse of stone, nearly blending in with its surroundings, came into view.

"I have not been here of late." Try as he might, he couldn't remember the condition of the interior the last time he'd been home. Had there been a leak? Or a puddle? His servant, Fionnlagh, was not overly ambitious, and Diarmuid had never been bothered by it. He might need to rethink that now.

After setting her down on the doorstep, Diarmuid shoved the door open and was met with a damp chill. Aednat preceded him inside.

"*A thighearna?*" Fionnlagh was quick to jump up from his pallet against the wall in the corner. "I did not hear yer approach."

Fionnlagh set about blowing the fire aflame. That accomplished, he lowered the torch from its bracket and lit it before returning it to the wall. "I beg forgiveness for my idleness. I did not expect ye back so quickly—"

His jaw dropped as he took in the sight of Aednat. The white-haired man's shocked expression was humorous, but he quickly recovered, lowering his gaze. "…or that ye would not be alone."

Diarmuid had always preferred to keep his home a

place for seclusion, not even bringing women here. He imagined the man's mind was working through a hundred different scenarios.

"This is my wife," he said, giving him a reprieve. "Aednat." The man's jaw dropped again, his eyes widening. He was quite speechless.

Aednat dipped her head in recognition but looked to be holding back a grin.

"Be easy, Fionnlagh. Go. Sleep with the others. I will see to my own needs. I wish to be alone with my bride."

"As ye will." Fionnlagh closed the door quietly behind him without so much as a backward glance. A good man, he would not return to Diarmuid until he was ordered back. He would also refrain from sharing their king's change in status until given leave to do so.

Diarmuid approached the hearth, rubbing his hands together and glancing around. Once the stone heated, the inside would be exceedingly comfortable. The walls were decorated with colorful tapestries in bright shades of red, green, and blue to keep the drafts out and the warmth in. He kept his eye on Aednat as she perused the single room, her arms wrapped about her.

"Are ye cold, Aednat?"

"I am fine." She rubbed her arms as she spoke, not looking directly at him.

"The stone quickly heats."

She paused to look more closely at the tapestries, even lifting a corner of one as if to see how it was made. The scenes of fjords and ice rather than the traditional forest and ocean must be strange to her.

"A gift to my grandfather from one of his Viking friends."

"They're lovely." She gave him a cursory glance. "And yer mother and sister? They are safe?"

"They are. They'd not been taken after all, but had thought to retrieve the missing sheep themselves."

Aednat turned a sharp eye on him, but he only smiled. "Then Astrid had a fall instead. She'll be fine."

"A fall? Should I see to her?"

Her expectant look nearly crushed him. Seduction was the only thing on his mind, and getting that lovely dress off was first on his list. He closed the distance to her, a hand to her cool cheek. "They are fine. Ye will meet them when 'tis time and not before."

When he moved in to kiss her, her wide eyes drifted closed. The yielding softness of those lips only made him more hungry for her. He wrapped his arm around her, pulling her flush against him. Despite an instant desire to grope that lovely arse, he resisted, deciding slow would be best. That her arms went willingly around his middle gave him definite hope that his abstinence was about to end.

Diarmuid broke the kiss and looked into her eyes. "I did not get to tell ye how lovely ye look in that silken *léine*."

Aednat blushed and smiled. A bashful smile. It gave him pause.

"Has no one told ye how pleasant ye are to look upon?"

"No." She nibbled at her lower lip before raising her eyes back to his face. "Not like that."

"Like what?"

"Like ye would prefer it no longer be on me." Her lips parted and she took a slow intake of air, letting it out slowly. "As if ye'd like to eat me up."

Diarmuid's chest tightened and he held her gaze.

"And so I would."

Ever so slight the gesture, she moved toward his lips. His exaltation could not be contained, and he took her mouth with exquisite tenderness, showing her the subtle language of a kiss while he denied his hands the access they sought. She bloomed before him, wrapping an arm around his neck and setting his lust aflame with her own pleasurable response.

Afraid he may ignite within her very grasp, he broke the kiss. She looked bewildered and opened her eyes as if she'd been somewhere else.

It took a moment for Aednat to break through the haze in her mind. His kisses had been that delightful.

"Yer embrace sets me on fire." His husky voice reverberated through her, pressed tightly together as they were. Just as his lips had sent heat to her nether regions.

"Why did ye stop?" Her face heated as soon as the question came out. Certainly that was not a proper question for her to be asking.

But Diarmuid smiled, his eyes creasing at the corners, easing her embarrassment.

"Sweet Aednat, ye learned too quickly how to set me aflame with yer mouth. And yer tongue." He groaned, tracing her lips with a single finger. "I had wanted us to move slowly in our passion."

Aednat's heart skipped a beat and she broke the contact between them. She had enjoyed his kisses. His gentle encouragement that she take over the kissing had excited her, and she knew by now how much she loved the feel of his hands on her, but lying with him…

She averted her eyes.

With a finger to her chin, Diarmuid turned her face

back to him. His gaze searching her own.

"Oh, my passionate love." He shook his head. "Ye have nothing to fear from me. Ever." His gaze traced her length, settling on her breasts, which suddenly seemed very heavy. Looking to one then the other before returning to her face, he swallowed. "I am a patient man, but I am a man."

The simple words set her pulse to racing, and her lips parted to ease her breath. She almost reached for him, but her body tensed.

Diarmuid must have recognized it because he closed his eyes and took a shaky breath. He put space between them, leaning against the wall opposite the table. She settled on the bench between the tall wooden trestle and the fire, rubbing her hands before tucking them between her legs.

Glancing about the room, she took in the tapestries again before shifting her gaze to the assortment of clay jars covering the shelf beneath, the weapons that looked quite old, and the bed. Raised on a platform and covered with bed linens, wool blankets, and a finely stitched coverlet of red squirrel that reached to the floor. She was struck again by his great wealth.

It wouldn't do to stare at the bed now, so she shifted her attention to the weapons.

"This is the home my grandfather built when he lived here with his Gaelic wife," Diarmuid said softly. "My grandmother." He crossed his arms about his chest. "He was a Jarl—very powerful—but he chose to remain here with her rather than return to his home with the Vikings." He glanced around. "A quiet home where they could be together. Raise a family. God willing, grow old together."

One weapon in particular demanded closer

inspection, and she went to it. She turned a questioning glance on him.

Diarmuid chuckled. "That is a weapon I do not understand myself." He came closer, his fingers brushing against hers as he removed the arm-length blade from her hand. "The design makes little sense." He held it up, showing the curve to better advantage. "Mayhap someday I will return to the land of my grandfather and ask them."

"Would ye really go so far as that?"

He shrugged. "Mayhap."

She wet her lips before sinking her teeth into the bottom one. He took her hand with a light touch and stepped back to extend her arm. "Now show me again this weapon of yers."

He released her hand and his gaze deepened in its intensity.

With no forethought, she reached down to pull up her gown just high enough to show the dagger wrapped around her thigh.

"Oh, sweet Aednat, please"—he indicated the bench—"sit. No! Do not drop yer skirt." He settled on his haunches before her. His large hand firmly covered hers, which gripped the material, keeping it just above the knees. The material rubbed along her leg as he pushed it higher. "Allow me to inspect it."

"But—"

A finger to her lips quieted her, and the touch of his hands gliding along her bare calves was excruciatingly pleasurable. While he watched her face, his eyes hooded, she struggled not to reveal her own desire for him lest he take her for a wanton and lose interest.

She could not have been more wrong.

Chapter Eleven

Diarmuid found his wife's passion to be much greater than he had ever dared hope—and yet she resisted her attraction to him, mayhap from fear. He needed to set that to rest. The mead sat just a few feet from the door even now, but he preferred she be overcome with passion and desire, not sotted with drink.

The silk of her skin beckoned to him. A hand beneath one knee, he gently lifted her leg enough so that he could slide his hands to where the *miodóg* lay against her thigh, held by a leather strap. With a gentle tug, the blade fell into his hand and he tossed the strap onto the table. She watched him silently.

"A formidable weapon." And he was not flattering her. He'd never seen a more well-made blade. He glanced at her. "From Sean?"

She beamed a smile and his breath caught.

"He had it made especially for me," she said.

Struggling with an unfounded bolt of jealousy, he realized from whence it had sprung. *He* wanted to be the one to put that look of absolute adoration on her face. "Very nice."

A glance back at her bared legs and his focus returned to seduction. Hidden in the shadows of her skirt was his final destination, but the red and puckered skin where the dagger had been secured to her skin required his immediate attention. He gripped the one thigh, massaging against the soreness the strap must have left in its wake.

"Does this please ye?"

"It pleases me." She winced. "I did not realize how tightly I'd tied it. I was in a bit of a hurry that morning."

His fingertips raked the skin, then pressed into it, edging into a larger circle, his eyes never leaving her face. "And why were ye in such a hurry?"

"To see ye of course."

Diarmuid's hand stopped. This would be the morning after their meeting in the woods... and the mushrooms. "Why would ye seek me out?"

Aednat turned away, her eyes finding the tapestries once again very interesting, but the color spreading across her cheeks and down her neck was sending a deliciously wicked sensation to his already hard arousal.

"Aednat?" He dared not remove his hand, but he did come up on his knees, pressing his chest against her so that his face was on level with hers. "Did ye seek me out because ye wished to spar with me?"

With a loud whoosh, she turned to face him. "I'd had the most intriguing dreams of us, and I wanted to see if ye were truly as handsome as I'd dreamed ye."

His breath stilled. More affected than he should be by her words, he grabbed her hips to slide her bottom closer to him, effectively placing himself exactly where he wanted to be. "Let me love ye, Aednat."

"Will ye steal my power?"

"Never! And if it comes on me, I promise to give it back to ye."

She closed the small distance to his mouth, her arms going around his shoulders to pull him against her. Her tongue danced with his as he sought to devour her. She pressed her breasts toward him, as if begging for their turn with his mouth. He did not disappoint, sucking one of her nipples through the silky material, tonguing it into a firm nub. His hands gripped her tighter until the apex of her legs was at his chest. The scent of her desire a sweet boon.

Dropping his mouth to one of her knees, he lifted her foot to rest on his thigh as he stroked the sensitive skin with his tongue. He traced along her inner thigh, pushing the material of her gown even higher as he went. Turning aside, he did the same with the other leg, moving slightly closer to her heat.

Before she had been pressing toward him like a nursing kitten and pulling him closer into her body, but it suddenly broke into his lust-fogged mind that she'd gone completely still. Her eyes downcast, she had ceased all motion.

He took a shaky breath and dropped to his haunches to search her face. "What is amiss, *a ghrádh*? Did I hurt ye?"

She shook her head, adamantly, but still refused to

face him.

"Then where is my fiery lover?"

That earned him a quick smile. Surely she was not upset with him. Her slippered feet still rested on his thighs. He had one idea. Going to her crippled foot first, he kept an eye on her face while he unlaced her footwear as he had done that first night. With a gentle tug, her foot was bared. He lifted the heel to his mouth and kissed it even as her eyes widened and her mouth opened in protest.

"Do not!"

He raised a hand. "D'ye tell me I may not lavish my love on my bride? I may not enjoy every bit of her?"

Her eyes narrowed as she considered his question. And while she watched him, he took her misshapen heel to his mouth and kissed it again, intently rubbing it with his thumb the way she liked. Closing his own eyes in enjoyment, he pressed it to his face, only turning back to find tears in her eyes.

"Is there pain?"

She shook her head, pressing her foot back down, and pushed herself onto his lap, hugging him as if she never meant to let him go. Her quiet sobs tugged at his heart.

"Look at me, Aednat."

Withdrawing slightly, she wiped at her nose and faced him.

"There is nothing about ye that is not beautiful. If anyone has told ye otherwise, they lied."

"I… I was cast out by my grandfather because of my foot. My mother and father died when I was very young. My grandparents were all that I had. They were my family. I think he had hoped I would die living in that cave."

Diarmuid stopped her hand just short of slapping her foot and shook his head. "Then yer grandfather was a fool! I have no shame in ye."

Aednat's expression softened and she kissed him. A passionate kiss. Her lips were soft, enticing, and she arched into him again.

He moaned. "I wish to make love to my wife."

"Take me." Her whispered words sent his heart soaring.

He pulled her to him, crushing her breasts against him before relaxing his hold enough to gather her into his arms. Setting her down on the side of the bed, he knelt behind her. He rubbed her shoulders with gentle hands, brushing her dark hair aside for better access to her long, elegant neck. When he kissed her there, she shivered and he slid his large hands along her arms, squeezing as he went.

His face close to her ear, he leaned forward and whispered, "Mayhap it is the cold that makes ye shiver. Mayhap it is yer own need for me."

She exhaled a loud breath. With a cupped hand he grasped one breast and then the other, nuzzling her neck again.

"Such lovely breasts." He whispered the words, and for a moment he wondered at his intense need for this woman. If this need persisted, how could he ever leave her? Even to see to his duties? "This gown has to go."

Together they removed the floor-length *léine*. As she stood naked in front of him, he feasted on the treasures before him. With little urging, she lay across the bed. Whipping his own shorter tunic over his head, he lowered himself over her, settling between her parted legs. His heavy cock was stiff with need and rubbed against her. The slickness of her entry was deceivingly inviting, but there would be pain this first time. There were men who thought it entertaining to deflower as many lasses as they could find, but Diarmuid usually preferred a woman with a bit more experience. One who knew what she wanted.

Looking into those mesmerizing eyes, he realized he'd found just what he'd unknowingly sought. He gripped one plump, glorious breast and traced it with his tongue, before suckling her. His other hand slipped lower, seeking her heat. Her moisture covered his fingers and he groaned. "Had I more time, I would show ye what a feast I could make of ye."

As if in answer, her hips rose to meet his hand and he slipped a finger into her wetness. She undulated against him, his need became unbearable. He wanted to ride her, long and hard, giving in to his desire. But he stilled and turned his head. She was a virgin, and he mustn't let her passionate response cause him to forget that. With a deep, steadying breath, he withdrew his hand and replaced it with his ready prick just at her entrance, praying again for control.

"A sting is all." He whispered the words right before his quick thrust tore her maidenhead.

Her hips stilled, and he looked into her eyes.

"There will be no more pain." He waited for her to release the breath she held. "Only pleasure."

"Are ye certain?"

"I am quite certain."

She exhaled slowly, and he gave in to the sweetest sensation of her tight grip around his cock. Exquisite. He would die if he didn't press into her, fully sheathing himself, and relish the pleasurable tautness.

It required all his concentration not to move. He dipped his head into her neck, a slow exhale.

"Oh, dear God in heaven. Is there pain?" He moved ever so slightly into that depth of bliss, then a bit more, before withdrawing.

Lifting his head, he watched her intently for any sign of discomfort. He eased into her again more fully, moving slowly. She inhaled and nodded, ever so slightly, as if giving her consent. He continued to press into her until he was completely surrounded by her warmth. And again. He exhaled slowly even as his need increased. When her breath quickened with his, he moved more insistently, steadily driving into her.

More than anything else he wanted to give her pleasure, so he kept a tight rein on his passion, reveling in the way her mouth opened in a silent moan each time he entered her. And when he withdrew? Her fingers gripped his shoulders as if to pull him back. And he obliged, entering her a little differently each time. Harder. Slower. Deeper. Her high-pitched breathing was loud in his ear as she moved closer to her release.

"Sweet Aednat," he whispered before flicking his tongue against her lobe at the same time he quickened his movements. "Let me know yer pleasure."

She made a guttural sound, her body relaxing, throbbing around him. And he impaled her depths repeatedly, prolonging her climax and ignoring his great need until he could hold back no longer. He pumped into her with deep, fast thrusts, then stilled, his heartfelt moan of pleasure surrounding them at his release.

Spent, he rolled onto his back, pulling her with him. He pressed her close to his side. A new experience for the man who usually couldn't get up and away quickly enough. Even exhausted, he wanted her near to him. He sighed in contentment, despite his strange musings, and kissed the top of her head.

"And how is that bump on yer hard head?"

She made some unintelligible sound, and he wasn't convinced she was still awake.

"Ye were killing me, setting me off each time this lovely round arse rubbed against me." He spoke in a quiet voice, reaching low to grip one firm cheek. "Ye were keeping me ready for ye."

Aednat made a sound that could have been a giggle or a snore.

And he was hard for her again in an instant. "And I want ye now, too."

He'd hoped to be able to set aside his need for her, at least for a little while, once he'd lain with her. It was not to be the case. She snuggled closer. Was she asleep or giving her consent? What was she thinking? What she was feeling? He wanted to know it all.

He dragged a hand over her hair, reveling in its silky texture, the sweet scent of lavender surrounding him.

"I'd never thought to take a wife." Rubbing the ends of her hair against his cheek, he continued his quiet words. "I am a solitary man. Except for my love of war and women, I could have been a monk. What need have I for a wife?"

"Or I for a husband?"

She startled him. Pausing before resuming his caresses, he tried to imagine why she would feel that way. He had thought every woman longed for a man to see to her needs. How else would they have children? A home of their own? For protection, if nothing else.

"Ye took care of Sean's children?"

She nodded.

"And ye never wanted children of yer own?"

She shrugged. "No one wanted to marry a woman whose body was not sound."

Diarmuid scoffed. "Pleased I am to hear how stupid the men in yer clan are."

She propped herself up and looked down into his face, her long hair, whisper soft, falling across his bare chest. "Ye are not afeard we will have children who are not sound?"

"It matters not! *We* will make them strong."

He pushed her hair from her face. A plump breast pressed into him. Bone weary though he was, the sight of her continued to stir him.

Aednat held his gaze, her eyes intent on him. "I am pleased with ye as my husband."

Did that mean she would stay with him? Marriages were governed by their law, not the church, and divorce was allowed at will. Was she giving her consent to the marriage after all?

"Happy I am to hear ye say that." He offered a quiet smile. "Mayhap I will not be a good husband." Pulling her face closer, he traced the line of her jaw to follow it to her lips and kissed her gently. "But I assure ye, I am a most diligent lover."

His hand cupping her neck, he drew her lips to his, determined to demonstrate the truthfulness of his words.

Chapter Twelve

The incessant knocking woke Diarmuid from a very relaxing sleep. His wife nestled against him, setting off an urge to wake her for more lovemaking. Still, the pounding continued. Aednat stretched her limbs. The sight enchanted him, one arm bent to her neck, and the rest of her nakedness sleek before him. He had taken the few minutes after that first time to provide her with water and carefully put away the bed sheet, storing the proof that she was a virgin no longer. She had shown her appreciation for his consideration. Appreciation she had not needed to show, but that he had enjoyed just the same. A passionate woman indeed.

And the pounding continued.

"Argh!" Diarmuid wanted to break some heads,

starting with his visitor. "Who is knocking?"

He grabbed his *léine* on the way to the door and then yanked the door open to his startled sister. Despite the shock on her face, it troubled him not in the least that he stood there naked.

"I see I have interrupted ye." She pointed to his rod. "Ye know I would not wake ye but for a good reason." She frowned. "And who have ye *here* to be in that condition?"

She pushed past him, searching out his house until she caught sight of Aednat, who had rolled away from the door and nodded back to sleep, her bare bottom peeking out from beneath the fur coverlet.

Astrid turned on him with wide eyes. "What have ye here indeed! Did ye steal a woman?"

Diarmuid yanked the knee-length tunic over his head before answering. "My wife. What d'ye here?"

"A wife? D'ye jest?" Astrid's expression of disbelief became quite comical. She even covered her mouth as if she were too shocked to even laugh. So Marcán had left it to him to share his news.

He waited for her to cease the hubbub, but she had more to say.

"Tell me true, brother. Who would wed *ye*?"

"I would," Aednat's quiet voice was a boon to Diarmuid. His appreciation of his new wife doubled with that answer, and he looked forward to demonstrating that to her. With only the bedclothes to cover her, he moved to block Astrid's inspection.

"Convinced?" Diarmuid asked Astrid. "So I ask ye again, what d'ye here?"

"What?" Astrid's confusion faded. "They have not returned. Neither the sheep nor the men."

"I left ye all there with the Meic Murchadha."

Securing his scabbard to his belt, he sheathed his sword and headed out the door. Astrid followed close behind, but before they made it more than a few steps, he stopped in his tracks. Retracing his path, he sat down on the side of the bed and caressed Aednat's cheek. She smiled. A lazy, satisfied smile.

"Good morning, *grádh*." He touched his lips to hers, still swollen from their earlier lovemaking. "Sleep if ye can. I will be back anon."

"Kiss me again." She wrapped her arms around him and they exchanged a tender moment.

Diarmuid had the strange sensation of being where he belonged. He pulled away, disturbed by the thought.

"If I am not to return anon, I will see that ye are not starving. I want ye well rested." He quirked a brow. "Just do not set foot outside this house."

Her eyes widened at the order. "Why ever not?"

"Because I want ye here, just like this." He tugged at the thin material she used as a shield, tightly tucked around her nakedness.

Diarmuid tensed as he watched the warring emotions dance across her face. When her lips curled up and her eyes creased with her genuine smile, he was relieved that her desire to please him won out. She would be safe.

"I will be here," she said.

He kissed her, crushing her against his chest, in a silent reminder of what he would be returning for as soon as he was able.

Astrid waited outside the door, a hand to her mouth and an expression of disbelief still on her face. "I cannot believe ye've married."

Diarmuid strode past her, intent on getting to the

stable and securing a horse. "Tell me how ye were separated. Did Marcán not return with ye?"

But she wasn't behind him. He'd forgotten about her injury and stopped to wait for her. She hobbled along, working to avoid stepping on her bad foot. When she winced in pain, he was reminded that his wife may know what to do to ease her pain. He put a fist to his hip.

"If I trusted ye, I would send ye back to Aednat."

Astrid stopped, a scowl on her face. "Ye do not trust me?"

"Ye will tell her all my failings and speak of things only a sister would know."

She hobbled past him. "I would enjoy telling those stories."

"Harrumph." Diarmuid had a sudden twinge of guilt. "Wait! Wait, Astrid."

She turned to face him, her wide blue eyes deceptively innocent.

"Tell me how ye came to be here ahead of Marcán."

"Pádraig brought me back."

His sister averted her eyes as she said it. Not a good sign. Diarmuid crossed his arms and studied her.

"Alone?" he pressed.

"We were on a horse!"

He nodded. Slowly. Allowing that I-know-what-ye're-not-saying look to take over. That expression she no doubt knew very well. "And did ye kiss him back?"

Her jaw dropped right before she slammed it shut. He could almost hear the sound of her teeth grinding, but he did not waver. Neither in his expression nor in his stance. He did not need his sister getting with child before she was taken to wife. Finally he spoke.

"Then ye must have enjoyed it."

Rather than respond to his accusation, she went on the offensive. "Marcán has been rude to me, acting like he is my king. I'll not stand for it."

"Not stand for it? If Marcán was protecting ye, I'll have to thank him since I should have been there myself. What were ye thinking, Astrid?"

Tears trickled down her cheeks and her chin quivered. "I do not understand how he could be so unkind to me. And in front of others."

"I'll not speak a word against the man, Astrid. Ye should think on what ye were doing for him to behave in such a way."

Her eyes rounded, but he pressed on.

"Marcán would never belittle ye. He's a good man, but he will protect ye even from yerself. If any of the lads there thought to make free with ye and he believed 'twas yer behavior encouraging them? He'd not just stand by and watch."

"Of course ye take his side."

"But I cannot understand why he allowed ye to go off with Pádraig alone."

Astrid tightened her lips, and she mimicked his stance, placing her fists on her hips. "I was not so obvious as that! I snuck off with him."

"And that confession will get ye a sore arse upon my return." He tossed her over his shoulder despite her objections and headed back to the stone house. A hard smack to that area had little effect on her flailing slaps and punches, let alone her complaints. "Ye'll return to my wife, and I will go to the Meic Murchadha. If all ye've said is true, something is still amiss, as Marcán has not yet returned with the others.

Ye best pray no offense has been taken and no blood has been spilled on account of ye."

The struggling ceased immediately, and she hung limp down his back. Out of consideration for her, he set her back on her shaky feet before going inside.

"Oh, Diarmuid, I would be beside myself if any blood was shed on account of me." Her sincere expression was convincing. "Please! Go bring Marcán back."

Marcán, was it? And no concern for Pádraig? Interesting.

"No doubt I will find them all passed out from overindulgence, and I will bring them home myself. The men, our mother, and the sheep. Ye will see my wife, the healer, and she will help lessen yer pain."

"She is a healer?"

Opening the door to find Aednat dressed in her gown, her feet still bare, dampened Diarmuid's exuberance a bit. "Astrid, meet my wife, Aednat." He stepped closer, lowering his voice. "We must discuss yer insolence. It pleased me to think ye awaited me in the bed. Naked."

Her eyes wide with innocence, she said, "I am here as I said."

He scowled, still addressing her. "*For now* ye may see to my sister's ankle while I retrieve the sheep and locate the men! Both of ye stay inside!"

When Diarmuid shut the door behind him, the walls seemed to close in on Aednat. Astrid's eyes took in all of her, and she was grateful she'd thought to dress, even if her husband was not.

"I am very glad ye have wed my brother," Astrid said at last, crossing her arms.

"Oh?"

"I thought he would never find a woman who could overlook his many faults."

"Has he so many?"

"Ahh!" Astrid poured it on thick, her expression one of sheer disgust. "Too many to speak of, but ye will learn about them all yerself, I am certain."

Aednat held back a grin. "I am certain."

Astrid finally broke into laughter and Aednat joined her.

Astrid said, "I must tease him even if he is not here to witness it." Wiping the tears from her eyes, she offered a genuine smile to Aednat. "Ye are very beautiful. He must have been pleased to take ye to wife."

"I do not know." Heat crept up her neck. "In truth, he did not have much of a choice."

Astrid gasped. "Tell me he was chivalrous with ye."

"He was! He just did not have a chance to say no. 'Twas for my protection. Sean—"

"Sean of Drogheda?"

"He *was* of Drogheda."

"Ah, I forget. I have not seen him much of late. He has always spent more time with my brother. How fares he? Is Thomasina big with child?"

"She is not. Lorccán is their last, and he is nigh on six years now." Sadness washed over her at the thought of Lorccán, but she tried to hide it. Even if she might never see him again and hadn't gotten a chance to say goodbye, she needed to be content that she was indeed safe.

Astrid sighed and settled on the bench as she spoke. "When I was very young, our clans would gather for celebrations. That was when my father was still alive. But I am not allowed far from here now. My mother keeps me close to her side. I also think Diarmuid does not trust me to not make a fuss. He leaves me behind for his own peace."

When she lifted her gown and revealed her wrapped ankle, Aednat gasped. "Who has done this to ye?" She turned the leg just the slightest bit to see the dirty, saggy covering that had been wrapped far too loosely around Astrid's ankle. "This is not the way to help it mend."

"Meic Murchadha's healer covered it up."

"May I see it?"

Astrid nodded.

Layer by layer, Aednat unwrapped her leg. "Does it hurt?"

The ankle was purple and black. It had to hurt, but Astrid only shrugged. "I am often hurting myself. My mother says I am clumsy."

After soaking the wounded ankle in water from just outside the door, Aednat set it with a firm binding soaked in spearmint oils she found amongst the jars. "That should ease the aching."

Astrid rubbed the covering. "A much better job than the Meic Murchadha's healer."

"Did she put anything on it?"

Astrid shook her head. "She was more interested in speaking of God's curse on me, saying it was my behavior alone that caused me to have so many accidents."

Many believed the terrible things that happened to people were because God was angry and they needed to repent. "Mayhap ye need to be more careful."

"According to her, 'tis irrelevant whether I'm

careful or not." Her expression softened. "D'ye believe it as well? That God is angry with me?"

"I do not know how God feels, but were ye walking at a steady pace? Was the ground sound beneath yer feet?"

"Oh, no. I was hurrying along the sheep trail that connects our land with the Meic Murchadha."

"Rutted? And well worn?"

Astrid nodded.

"Then it would seem ye put yerself in harm's way by not giving the path the diligence it required."

Astrid wrapped her arms tightly around Aednat. "My thanks! I do not like to think God is angry with me whenever something bad happens."

Hugging her back, Aednat said, "Is yer behavior so terrible that ye deserve God's wrath?"

Astrid shook her head and pulled away. "No! It's just that—" She wiped her tears before continuing. "I am of marriageable age… and… well, I wish to be married! Why would my brother not see to it? Am I never to be a wife?"

Aednat guessed Astrid was younger than herself, but if truth be told, she would have thought about marriage long before now had she not been so certain her crippled foot would make her undesirable as a wife. She had convinced herself not to want what she thought she could not have.

"D'ye seek out men on yer own then?"

"I enjoy their attention when they talk to me, but they seldom do."

"And all ye do is talk?"

Astrid's eyes widened. "I remain untouched!"

Aednat wondered why a woman as beautiful as Astrid, with her long blond hair and bright blue eyes, was not fighting off droves of interested warriors. Then again, it would be Diarmuid doing the fighting. She suddenly understood the girl's dilemma. It was her brother she needed to convince she was ready to be wed. No doubt he was putting off any interested men with a fierce growl.

"For good measure, go to the priest with yer confession, and be sure Diarmuid is aware of it." Aednat grinned. "And be more careful of yerself. That starts with being mindful not to walk on yer injured leg overmuch. It needs to rest to be healed."

"My thanks." Astrid rubbed her hands over the clean cloth in a thoughtful way before looking up. "How were ye in need of protection?"

Aednat hesitated, not sure how much she should share. "It is enough to say that Sean arranged this joining. He trusts Diarmuid very much."

"My brother is trustworthy. He will do whatever his overking asks of him," Astrid said. "A natural leader, though he prefers not to be dragged into everyone's disagreements. As their king, many of the squabbles he must settle irritate him to no end. He'd prefer a peaceful life." She looked around the room. "He sought to have another become king, but the *derb fine* decided on him. A great honor for most." She shrugged. "There is no man like my brother."

With each pronouncement, Aednat cringed a little more inside. The man his sister described did not sound like the sort who would willingly marry. She remembered his earlier words. *"I am a solitary man."*

If Sean had asked him to jump off a cliff, would he have done it?

Though she'd gone into this knowing why they were marrying, it stung to think that her husband would never have sought her hand under different circumstances… although he'd seemed pleased enough with her last night. Even wanting to make love again early this morning.

But would he prefer not to be married to her? Not to have to defend her against other men who sought to take her? If she could make his life more pleasant, mayhap he would see the other benefits of having a wife.

"How does yer brother like to break his fast?" she asked.

Astrid scrunched up her face. "He takes what he is given. He is not one to complain."

Worrying at her lip, Aednat realized his sister must pay little attention, or she would know these things. Surely he had a preference, and she vowed to learn it. She would take his likes into consideration at all times.

"Are there hens for eggs?"

"We have several hens!" Astrid leapt up and immediately fell back onto the bench, her face tight with pain.

"Oh, ye must not move so quickly. Do stay off yer foot, Astrid! It needs to heal." Aednat dropped down beside her and then bent to feel her leg beneath the bandage. "Tell me where I can find the chickens, and I will retrieve some eggs."

"Down the hill, along the tree line." Astrid hobbled to the pallet. "And I will rest until ye return."

Rummaging along the shelves in the corner, Aednat found a small basket and went off in search of the eggs. She followed the path that led back the way Diarmuid had brought her, moving toward the open fields. The smell of hyacinths carried to her, and she paused, unsure which way to go. Choosing left, she was soon at the top of a small rise, the stone tower in the distance. A lovely little area. She sighed in contentment. Certainly she would be safe here.

Chapter Thirteen

The sun was high in the sky, and Aednat was surprised they had slept so late. Fortunate to have found a few basic tinctures amongst the assorted clay jars in Diarmuid's house, Aednat kept her eyes open for any herbs she could come back for once Diarmuid returned home. Mayhap Diarmuid's grandmother had some healing knowledge as well.

The sound of annoyed chickens made them very easy to locate even though they were a bit further down the hill than she'd expected to go. The dark of the trees offered protection for the brood. It also gave the area an ominous feel. Diarmuid had asked her to remain inside, but surely he had not meant that she could not gather food.

A twig snapped a short distance away, but try as

she might she could see no farther than a few feet into the darkened woods. The chickens surrounded her as soon as she climbed within their enclosure.

"And how are ye, ladies? I have nothing for ye." She dropped down to the straw, working her hand beneath their empty perch. "D'ye have any eggs ye wish to share with me?"

Something rustled behind the wooden fence and a chill passed up her arms. Wolves were not a problem for her clan, and she wondered if they would be here. She had not thought to ask. The chickens showed no reaction, so she continued her search, finally placing three brown eggs into her basket.

"This will make a fine meal for my husband," she said to herself softly as she made her way out of the enclosure.

"And what d'ye have for me?" A large man ripped the basket out of her hand and yanked her to him. "I'm thinking I'll settle for nothing less than *ye*."

"NO!" Wrenching away, she screamed the word at him. The hard slap across her cheek snapped her head back, disorienting her, and she was turned about.

A burly man with black hair and beady eyes covered her mouth in a bruising grip. Aednat's head smacked back against his shoulder, and her eyes watered from the force with which his fingers dug into her cheeks. The smell of shite and sweat wafted to her nose, making her gag.

"Get something to cover her damn mouth!" Bending her arm up behind her, he muffled her screech of pain with his large palm. There were at least three men. She did not recognize any of them. Warriors all, with fierce sidearms and heavily bearded faces that made them seem oddly soulless. Their filthiness added to their wild appearance, making them look more like animals than men.

A smaller man sheathed his *miodóg* at the command and came toward her. His dirty hair, the color of rust, hung in thick, filthy clumps. A length of material dangled from his hand.

"Too bad ye had to be such a hard-to-find bitch!" Rusty's growling tone matched the harsh scowl on his face. He peered at her through narrowed eyes, his mouth close enough that she could smell the fish on his breath. "It will not go easy for ye now."

The bigger man released her mouth, still keeping a hold of her wrists. She jerked and turned her head, struggling against Rusty when he tried to shove a piece of cloth into her mouth. That got her another hard slap to her ear, setting it to ringing. She was unable to resist, and he tied the long piece of cloth around her head in short order. When he moved behind her to bind her hands, panic set in, and she twisted against the restraints, despite the pain that blackened the edges of her surroundings.

The big man reached down to clasp both of her hips and threw her over his shoulders with an *ugh* just before she would have passed out. Her feet locked against him, she shifted as much as she dared with her upper body and knees. If they got her away from here, she had no chance of escape.

She was dropped to the ground with a thud, the wind knocked out of her. The burly man covered her with his heavy body, his knee shoved between her legs and his face up against hers, leaving her no doubt of his intentions.

"I'd as soon take ye right here, healer, but Oengus would not be pleased, since he wants ye first. Give me more trouble, and I'll have to explain to him why I decided not to wait."

Aednat stilled her fighting, unable to take a breath, and fought down overwhelming panic. These were not just troublemakers from a nearby clan. These were the men who had been hunting her down. And now they had her. All that work trying to get her away. All for naught.

The burly brute tossed her back over his shoulder. The truth of her situation took hold, and her body started to quake. They were going to rape her. She certainly would never willingly lie with any of them.

If Aednat told them she was wed, would they let her be? Did they have any kindness in them? The sudden darkness of the forest brought her out of her troubled thoughts. He was leading the way to a few horses just within the tree line. With no thought for her discomfort, he tossed her up onto the mount, facedown. When the man got up behind her, he laid a heavy hand across her arse.

Leaning over to look into her face, he smiled, revealing three missing teeth and black gums. "Now that's the way I like my woman. Easy to handle and arse up for a good swiving."

Grabbing her buttocks with a hard grip, he laughed, a belly laugh that had the horse shifting beneath them. "A fine arse 'tis, too. I'm thinking I do not mind the trouble she's put us through. She'll be a fine tumble indeed. What of Oengus, William? D'ye think he'll be pleased?"

The third man, this William, had not spoken a

word. Aednat found herself straining to hear his voice. The other two had been so physically abusive to her; while this other man could very well be the same way, she held on to the slightest hope he was not. All she heard was his grunt, and then he was riding off past them on a gray steed.

The one holding her jabbed his heels into the courser, and they were galloping off, too. Aednat was tossed about with every step, despite the man's hand pressing hard against her back. His knee smacked into her face more than a few times. Try as she might, she wasn't able to keep her head clear of him. It was near impossible to follow where they were going. They talked, but she couldn't make out what they were saying. William kept to himself, riding in the lead.

After hours of sheer agony, a numbness began to take hold of Aednat's body, and she was soon drifting off despite struggling to stay awake. They'd tied her arms behind her back so tightly that she could no longer feel her hands, and her shoulders ached for release. Tears dripped into her hair. Her throat was so parched, swallowing became impossible. Just when she believed she would pass out into blessed oblivion, they jerked to a stop.

She squeezed her eyes shut and pushed her shoulders back against the hands that used her arms to yank her off the horse. Pain shot across her back and chest. She crumpled to the ground at the whoreson's feet, unable to move, and prayed she could get clear of his feet if he decided to kick her.

"That's where I like my women."

Anger jerked her out of her exhaustion. Without success, she struggled to get up to her feet. Repeatedly. But with her arms trussed up behind her as they were, she had no hope of keeping her dignity. An arm's length in front of her, the man only laughed at her efforts, offering no help. Suddenly, he dropped to his haunches in front of her, holding a mean-looking dagger near her face. Did they mean to kill her?

"Turn around." He barked the order. She tried to move, but she stumbled, falling against his bare leg. Side stepping, he allowed her to fall facedown into the dirt. Her bindings were cut, and a prickly pain coursed up her arms. Once she could feel her arms again, she forced one of them up to pull the material away from her mouth.

"Ye devil spawn!" At last able to speak, she screeched her uncontainable outrage. "My husband will kill ye for this. Ye impudent dogs!"

Whoreson, still squatting down in front of her, stared at her with a speculative look on his ugly face, and she cowered back, expecting him to slap her again.

"When we're done with ye," he began, his voice menacingly quiet, "I'm thinking he'll not care to have ye back, so ye best watch how ye speak to us."

With a lift of his chin, he indicated for Rusty to put the gag back in place. To her horror, tears slipped down her cheeks. When Rusty squatted before her, she begged with her eyes and shook her head.

"Please. Do not!"

But he put the cloth into place and then retied her hands in front of her.

Aednat cried out in pain, but it was muffled by the thick material. Surely her arms were being ripped right off her body. None of the men around her seemed to care if she made noise. William stood off by the horses, never saying a word, but she could feel his eyes on her. She feared for her life. If they knew she'd lain with her husband, would they just kill her? How could they return her now? There would be hell to pay.

William was her only chance. If she could speak to him, convince him to be merciful to her, he might be able to sway the more violent pair.

Tall and thin, William was dressed like the others, but his threadbare clothes hung off him. He leaned against a tree eating an apple. She was more thirsty than she'd ever been. Desperate to convey that message, she turned toward him with her most pleading expression. When he noticed her, he stilled and watched her with dark, brooding eyes before he spoke.

"What is she about?" He took a bite of his apple, paying no mind to the juices running down his bearded chin. "Make her stop."

Whoreson yanked her around so she could no longer face William. Shamelessly, she gave him the same look.

He scowled. "What's that all about?"

Rusty came over to stand beside her, both men looking down at her like she was some oddity or a dead body. "Mayhap she needs something?"

"Well, I've got a need." Whoreson gave her a shove hard enough to make her fall backward and yanked up her gown right before he lowered his filthy body onto her. The cold air on her skin was better than the feel of his hand between her legs. He yanked down his hose, freeing his stiff prick, and smiled down at her. "And ye can see to it just fine."

"STOP!"

It was William who spoke. A commanding voice but not angry. Whoreson halted his movements, his breath still heaving close to her ear. An involuntary shiver climbed up her legs and he leered down at her. Her stomach heaved.

William tossed the apple core into the bushes and sauntered over as if he had all the time in the world. She wanted to scream to him to hurry up, to get this man off her. But she wasn't convinced that was what William had in mind. He didn't seem overly concerned. Mayhap he just wanted to get a better view of the event. Bile filled her mouth. The engorged cock lay heavy against her thigh and exceedingly close to its target. If he moved any closer, she was going to be sick.

"Get off her, Réamann," William said, and raised both brows to make his point. "That is not for ye."

Relief flooded her.

Whoreson shrugged, clearly irritated, and got up. None of the men did anything to cover her or help her sit up again. And the man now standing beside her? He had stopped Whoreson, but for what purpose? His cursory glance over her body ended at her feet. The other two were nearly salivating, and their expectant expressions gave her little hope. William glanced at her matted hair and rubbed his lips together. When he finally met her gaze, there was no expression in his eyes. Neither lust nor pity. Nothing.

"She's a pretty thing." His voice was low and he hunkered down beside her head, but his eyes continued to venture lower. "So, are ye still a virgin?"

Aednat waited until he finally looked at her face, and then shook her head once as hard as she could. William nodded, his doe-skin glove making a rasping sound where he rubbed it along his chapped lower lip in a thoughtful way. A contemplative expression. He glanced lower again and she tensed. His eyes met hers for the smallest second, and surely it was her own exhaustion, but she'd swear he gave a little nod. Her breath caught.

"Malcolm? Réamann?"

They took their eyes off her naked legs to glance at their leader. Whoreson's and Rusty's leering grins remained in place.

"There is no need for the two of ye to stay," William said. His voice sounded pleasant. Affable.

Whoreson's crestfallen expression confirmed her fears. This other man, the one she'd hoped would be her salvation, meant to slake his own need with her.

William looked at his open glove before making a fist. He looked down at her and said, "I will see to this one myself."

Aednat dared not breathe. Tears threatened, but she flattened her lips together, swallowing them down. She would not cry. She would scream as loud as the gag permitted if he dared to touch her.

Whoreson and Rusty did as they were ordered, mounting their animals without another word. The big one approached as if to peruse her body from the higher view, but he simply tossed William a skin of water and a sack before turning his horse back toward the trail. The cloudy sky made the trees look dark and ominous. Rain threatened, and it occurred to Aednat that it would be a welcome relief to wash away the filth of what was about to happen.

When the two reached the trees, Whoreson stopped suddenly and jerked his horse around.

"Should we continue to make haste to Black Oengus?" he asked. "Or would ye have us travel more slowly so ye can catch up with us after… ye're done here?"

Even that dirty pig couldn't put into words what this man was about to do to her. Her throat tightened.

William's eyes never strayed from her face. "Take yer time."

Chapter Fourteen

The sound of the horses retreating into the distance carried to them, but Aednat dared not release the breath she was holding. William's eyes were still on her. Dark and unreadable. Her trepidation increased three-fold. He yanked the material from her mouth, and she shoved it down further with her shoulder.

"Please!" She swallowed. "Please untie me. Let me go back to my husband. I am of no use to ye."

He watched her, his expression still thoughtful, inscrutable, then sliced the bindings with his dagger. He didn't turn away when she yanked her gown down around her feet and sat up, but he made no move toward her.

"Husband? Hmm. That's a problem."

There was no emotion in his voice, but she feared

this calm facade. She did not know what he was playing at.

"Is it a ransom ye want?"

His interest now piqued, he asked, "Would he pay a ransom for yer return?"

Aednat didn't know the answer. "Of course he would. He is very wealthy. And he would give ye even more if ye left me untouched."

William nodded, flattening his lips. His quietness set her heart to fluttering even faster. She needed to distract him. Surveying the area, her eyes landed on a stone that was the perfect size to smash against his head. It was just to her right. If only…

"I'm—I'm very thirsty. May I—"

He dropped the skin into her lap. Her hands were stiff, and she struggled to bring the vessel to her lips. She drank the warm water with her eyes on him. His eyes had still not wavered from her.

"Ye're a healer? But a virgin no longer?"

She stopped drinking to wipe her mouth before nodding her head.

"Well, Oengus wants ye still."

Her breath started in little pants, making it hard for her to catch her breath. "He'll know—"

William put his hand flat on her back. "Blow out a breath now, Aednat. That's it."

Her lungs immediately filled with air, and she watched him with narrowed eyes. No one else had called her by name. "The power comes from an untouched healer."

Lifting his shoulder, William grinned. "He'll assume that part of the legend is wrong." His dark eyes brightened, and he fumbled with removing his gloves. "He's taken enough of them. Traveling from group to group to find any healers he can. The presence of their maidenheads seems of little interest to him. Ye've grown into a lovely woman."

"Please! Bring me ba—What did ye say?"

He dropped the first glove into his lap. "Ye've grown into a lovely woman, Aednat."

The way he said her name seemed familiar, but she did not recognize this man. He was filthy, a recluse to be certain. She ground her teeth from side to side, as frustrated by his familiarity as she was by her own inability to place him.

"Yer hair has lost most of its curl." The last glove dropped, revealing fingers hacked off at the first knuckle. He picked up her hair with the stubs. "I loved yer curls."

She gasped. "Will?"

She was overcome with a range of emotions, from disgust that her Will could be with these men ready to rape her, to joy at knowing he still lived. Settling on outrage, she began to pummel his chest as hard as she could.

"Ye bastard! How could ye! Not my Will! Ye cannot be!"

He pulled back, a scowl on his face, grabbing at her flailing hands quite capably, despite the missing fingers. "Easy woman!"

"How could ye!" Her uncontrollable sobs made her feel so vulnerable, but the pain in her chest was all encompassing. Her Will had always been so kind and considerate. What had become of him? "How could ye allow them to be so cruel to me?" she wailed.

"I did not know it was ye, Aednat." William's voice was quiet as he gathered her hands between his palms and pressed them against his chest, his earnest expression indeed familiar now. Even more so the soft brown eyes. "When I figured it out, 'twas too late and they'd already stolen ye."

"So ye did not mind helping them to steal a different woman?"

He shrugged again. "It is not what they normally do, but I am not one to be listened to overmuch. I was not going to let them have at ye, though."

"Ye did not seem inclined to stop them!" She turned to get up, but he yanked her back, pulling her up against him.

"Play along," he whispered the words before he covered her mouth with tight, firm lips.

Shocked into silence, she didn't move. She didn't breathe. Then she heard the horse, and she closed her eyes, afraid for what was about to happen. Grasping her shoulders, Will made movements that could have resembled passion, but he touched only her lips.

"William!" Rusty called, stopping a bit away but remaining mounted. "Oengus is on his way."

William broke the kiss, leaving the barest space between their faces, his eyes wide. "That's going to make this a bit harder."

Aednat's soaring hope dropped like a rock. "Please, do not let them take me!"

When Diarmuid returned home, it was the lack of any smoke over his house that set his heart racing. Heavy storm clouds hung in the sky. A deluge would come at any time. Dropping from the horse, he threw the door open to the little stone building. Astrid sat up from the bed, her eyes still heavy with sleep.

"What are ye…" She looked around. "Yer wife takes a long time to fetch eggs."

In two strides, he was at his sister's side, bearing down on her. "Where is Aednat? Where did she go?"

Astrid moaned, pushing the hair out of her face. "I must have fallen asleep. She went to get eggs."

"Ye let her go out alone?"

"'Tis just down the hill, Diarmuid. Why would she not go alone?"

Diarmuid ran out the door, mounted his horse, and raced to the chicken enclosure. Standing alongside the cackling birds, he scanned the area for any sign of her having been there. It took three sweeps of the area for him to find it. The basket lay hidden by the tall grass, its contents crushed on the ground. She'd been there. She'd been taken.

Remorse flooded him. His first mistake had been trusting she would take his words to heart and obey him. She was strong-willed and would do whatever she pleased. His second mistake had been to believe his home would be a safe haven. It was only safe when he was here to guard it, and the relentless bastards had tracked her down even to this remote place. His third and biggest mistake? Being swept away by the emotions of satisfaction and gratitude and the belief that things could be different.

They could not.

Throwing the basket to the ground, Diarmuid ran a rough hand over his face. He should have been more careful with her. He whistled, long and loud.

Astrid finally caught up to him, her stride uneven and slow. "What has happened? Where is she?"

Diarmuid clenched his jaw before responding.

"Men have been chasing after her. I thought to protect her. I was careless, and now she's at their mercy."

Three men came running across the field toward him.

"Sweet Jesus." She grabbed his arm in a tight grip. "What can I do?"

"Use the horn and call the others."

"And what of Marcán?" she asked.

"It was as I said. They had passed out in a cave, though he swears they were not drunk. They will be here anon. Our mother as well. Marcán especially desires to speak with *ye*." He mounted his horse and signaled the others to come with him. "Have them follow me. I will track her down."

"I did not know I needed to watch out for her, brother." Her eyes filled with tears.

"Wheesht now, Astrid!" He had no time to comfort her. "I will find her. Do as I said!"

It was his fault alone. His wife had deserved a better protector. Just as his little brother had. Diarmuid had witnessed how their mother coddled Fergus, and even though he'd known right along it would come to no good, he'd still left his brother behind with her instead of taking him along to visit the outlying warriors guarding the bounds of the *túath*.

"Go. Now!" His words were unsympathetic. He had no time for her foolishness.

Astrid nodded, sniffling as she hobbled back toward the roundhouse.

Their trail was hard to miss and that arrogance galled Diarmuid. Did they believe he cared nothing for what was his? As if he would not immediately begin searching her out? The business with the Meic Murchadha was growing more suspicious, although they were not so foolish as to become involved with such a scheme willingly. Marcán had assured him there had been no falling out, and he had not over imbibed, only awaking in the cave with an aching head. Had Diarmuid underestimated the cunning of these superstitious warriors tracking Aednat?

The rain clouds opened up and he was soon drenched. Slowed by the fact he couldn't see beyond his horse's muzzle, he kept riding restlessly, leading the way. Seven more of his men had joined him, all attentive for any shift in direction.

It took half the day until the trail disappeared.

Diarmuid leapt from his horse, beside himself with rage. Only Marcán dared approach him, his furrowed brow mirroring Diarmuid's own anger.

"The longer we take to find my wife, the greater the chance they will have taken what they wanted." His nostrils flared and he fought to control his temper. "We must have missed their turn."

He scanned the trail behind them, the ground sodden from the drizzling rain.

"Find out where!" His booming voice startled the mounts, and the men worked to calm them.

The three men Marcán sent back looked relieved. Diarmuid's anger unleashed was not pleasant for any of them, he knew that. But he had not the first idea how to ease this gut-wrenching anger.

"Verily they have outfoxed me again. This is unbearable!" Diarmuid fisted his hands, unable to think clearly, overcome with fear for his wife and the abuse she may be suffering at their hands. "They snuck in by setting a trap for me, and then stole her away by leaving a blazing trail that leads us nowhere." He turned his scowl on Marcán. "Is there any place they could be hiding with her that we have not considered? How far could they have gotten?"

The man shrugged. "The coast? If that was their destination. Lough Derg if they headed that way."

Diarmuid held up a hand. "Lough Derg? The exact opposite of the direction we've been traveling. A clever ruse. The rampant lawlessness there would provide the perfect cover for hiding a hostage."

"A hostage? Ye think they could be bargained with for her release?"

"I would pay any price for it."

Marcán's eyes pierced him. "Diarmuid, they may have taken what they wanted by now. We do not know what they would do with her when they were finished."

Diarmuid's blood turned cold. "If they've touched a hair on her head, I will gut each one of them from groin to neck, cut off their ballocks and stuff them in their mouths, then hang them from the highest tree."

"So do we head to Lough Derg and pray for the best?"

A course of action for his intense rage helped to clear his foggy thoughts. He blew a breath. "*I* will go there—alone. *Ye* go quickly to the ocean looking for any sign of them. Ye three," he addressed the remaining men, "go with Marcán, and the rest of ye head east. We will pick up their real trail and not rest until we do. Send word if ye find her. If ye do not, ride like the wind to me. D'ye hear me?"

None questioned his orders. Marcán held him up. "Do we bring the men to ye if we find her?"

"Drag them from yer horses if ye must, but bring them back, and I will deal with them myself."

Diarmuid set off toward Lough Derg and knew in

his heart that the lough was where he would find her. What condition she would be in, he didn't dare guess, but the men who'd kidnapped her would pay dearly for taking what was his.

Chapter Fifteen

When Oengus arrived, he gave her a cursory glance, then hitched up the belt at his waist and ordered everyone to mount up. Aednat had been allowed to ride with Will even though they had no idea what a relief it was for her. He remained quiet during the long ride, his mere presence a boon. He shot her a small smile, the only reassurance he dared offer with the other men surrounding them. She dozed off several times but would jerk awake, disoriented. He'd put a hand to her once to calm her, then glanced around nervously to be sure no one had witnessed the overture. They traveled at a leisurely pace, ten or so men with their group.

It was well past dark by the time they arrived at the camp. It lay in a narrow meadow flanked by a brook to the west and nestled against wooded hills to the east. There were twice as many men lying about as traveled with them, and no alarm had been sent out to signal their arrival. Completely out in the open and no watch? It was as if they had nothing to hide from.

Few seemed to notice her, or mayhap they were too deep in their drink to care. Scruffy, from the group that had attacked her and Diarmuid at the lough, made a point of sneering at her as he walked past her.

"'Bout time ye caught that bitch," he said.

Rusty had dismounted and moved up closer. He nodded in response and held a gold coin in front of his nose with a wide, beaming smile of pride.

William ignored the others as he helped Aednat off the horse. He gave her tied hands a shake as if to ensure they were not too tight.

"No one said nothing about untying her." Rusty's scowl stretched across his ugly face as he looked down at her.

William straightened his shoulders and leveled a gaze at the man. It was enough to send Rusty skittering away like a scorched insect. After glancing around to ensure they were not watched, Will shot her a smile.

"That's the one!" A tall man, far too young to be as hunched over as he was, staggered toward them. It took a moment for Aednat to realize he had been at the lough as well. "The man said 'twas his wife and not a virgin."

"He lied!" Another little man sat on the ground, his arms about his legs. "*I* knew sh-she was the one he wanted."

"Ye knew?" The tall man turned back. "Why did we not take her, Father?"

"*We'd* have the coins now, Eoghan!" Scruffy sounded ready for a fight.

Eoghan opened his arms to reveal his wound, still wet with his blood, and his son immediately sat beside him again.

"She's s-ours s-now." The blood soaking through the little man's shirt was no doubt the reason for his slurred speech. The fools hadn't even bandaged it. Aednat was surprised he was still able to stand. Left alone, he'd be dead by daybreak.

A single fire glowed at the center of the camp with women tending to the cooking of a foul-smelling repast. A few turned toward them as they entered, but none gave more than a cursory glance. Filthy children ran around with a mangy dog chasing after them. It appeared Aednat had been brought to their home, such as it was, to be raped.

Oengus was a stocky man with long clumps of gray hair that lay flat on his head, away from his face. He and his men started across the camp, and Will followed with Aednat, leading her past the fire and to the far side of the camp. They passed a few lean-tos that appeared solid and stable, secured by poles with large animal skins draped over them, creating an enclosure. The one nearest the trees was larger with a few weapons and miscellaneous supplies piled alongside and at the ready. Oengus's?

Oengus ducked inside, and the others all stopped to wait for him. When he came out, he carried a length of cloth and a horn, which he drank from greedily before wiping the liquid from his mouth with the back of his hand. He moved past Aednat as if she didn't exist, settling instead before the fire. Will motioned for her to sit. It wasn't until she sat down, and was immediately cast into darkness, that she realized he'd chosen a spot in the shadows to help conceal her from the others.

A woman hurried up to refill Oengus's horn. Another came with some sort of meat that he ate with relish, belching loudly and calling for more ale. The others were all drinking, eating, and talking. Will stood beside her, seemingly at ease, but he continued looking to the left and right, scanning the others. She prayed he was thinking of a way for her to escape.

"William?" A lass a bit older than Aednat with long, auburn hair and a light smattering of freckles across the bridge of her nose came to stand beside him. She offered a shy smile and handed him a horn. "Ye must be thirsty."

"My thanks, Merewyn."

"I have missed ye, William. D'ye need some meat? They caught a deer this day. I can get some for ye."

"No. Some water for the prisoner?"

Merewyn frowned, seeming a bit disappointed that he'd request something for the healer, and gave a curt nod.

Returning with a wooden cup, she shoved it toward Aednat. When Aednat tried to take hold of the cup with her tied hands, its contents sloshed over the top, dowsing her clothing. Will glared at the woman and dropped down beside Aednat to hold the cup to her mouth. The water was warm, but nothing had ever tasted as good.

"Ye know ye were treated the same as this, Merewyn. Tied up and all," Will said, his eyes remaining on Aednat.

Merewyn had turned away, her eyes scanning the

men gathered around the fire. When she brought her attention back to William, he stood and handed her the empty cup.

"And I came to ye and offered ye water. D'ye not remember that?"

Merewyn looked askance at him. "I do."

"Then why would ye not do the same for another in need?"

She pressed her body against him, nearly stepping on Aednat in the process. "Because I know ye wanted to bed me."

William shook his head. "I was showing ye a kindness."

Showing a kindness.

Aednat's memory sparked and she could hear the same words in her grandmother's voice. A lesson she, Cad, and Will had learned all too well. Her grandmother had made it a point to teach them kindness. Outcast at so young an age, it would have been easy for them to be cruel to others. It was all they knew *from* others.

"Then why did ye take me to yer bed?" Merewyn almost purred the words.

William said nothing but held her gaze. Aednat sensed the tension between them. In part, it was the way they looked at each other, as if they had an unspoken attachment. Will's lips curled up and he gave her a swat on her bottom. Merewyn smiled, glanced down at Aednat with contempt, and moved away to the far side of the fire.

He turned toward Aednat, who raised both eyebrows.

"What?"

"Well? Were ye showing a kindness?"

"I was more kind than the others, who would have just used her and then paid her no heed until they wanted her again." He glanced toward Merewyn and his expression softened. "But I *did* take her to my bed, and I've cared for her, besides. That gives her my protection. As our slave, the kindness was not necessary."

"I am not certain Grandmother would agree it was a kindness."

Will turned toward her. "I think of her often. She was very good to me. How does she fare?"

"She died a while ago. I miss her very much."

"But now ye are married?"

"I am." The thought of Diarmuid searching for her, in a blind rage toward her attackers, was her only solace. And with that solace, the truth that she was yet again ruining the peace he sought.

"Ye sound sad about it. Are ye not pleased with yer husband?"

She'd swear he seemed to take some pleasure in the thought she might not be happily married. "I was wed to Diarmuid for protection against Black Oengus." She gave him a pointed look.

"He does enjoy that title." Will nodded. "But he is growing older, becoming more feeble, and that is every king's fear, overking or a lesser king. If he cannot continue to lead a warband, he is of little value. *Anything* that might give him the power he seeks is worth trying."

"And d'ye seek his title?"

Will sneered. "I have no such ambition." He glanced at her. "And what of yer ambitions? Is Diarmuid the man ye would have chosen for yerself?"

Being settled in the dark beside Will felt oddly

familiar. He was her confidant once again. "He is a man I can respect."

"And when he takes ye to his bed?"

Aednat turned to Will, her mouth hanging open. "Ye cunning fox! D'ye believe I lied about no longer being a virgin?"

"We may all know soon enough." His regretful tone did nothing to soften the words. She shivered.

"Will he just force himself on me here? In front of his entire clan?"

"He shows his prowess in doing so."

She squeezed her eyes shut, and the first image that surfaced was Diarmuid's tender expression when he had taken her that first time.

"Diarmuid is a good man and finds me desirable," she said quietly, almost as if reminding herself.

"Still questioning yer worthiness, Aednat? Surely ye must realize what a lovely woman ye've grown into."

She glanced down her leg. "And yet my foot continues to be the first thing anyone notices about me."

The low flames cast strange shadows on the men sitting around the fire as they drank and laughed.

"How long did ye stay in the cave? I thought with my grandfather dead, ye'd have been welcomed into the clan again."

Shrugging, Will said, "'Twas not so simple. They believed him when he told them we should be kept separate. We stayed in the caves until Ulann died."

"Ulann! The old man who told all the stories! I had forgotten his name."

"How could ye forget Ulann?"

"I did not forget the man, just his name."

"He taught me and Cad how to make weapons, hunt, fish, and defend ourselves as much as we were able." He turned to her, holding his hand up to wiggle his shortened fingers. "Even how to shoot an arrow despite this. When he died, there was no reason to stay. Ye were gone. Grandmother was gone."

Aednat heard the loss in his voice. They had been his family. "What of Cad?"

"He died of a fever two winters past."

"Is that when ye came here?"

"We came here together. Oengus took us in. Saved us."

Aednat harrumphed. She saw nothing redeeming about the man.

Will stiffened, his lips barely moving now. "Oengus is looking over here."

Oengus approached from his spot of honor before the fire, walking tall with his shoulders back, commanding the attention of all. The long length of material he'd retrieved from his lean-to remained in his hand, not quite forgotten. Aednat's stomach dropped and she averted her eyes.

"William! Go feed yerself. Ye've worked hard." Oengus patted his shoulder as he walked away, as if abducting women was a good day's work. An everyday occurrence. That fact hit Aednat like a punch to the gut.

When William crossed to the fire, he did not glance back. Merewyn met him part way with a trencher and a wide smile.

"And so ye're here now. The *Great* Healer! I tried settling for any healer, but the legend has it that only a *Great* Healer holds the powers of the ancient ones."

Her reputation had indeed preceded her. Those poor women he'd tried "settling" for. A shiver of repulsion worked through her.

"Ye needn't fear me! Unless ye mean to make trouble." Nodding, he glanced around the camp. "No one here will help ye. Not even the slaves. They obey me alone." His gaze turned back to hers as he lifted the cloth. "In my infinite mercy as *thighearna* here, I'll give ye one chance to forego the gag. D'ye promise not to make a fuss?"

Aednat's chest tightened with the overwhelming urge to laugh. Did he expect her not to fuss when he was raping her? Or when he was tying her up? Or when his men were raping her? She forced down the panicked thoughts, filled her lungs and held her breath, and nodded once before slowing exhaling. He tucked the material into his belt, no doubt keeping it at hand in case she could not stop from screaming.

With a snap of Oengus's fingers, one of the women came forward, her expression vacant. The black-haired woman hunkered down before her and tears pricked Aednat's eyes as the small fingers gently loosened the thick knots. Arms akimbo and his big belly sticking out over his leather belt, Oengus looked on as the bindings were removed. When the woman blocked his view, Aednat took a chance.

"Will ye watch them rape me?" she whispered the words.

The woman lifted her eyes from the rope for but a moment. Her eyes focusing on Aednat's lips almost as if questioning if she had actually spoken. But there was no reply. The woman finished her work and walked away. Aednat clenched her teeth, fighting down the despair that threatened to swamp her.

Oengus moved closer, taking the woman's place, and yanked Aednat to standing. Her legs threatened to buckle beneath her, both from fear and her misshapen foot. He gripped her chin, dark eyes narrowing as he turned her face one way and then the other. Then he released her and walked around her in a circle. Inspecting her as he might a new horse.

Aednat blocked the man out, instead scanning the many faces surrounding her. Whoreson at the forefront with Rusty close beside him, his beefy arms about his chest. Will stood a little farther back, eating, Merewyn hanging on his arm as she spoke to him. Though he appeared to be listening, Aednat could see his focus was on her. It gave her much-needed support.

"She does not look so special to me," Oengus said.

He had stopped in front of her, but the comments were clearly intended for his audience. They responded with laughter and jeers, exchanging quips, all having something to add. The level of excitement increased. This was their entertainment! *She* was their entertainment.

One woman shouted out, "Mayhap we should see what she can do?"

It was the black-haired woman who'd removed her bindings. Aednat locked eyes with the woman, feeling betrayed.

"Let her heal Eoghan!"

It was a man's voice this time, but Aednat's eyes remained on the woman, following her slow movement toward the tents. Dropping down beside the pile of supplies, the black-haired woman shifted a few things about. When she yanked out a length of wood, her eyes met Aednat's for the smallest moment before she vanished inside the tent.

Aednat's breath caught and hope surged in her chest. With a weapon, mayhap she'd have a chance to escape. It was only a short distance from her and the handle was even closer now. She flexed her hands into fists, steadying her breathing, and shifted ever so slightly closer.

Oengus glanced around, paying little attention to Aednat. He was much more interested in provoking the crowd, nodding in agreement with all the crude remarks being tossed about. Not knowing how long she had, she shifted as if uncomfortable on her feet, edging closer to the weapon with each slip of her foot.

When Oengus's gaze returned to her, she froze. His gaze dropped lower, and he reached to pinch her breast. She cried out and jerked away. That got her a slap hard enough to turn her face. He grabbed her chin in a bruising grip between thumb and forefinger.

"No!" He spat the word at her. "*Ye* will not speak. *Ye* will not make a sound. Unless ye wish to be tossed to my men after I am done with ye."

So she had a choice? Oengus waited for her answer, his eyes widening the longer she refused to respond. It was his hands curling into fists and the sudden realization that he might hit her again and again and again that forced her to shake her head. His ugly face relaxed into a cold, smug smile. "Not special at all."

Turning toward the crowd, he looked out over the sea of faces. "Bring Eoghan forward."

Aednat had seen the way the man was still bleeding. If the wound had gone untouched since the day of his injury, there was little she could do for him.

It was the younger man who helped him up, probably his son, settling him before her. The stench of rotting flesh was overpowering.

Oengus clapped a hand on the younger man's shoulder in a reassuring way before turning to Aednat. "Healer? D'yer best!"

Hesitating but a moment, she stepped toward the man, which also brought her closer to the weapon. His eyes, dark and angry, never wavered from her face. With the gentlest touch, she pulled at the tunic soaked in his blood, but it resisted. She yanked on it and the man cried out in pain.

His son shoved her, knocking her on her arse and away from the weapon. "Do not hurt him more!"

She clenched her teeth to hold back her scream of frustration. The son used his one good hand, lifting the material the rest of the way for her. Aednat moved around to the other side of the man, as if to better see the wound, again closing the distance separating her from the weapon.

She gasped when the condition of the wound finally registered and gaped up at the young man. "This wound has not even been cleaned."

"Water would kill me." Eoghan's frail voice barely reached her.

Like many, he had a fear of water and cleanliness. A fear that came from some long-ago belief Aednat had never understood. The slice was not deep and could easily have been sewn together days ago. Now the ends were black and shrinking away as they died. Removing the material had been necessary, but it had also increased the bleeding. Her husband had done quite a good job with little effort. "I need some water heated."

"Did ye not hear me?" Eoghan's tone was insistent.

Oengus raised a hand at the son's outraged bellow. "Let the healer work."

Merewyn brought forth a wooden bowl of hot water, sloshing it slightly when she put it down. The young girl's eyes were wide as she settled in beside Aednat.

"A cloth?" A filthy rag was tossed to her and she soaked it in the water. "This may sting, Eoghan."

Eoghan's eyes bore into her and he clenched his jaw shut. When the water touched the wound, he inhaled sharply. His son fought to hold himself back, fisting his hands and shooting her angry glances whenever she wiped at the blood. She needed to see the wound before she could assess what to do, but with each swipe, more blood flowed forth, concealing the damage.

Because it was a clean cut, she could still try to stitch it up, but the man's face was pale and his eyes were no longer focusing.

"Is there any yarrow?"

Merewyn jumped to do her bidding, returning with a small clump of the plant. She offered her a small, well-worn satchel. "Ye can use this as well."

Aednat smiled her thanks and took out a handful of the crushed leaves, not only yarrow but valerian root as well.

She eyed the girl and said, "If ye know what to do, why did ye not attend him?"

Merewyn glanced toward Oengus, who only frowned at them, either unaware of what they were saying or uncaring, before guzzling more mead. "Being a healer does not bode well in this clan."

"I am not sure I can heal him."

Merewyn glanced at the onlookers. "I do not believe it can get any worse for ye."

Using the only water available, Aednat worked the powders into a paste and gently smeared it over the man's chest. His eyes rolled back into his head. Merewyn offered her a horn filled with water before she asked for it, and Aednat dropped some of the leaves into it to make a drink.

"Mayhap ye should return to William so they do not turn on ye," Aednat said, pressing the drink to the man's lips.

Merewyn nodded and disappeared into the crowd of onlookers.

"He's passed out." Rusty's words rang out and Aednat saw the truth of the words.

The man's son lowered him the rest of the way to the ground, hovering over his body. "Ye've killed him!" he cried out in despair.

An immediate outcry rose up from those around her, but Oengus raised a hand to settle them.

"I did not kill him!" Aednat said. Reaching down to feel the man's heartbeat, she found none. The liquid dribbled out the side of his mouth.

"Ye did!" Outraged, the son stood now, his wrist at an odd angle. "Ye are no great healer!"

Aednat stood as well, Oengus's eyes on her, and trembled in fear. The sight of that weapon's handle taunted her. Finally turning to face him, she shook her head, and Oengus lowered his eyes as if in understanding.

"Settle yerself. Réamann! Come forth." Her burly abductor did as he was bidden. "Remove the body."

The coldness the man showed toward one of his own held her there, staring at him, her eyes wide in disbelief. He cared so little for his men. How would he treat her? She wanted to explain, to defend herself, but she had no words. The man should not have died this quickly. There should have been some chance. Stopping the blood would have given him at least until the break of day, but she hadn't been able to do even that.

With the tilt of his chin, Oengus directed Rusty to her and she stepped back in fear. Were they going to beat her now? He stood close, peering down his nose at her, then began pushing on her shoulders. She gritted her teeth, resisting until she had no choice but to drop at his feet, but she refused to go to her knees again. Instead, she fell into a seated position, legs to the side. This devil's spawn would have to work harder than that to get her to her knees before him. Still, humiliation worked its way through her body, and her face heated. The corpse was dragged away with little fanfare, the crowd parting only long enough to allow its removal.

Oengus stepped toward his hut, a leering smile on his face. He removed the wolf skin draped over his shoulders with great ceremony, knowing all eyes were on him. His belt and battle axe came next, removed by the same black-haired woman.

When he turned back, his menacing expression held Aednat frozen in place. Her stomach tightened, and she fought the nearly uncontrollable urge to scream. She could not scream now, and she dare not even glance toward the weapons. If she was unable to reach them, her silence now might at least limit the number of men allowed to touch her. Of course, this awful man might not stand by his word, but she had to believe him. The situation she'd found herself in was horrible enough.

"Stoke up the fire, lads. Nice and bright. I'm going to enjoy this."

The crowd cheered, already forgetting about the death of one of their own, and his orders were seen to. Oengus took the few steps toward her with purpose, his body casting an ominous shadow over those moving in closer still to watch. Women and children alike.

Her breath hitched. The man halted, stroking his manhood through the threadbare material of his *léine*. Aednat searched her brain for anything to say to get him to stop this. Then he dropped to a squat in front of her, his face close, his gaze taking in every bit of her. His lip twitching as if already envisioning the act he would perpetrate against her.

"I do not know she is such a *great* healer."

William's voiced startled Oengus out of his dark thoughts. Aednat could see it on his face. When his eyes refocused, he turned to William, who now stood alongside him.

"William?"

"I would wish for ye to have some enjoyment from this."

"Any time a woman spreads her legs, I receive enjoyment." Oengus's guffaw sparked the other men to join in.

William shrugged, his expression blank. "She was like a limp rag the whole way. Even now."

Oengus pushed up from his squat, his eyes assessing.

"I'm thinking the power may be out for this night. That must be why Eoghan died." William snorted. "Look at her."

All eyes shifted to her, intently doing as Will had suggested. The men, even the drunk ones, had wide, staring eyes. Some had expressions of awe. Others, expressions of lust.

"She is not much to look at." His voice flat, Oengus repeated his earlier assessment. "But she saved that drowned man. Brought him back to life. Only a great healer could raise the dead."

William nodded as if considering the words. "But this power? It may come and go. Mayhap it has drained out of her. Giving her time to rest may bring it back."

"I do not want to wait." Oengus wailed his displeasure. "I would prefer to see this done with now."

"Then look at this!" William snatched up her skirt, exposing her foot.

Aednat gasped, betrayal slashing through her.

William grabbed at her foot and she tumbled backward. "This foot is not right!"

Murmuring erupted. As one, the sea of faces vied for a better look. Aednat reached up to push William away, clawing and yanking at the material gripped firmly in his hand with little success.

"Are ye certain 'tis power ye'll be getting off her and not a curse instead?"

The children's expressions of disgust when they turned away danced before her tearing eyes.

But Oengus only nodded. The man was considering William's words, taking them to heart.

Oengus smoothed his fingers over his prick in a loving way. "I am not even sure I can find it in me to take her."

"No doubt she has placed a curse on yer prick."

William released the material and turned toward her, his face expressionless. "Look at her face! Her eyes are full of witchery."

The leader's eyes widened as he peered more closely at her, the advancing panic obvious.

"Get Bodhmall! Bring her here!" Oengus called over his shoulder, fear and anger thick in his voice. But he kept his eyes on her, his hand covering his groin. "The *bandruí* will protect me. A witch will know what the healer is about." He shifted uncomfortably. "I think she may have cursed my prick. Turn her away from me."

William jerked her around so her back was to the others, who continued to discuss her malady with words like "disgusting" and "gross." His caress against her cheek, wiping the tears away, only made her cry harder. She dropped her face into her cupped hands. Exhaustion was overtaking her and she couldn't think straight. Had Will meant to be cruel, or was this a ploy to protect her? He stood behind her now as if shielding her from their view.

"I do not know." William spoke with the same calm tone. "Even Bodhmall may not know what to do."

Growling sounded behind her just before William tumbled over, brushing her shoulder as he landed flat on his back in front of her. "Ye shut yer mouth! I'm believing everything Bodhmall tells me and ye better believe her, too!" Chills spread across her skin. Who was this woman they were bringing to look at her?

When she moved to see if William was hurt, he flashed a warning grimace and pulled himself up. Barely within her line of sight, he stood to her left wiping at his bloodied lip. He shrugged. "It feels like she makes it up sometimes."

"That is because the thoughts come upon her from someone more powerful! Not from her own mind."

The crowd quieted, and Aednat's tears ceased while she listened for any sound behind her. The shuffling of feet pricked her ears, but she dared not turn.

"Oh, Bodhmall, come. Come. See what I have."

Aednat hadn't realized she was holding her breath until the burly man yanked her halfway to her knees to face them. Her knees burned where they'd already been ripped open by the stones in the ground. The smallest woman she'd ever seen stood before her with wild gray hair and large, hanging bosoms. Something about her eyes seemed familiar.

"Here's the Great Healer!" Oengus pointed to Aednat and spoke in a hushed tone. "Will she give me what I seek?"

Bodhmall made a face at him then moved in closer. The old woman sniffed at her like a dog. Aednat glanced at Will, hoping he would allay her fears, and was met with a stone visage.

"She smells like a great healer indeed!" The woman's smile revealed black gums, her breath hot and stinky. Aednat had no idea how she could smell anything beyond her own stench.

When the woman returned to Oengus's side, he wrapped a meaty arm around her shoulders. "Have I satisfied yer gods, Bodhmall? Is this the woman they seek?"

That was the first time he'd ever sounded pleasant. She had to stop from once again turning questioning eyes on Will. The rest of the men remained ready to act, but they kept their distance now.

"Ye take her! Take her now!" Bodhmall's squeaky voice matched the excitement on her face. "Now!"

Aednat scooted back, but the woman grabbed one arm with a surprisingly strong grip. "No!"

"But I am not a virgin healer!" Aednat blurted the words out. Surely a quick death would be better than this.

"We do not believe that lie!" Bodhmall said, her words all running together.

"It is no lie."

Bodhmall's fierce look of disbelief sucked all the air of Aednat's lungs. "A man has taken yer maidenhead?"

"My husband!"

"'Tis the maidenhead that holds the power!" The woman backhanded Aednat, knocking her to the ground. The sound of the others shuffling out of the way and the strange noise from the woman just before she launched herself at Aednat spurred her fear. She curled into a ball and covered her head in protection against the attack. Bodhmall kicked and slapped at her head, her body, wherever could make contact. The old woman had a million hands, and Aednat could not protect herself.

"Stand clear, William," she heard from a distance. "Let Bodhmall decide what we do."

Pain shot through every part of Aednat that the woman was abusing. The din of the men getting louder, cheering the old crone on, barely registered. Struggling to pull her knees up beneath her was taking all her concentration. With a heavy lift, Aednat finally shoved herself fiercely to standing. The crazed old woman fell face first alongside her. Bodhmall merely rolled onto her back, hands and legs up in the air shaking, and cackled with laughter. "Ye've missed yer chance!"

The fear of an even more painful death forced Aednat into immediate action. She lurched toward the staff the black-haired woman had pointed out to her. Lifting the heavy pole, she jumped to her feet. The wood, smooth from wear, fit perfectly in her grip. Extending it before her, she swung it around to keep them back.

A triumphant smile on her face, Aednat brandished the weapon before her. She shifted her hands along its length to assess the best placement, her belief that she could indeed defend herself making her brave. One man rushed forward, his *miodóg* extended, but a strong swing from the left disarmed him, and she shoved him away with the blunt end. The length was perfect for her. That he stumbled was an added bonus. All sound ceased in the camp—the men no doubt reassessing her ability with the weapon.

In her mind, she heard Sean as she surveyed the men before her, watching for any movement.

Remember to place yer weight on yer back foot, that's right.

Not too high now. Ye've got more power if it's lower.

Watch that Rusty. He's got his sights on ye. Keep him back.

Rusty rushed her with spread arms, but it was as if he moved in a dream, his movements were so sluggish. She swung the wood to his face, making contact, the full force of her body behind it. The weapon shook in her hand, vibrating up her arm. The force of the impact knocked the weapon back a touch, whipping her around into the ready position as he dropped onto his back.

"She's bloodied me!"

With surprised expressions, the men glanced at each other. Blood flowed from Rusty's nose as he sat up. Broken, no doubt, but she had no desire to stanch its flow for him. Let him bleed to death!

Oengus helped the *bandruí* to her feet with the gentlest motion. His warm gaze on Bodhmall, he tenderly wiped away the dirt from her face with his own *léine*. When they turned as one toward Aednat, his face was twisted into a sinister expression, but the small woman merely smiled. A satisfied smile.

Keep yer weight shifting, lassie, foot to foot.

Oengus threw the cloth he'd brought to gag her to the ground and walked toward her with angry steps.

Lower it now… and swing!

Had her mark been true, Aednat's upward motion would have cracked his skull right open with the force of her swing. Her need to escape was giving her strength she didn't really have. Instead, she caught his shoulder. He only ducked forward with the pain, but that gave her the chance to jab his unprotected side, dropping him to his knees. When she pulled back the pole, preparing for a second jab, he shoved forward, wrapping his arms about her waist and knocking her flat on her back. A fist landed to her gut, sending waves of excruciating pain through her, but she squeezed the wood tight. If she lost that, she'd lose everything. He heaved them both upright.

Grasping for breath, he glared at her, his eyes black with rage. "Ye rotten whore! Ye'll receive no mercy now!"

Do not listen. Deep breath. Steady now.

With all her strength, she fisted the pole to shove

toward him, but he reached his hands past the arc to grip her throat.

No! Yer arms are too far from yer body. Ye need yer body weight. Yer arm without it is too weak.

Damn. He turned away, easily avoiding the contact, tightening his hold. Her staff dropped uselessly to the ground, and she clawed at his hand, desperate for air, the world around her turning dark. Oengus's eyes were wild as he squeezed the life right out of her. The sound of laughter carried to her. She let her eyes flutter shut, not wanting his ugly face to be her last sight.

A hiss sounded nearby and then a *thump*. Followed by another. Pained groans filled the air. Aednat opened her eyes in bafflement—just in time to see Oengus's own eyes widen. His hands went limp and he dropped with a thud—face first, flat to the ground. She scrambled clear of him, gasping when she saw the arrow sticking out of his back. Pulling on her throat, she gasped for air.

Diarmuid rushed toward her, his face the only clear sight in the darkness eating away at her vision. She must be dying. The precious air eluded her still. The strength of his arms enclosed her as he picked her up. He held her solidly against his chest, enough for her to feel his own labored breathing. At least she would die in his loving arms.

The hissing of arrows was replaced by the sound of a warrior's yell. Chaos erupted around them as more men streamed in from the trees. She caught sight of Will and tried to sit up.

"Hush, now. I've got ye." Diarmuid held her tighter as he made for the woods, dodging fighting men and rearing horses.

Aednat struggled against him, watching over his shoulder. Her raspy throat refusing to make any audible sound even though she mouthed the word. "Will."

Heaving in a breath at last, she pulled herself out of Diarmuid's arms.

"Will." Her throat burned from the effort.

Aednat searched the area, pandemonium all around. People frantically running. Wailing children being snatched up by their mothers, their faces a mask of fear. Then Will. He ran toward the cover of the trees. She pointed with frantic motions. But Diarmuid's eyes never left her face, his concern for her alone. The willowy profile of her friend dropped to the ground.

"No!" She screamed the word, and all around her went black.

Chapter Sixteen

With his men all gathered around him now, Diarmuid watched on with horror. The sight of Aednat kneeling before Black Oengus, wide-eyed and trembling, had turned Diarmuid's blood to ice. He'd decided then and there that seeing the man stuffed with his own testicles would abate some of his fury—though only if the man was still aware when he did it, as much as one can be aware after a part of one's body has been hacked off.

Diarmuid would have advanced, but Marcán jerked him back. A saving grace indeed. Waiting the few minutes it took for his men to spread out, some mounted and some on foot, and surround the camp and ready their weapons had been the only reason their attack had been a success and the death toll so high.

Sitting beside Aednat as she finally lay settled in his bed, Diarmuid prayed he'd have the opportunity to make it up to her. She was an amazing woman, even more so than he'd realized. Her eyes, closed as if in sleep, and the paleness of her skin were cause for concern. Worse, the fighting had ended two days ago, and she still had not stirred. Not on the trip back, though he'd held her in his arms the whole time, hoping, and not when he'd carried her into his house.

"*A thighearna?* Would ye prefer to have me see to that?" Maeve stood behind him, and he could almost hear her wringing her hands. She had assured him that his wife's neck was not broken, bruised only, and she would recover. That the old healer had no idea why Aednat had not yet awoken had already caused Diarmuid to bellow for the woman's removal. No doubt she feared his anger now.

"I will see to my wife myself." *As I should have done from the beginning.*

"As ye wish, a *thighearna.*"

The woman collected the dish. The sound of the door quietly shutting behind him was a relief. Getting some broth into Aednat had been a challenge, and he'd required help, but now he wished to be alone with his wife.

Diarmuid squeezed the warm water from the cloth. Her captors had treated her worse than a dog. With a gentle touch, he cleaned away the dried blood and dirt from her face. Not even bruising could mar her beauty. He moved the cloth to her hands, her delicate fingers embedded with dirt. A sliver protruding from her palm.

The way she'd dived to grab the staff… Diarmuid had hardly believed his eyes. And she'd brandished it like someone who knew how to use it. If not for his own experience with the many things that could go wrong in battle and the fear coiling in his belly, he would have been awestruck. As it was, he was duly impressed. Her manipulations of the solid piece of wood spoke of both practice and skill. Her stance, even to the point of staying on the balls of her feet, marked her as an experienced fighter. He'd scoffed at her ability to protect herself, but she hadn't been lying. Shame washed over him at the memory.

Rinsing the cloth, he turned back to her legs. The scabbing at her knees suggested her captors had dragged her along the dirt. He wiped away every last speck of her abuse, and as he ministered to her beaten body, his anger only increased. Anger at himself. Anger at the men who had taken her.

"She still has not stirred?" Marcán spoke in a quiet voice from the doorway of the tiny stone house.

Diarmuid simply nodded, refusing to take his eyes from her.

"Ye cannot deny ye're enamored of the girl. Ye've not left her side once."

Diarmuid ignored the man and pulled the coverings up to her chin, tucking them tight around her still body as if they could keep her protected. Marcán put more peat to the fire. The sound of the sparks and peat colliding, along with the thud from the pot of fresh water being deposited beside it, were merely background happenings. Unimportant. Especially unimportant compared to the willful gaze Diarmuid focused on his wife. She had to recover and soon. He refused to consider any other possibility.

"If ye do not take care of yerself, ye will be of no use when she does awaken."

Diarmuid knew Marcán meant well, but he could make no adequate response. His friend had no understanding of his inner turmoil, of the galling sense of inadequacy clawing at him. He had been unable to protect her. And the guilt! It traced right back to his planned assault on the Meic Murchadha. She'd asked to accompany him, and he'd laughed at her. If he had only brought her with him, she would not be here now at death's door.

Leaving the matter in Marcán's hands had gone against Diarmuid's instinct. Despite his desire to avoid leadership, once proclaimed king by the *derb fine*, he had accepted all the responsibility that went along with the title. Under different circumstances, he would have remained with the other clan himself. Instead, the need to be with her had pulled him away—and then the need to fulfill his leadership role had pushed him back—setting up the situation that had allowed his bride to be taken.

He dropped his face to his hands, rubbing the painful memories away. They had raced again and again through his mind since her injury. He was flooded with regret. The other memories that wouldn't leave him were her moans of pleasure, his insatiable need to again hear her gasps, the sound of his name on her lips, and to see that spark of passion on her face—

The hand on his shoulder startled him.

"Get something to eat and some fresh air. I will stay with her," Marcán said.

With a heavy sigh, Diarmuid rose from the bench. He was surprised to see the sun setting yet again. "Have ye spoken to the women?"

"They've given us no indication where the men may be hiding. They say Black Oengus was the son of a king but with no land of his own. That is why they live the way they do."

Rage tightened Diarmuid's chest, making each breath more labored. "I want every last man accounted for. Not even one will be allowed to slip away. Mayhap their pagan gods are laughing at us even now."

Marcán's shocked expression was barely contained. "Ye cannot believe that blasphemy."

Diarmuid turned to his friend, his mouth clenched with fury. "I should have stayed to fight. No man would have escaped my wrath."

"Ye needed to see to yer wife. Stop torturing yerself! Go." He turned him toward the door with a shove. "Get yer mind clear and then return."

"Ye will call me as soon as she awakens?"

"Immediately."

Marcán waited for Diarmuid to close the door behind him before dropping to the bench. Aednat was not improving, and he feared the worst. Marcán could not bear to think about how his friend would handle it if she died. The memory of Fergus's body being found those many years ago still tormented Diarmuid. He had blamed himself then for not seeing to his little brother's protection. Diarmuid's guilt now would be even greater. And the loss would be devastating to the whole clan.

"Sweet Aednat." Marcán took her hand in his. It was cold as snow. "How long must we wait on ye? We wish to celebrate yer return. Yer joining! Open yer eyes and look at me."

When Aednat's eyes opened and she turned to him, Marcán's breath caught. He waited. Her eyes appeared unfocused. Vacant.

"Aednat?" He spoke with hushed tones.

Her expression remained unchanged.

"Can ye hear me, lass?"

She stared at him, but not as if she were seeing him, and then she turned back and her eyes closed again.

A cold breeze passed over Marcán, and he shivered.

He knew of people nearly killed in battle who were never right in the head again. Some said they were there in body but not in spirit. That they sat at death's door, biding their time until they were allowed in. What would Diarmuid do if that were true of his wife? He was in love with her. Marcán could not imagine how his friend would cope. And that scared him most of all.

Diarmuid's mail was caked with thick mud and splattered with blood. He stood beside Aednat's bed. Even now, she lay unresponsive. He and his men had managed to track down the lair of the rest of Oengus's warriors. The desire for revenge against the surviving outlaws had come to naught. They were landless with nothing of their own. He had shown them mercy by merely imprisoning them. Mayhap later he could decide how best to put them to use. They would remain hostages and never be freed again.

Maeve had come and gone with no further understanding of why Aednat still slept. Like a dog returning to its vomit, Diarmuid's dark thoughts returned again and again to his hasty dismissal of Aednat's offer of help. It tortured him. Imprisoning him with his own unrelenting guilt. If only…

Falling to his knees beside the pallet, he dropped his mouth to his folded hands.

"Sweet Aednat, why will ye not come back to me?" The silence ripped him apart. "I am here waiting for ye." He stared at her still features. "I want to take ye in my arms. I need to love ye again and show ye how I've missed y—"

"Diarmuid?" Marcán spoke from the doorway, a stern tone.

Diarmuid had been so intent on Aednat, he'd not heard the door open. Without turning away from her, he spoke over his shoulder. "I wish to be left alone."

"And we have heeded yer wishes, but now there are things that must be seen to. The hostages?"

Aednat's blank expression shifted.

Diarmuid paused. He stared at her.

"Diarmuid?"

Diarmuid sat up straighter, willing her to do it again, and played the expression over and over in his head. It had happened—he was certain of it.

"Marcán? Did ye see that?" His exhilaration came through in his voice.

"Diarmuid, ye're not listening to me." Marcán's anger was apparent, but Diarmuid waved a hand at the man, hushing him.

"She moved!"

"And Sean will be here by week's end. He will expect to meet with ye."

Diarmuid's beautiful wife, who had lain motionless on the pillow for nigh on eight days now, turned toward him.

"Aednat?" Diarmuid whispered, awed and nearly dumbstruck. He stood, his face a mask of amazement as he turned to Marcán. "Look at her, Marcán."

Diarmuid's excitement could barely be contained as he gestured toward Aednat with both hands.

He waved his friend closer. "Aednat?"

"Diarmuid, stop!" When Diarmuid dropped back to his knees beside the bed, Marcán yanked at his shoulder. "Ye can do nothing for the lass."

"No! Look, Marcán! Her eyes."

Aednat's eyes fluttered open. One look at her, and Marcán took a step back toward the door.

Diarmuid stood and turned to him. "Why d'ye look so frightened?"

"Heed my warning. She may not be right in the head."

"What?" Outrage ripped through Diarmuid's gut and he bellowed at his friend. "Be gone!"

Marcán backed out of the house, slamming the door closed behind him.

Diarmuid held his wife's small, pale hand in his. Her eyes were again closed. "Aednat? Ye have so much to come back to us for. Sean and Thomasina are coming."

There was no response. His chest tightened.

"Please, my love." His breath caught at the endearment he'd never thought to use. He kissed her palm. Odd that this woman, his perfect bride in every way, sat at death's door because of his own failings. "Sorry I am that I've allowed harm to come to ye. I'd never wish that on ye. Not on anyone that I love."

Thoughts of his brother raced through his mind. That sunny spring day Fergus had tried to follow Diarmuid. Their mother had been lax, coddling him and believing he'd never do a thing without her consent. That she had him well trained. But Fergus had the heart of a warrior. He'd heard the stories of the great high king of Ireland and couldn't wait for his big brother to show him where the *árd rí* Brian Boru had stayed.

Movement behind her eyelids caught his attention. "Aednat?"

She seemed to be dreaming now, her face twitching with some unknowable emotion.

"What does the healer order for herself? Will my love strengthen ye and bring ye back to health? My kisses." He leaned closer to lay a gentle kiss on her forehead, cool against his lips. "Will my arms surrounding ye warm ye through to bring ye back to us?"

With great care and still weighted down with his filthy mail, Diarmuid took her into his arms as he stretched out on the bed beside her. He kissed her brow. "And yer hard head? Surely nothing could damage that skull of yers."

Aednat snuggled against him, her hand at his chest and eyes still closed. He held her tighter, his own cheeks damp.

"Sweet Aednat, come back to me. I vow to learn be a good husband to ye. I need only a second chance."

A chance he'd never had with his brother.

At some point he drifted off to sleep. In his dream, Aednat was wholly recovered. Naked beneath him. He held her in a loving embrace and kissed her with all the passion she sparked in him.

"Ye are like no other woman I have ever known. If I had a lifetime to show ye my love, it still wouldn't be long enough. Sean and Thomasina were wise indeed."

"Lorccán?"

The whispered word seemed to come from his mind. He rested his chin against her head, his eyes slowly opening. She lay against his chest and her hand was at his side, squeezing him.

"Aednat?"

"I am here."

Afraid to believe his own ears, he tipped her chin so he could look into her wide eyes.

She returned his gaze, her eyes clear.

"Are ye back with us?" His breath trapped in his chest, his voice sounded so small.

"Where have I been?"

Diarmuid worked his way off the bed, helping her sit up. "Ye have been so sick. So very sick." He wiped a gentle hand across her brow. "I was sore afraid for ye. How d'ye feel?"

"It feels sore here." She rubbed at her throat. "Mayhap a bit thirsty?"

Standing beside the bed, he offered her a cup of water, helping her to bring it to her mouth. "Ye have been quite sick."

Aednat concentrated on finishing the water, her throat working as if she were still in pain. He refilled it for her.

"Where are we? I do not remember this place."

"What d'ye remember?"

She shook her head, a deeply furrowing brow marred her lovely face. "We were trying to escape… we were in yer grandfather's house."

Her hand warm in his now, he willed her to remember more. With all his strength, he willed it. He did not want Marcán to be correct.

Glancing around, her eyes brightened, and with

the trace of a smile, she said, "And that is where we are now. And we…"

When she raised her eyebrows and turned to him, the blush working across her face made him smile.

"We are husband and wife and this is the house where we made love." Squeezing her hand, he kissed it. "And I have missed ye."

"How long have I been lying here?"

"More than a week's time."

She gasped, her eyes widening, and sat up straighter. "Did ye say Sean was coming?"

"I have just received word." His joy could barely be contained. "And Thomasina and Lorccán as well."

"Pleased I am to be able to see them again."

"Did ye believe I was an ogre to keep ye from them?"

Her expression clouded, as if she was searching her memory for something, and then her face lit up. "Oengus! Ye killed him! What about Will? Did ye spare Will?"

"Shh." He added some wine to her cup, waiting for her to take a sip before continuing. "I do not know this Will, but some of the men did survive."

Clearly agitated, she began to slip her feet from the bed, but he stopped her.

"No!" He tucked her feet back in. "Ye cannot get out of bed! 'Tis too soon!"

Her expression turned to disbelief. "Ye do not understand! My Will! I must find him and make sure he is unharmed."

Unsure if her mind had indeed been affected, Diarmuid fought off a wave of a fear. "Tell me of this Will."

Blowing out a breath, she collapsed again on the

bed. "Will was my friend. He was a boy I knew long ago, back when my grandmother and I lived in the cave. He and I would play when the villagers were at meals. The only time we could be out and about without fear. Otherwise we remained in the cave.

"My grandmother cared for us. And Cad, another boy. She saw to our needs as best she could. I did not even know I had missed anything until I went to live with Sean, where I had a pallet of my own and there was always a fire at night to keep us warm. Even so, I never remembered feeling cold with Grandmother.

"We had another friend who was big and strong. A giant, really, and he'd bring us whatever we needed." She laughed, a conspiratorial little laugh. "My grandfather had no idea all the things he used to bring us.

"Tisa spent time with us, too, after she came to live in the village. She was married to my uncle then. But"—she turned to him as if just noticing him—"he never came to the cave with Tisa, and I think it hurt my grandmother that he didn't come to see her. Will would always try to make her laugh when she was sad."

The tenderness in her voice sent a surge of jealousy to his gut. "Was this Will one of the men who took ye?"

"He was one of the men… but…" Her intense concern for the man was undeniable.

Itching to bellow his outrage, Diarmuid was suddenly hit with just how spent he felt. He swallowed it down and forced an even tone. "He was one of those who held ye captive? And ye want to know that I spared him?"

Her wide, innocent eyes had dark circles beneath

them. She was exhausted, but it was obvious she would not rest again until he gave her news on one of the captors.

"Why would I spare him? I saw how ye were treated! He does not deserve to be spared. None of them do."

Despite his attempts at a reasonable voice, her eyes rounded in her upset. Deep feelings she had for this man. He struggled to keep his anger in check, his breath quivering in his chest.

"Forgive me, *a ghrádh*." He knelt beside the bed and took her hand. "I wish to understand yer concern, not upset ye."

Aednat moved her face in closer to his. "He was my friend and always kind to me. I value him greatly, and he did what he could to protect me from Oengus. Please find out if he lives?"

The sound in the room seemed to stop. She cared for this Will. Valued him greatly.

Is there another ye would marry?

She'd had no answer at the time, but perhaps now she would change her mind.

"I am sorry to disappoint ye, but I will see to *ye* first." He stood, stiff and controlled, and moved to call from the door, "Get Beibhinn!"

"Yer mother?"

"My mother."

She smoothed down her hair. "I've not met her."

"She has met ye." The woman who always thought of herself first had shown great concern for Aednat, stopping by several times a day to ask about her. "She feared that ye might soon die, and she would never meet the woman I took to wife."

Surely she could stay with his wife without causing

trouble. Besides, Astrid needed all the other women to help with the preparations for Sean and Thomasina's visit. Keeping Beibhinn here and away from the others might help things move along more smoothly, since she always managed to offend someone with her sharp tongue.

Aednat reddened.

"Diarmuid?" Beibhinn paused in the doorway. A small woman with soft gray hair flowing around her shoulders, her expression a perpetual state of alarm.

Diarmuid sighed and directed her toward the bed. When she saw Aednat was awake, her face brightened and, naturally, her eyes filled with tears.

"Oh! Diarmuid! She is awake!" Crossing to the bed, she moved into the place he'd vacated moments before and took his wife's hand. "Ye are so lovely."

Aednat visibly swallowed. "Thank ye. Pleased I am to meet ye."

"Oh! But ye look so tired. How d'ye feel?"

Diarmuid had a hard time holding back the comments that came to his irritated mind as the two exchanged pleasantries. His mother's tears were unstoppable, but he was proud of his Aednat that she did not join in, even though it was *she* who had been injured and mistreated. He cleared his throat.

"I must interrupt ye now." He grasped his mother's shoulder, turning her toward him. "I wish ye to stay with Aednat."

Beibhinn turned back to Aednat, her tears apparently forgotten. "Sean and Thomasina are coming to see how ye are faring here. 'Tis a great honor. There are preparations to make for our *ri túath*…"

Diarmuid would have preferred not to worry his recuperating wife about such things, and the look on her face cut through his gut. Sean did not know of her abduction and would be beside himself with anger, no doubt. But Diarmuid would deal with that.

"*I* will see to the preparations, Aednat. Rest. My mother will stay with ye." He turned stern eyes on Beibhinn. "And she will not tire ye out or cause ye to become more distressed."

His mother wiped at her face, bobbing her head as if she were the agreeable type. "Of course. I know what I am about."

"Speak of pleasantries only." The words, which he'd repeated to her often, and to no avail, were delivered in a low voice. His mother had a knack for choosing topics that created arguments and mayhem. "Aednat requires rest. Send word if anything changes."

He glanced back at Aednat. Her eyes were brightening, so mayhap the worst was over. Diarmuid wanted to take her in his arms and kiss her. Her concern for this Will still foremost in his mind, he hesitated.

Glancing at Beibhinn, he added, "See to her needs. The wine. The water. Some repast."

His mother followed his hand as he directed her. When she faced him again, he was met with a stern expression.

"This is the food I brought for *ye*, Diarmuid. Ye must take care of yerself."

He held up his hand. "Do not speak yer complaints, woman. I will take care of myself as I always have. See to my wife! Do not upset her."

Diarmuid left without a backward glance. His preoccupation with Aednat had caused him to shirk his duties, and there was much to do. When he reached the roundhouse, a few of his men remained. "Is Marcán with the hostages?"

"He stands guard, warning them off of their aggression." It was Gréagóir who spoke up. He set aside his whittling.

"Have ye spoken to them?" Diarmuid asked.

"Marcán has. We were not sure what ye would have us do with them." Gréagóir stood up straighter. He took his job seriously whenever left in charge. "There are only five left."

"And the woman and children?"

Peter, one of his other guards, answered the question. "They have been taken as slaves and distributed as such. We saw no reason to treat them any differently." He leaned against the wall beside the hearth and took a sip of the mug of ale in his hand. "There was no sign of the witch ye saw."

"She is called Bodhmall," Gréagóir added.

A common name for one who practiced the dark arts. The vision of the woman attacking Aednat was burned in Diarmuid's memory.

"And all the women insisted 'twas Bodhmall alone who told Oengus about the legend of the healer. They claim many of the men tried to turn him from the idea, but Oengus held the old crone in high regard."

"They tried to turn him from hunting down my wife? A fine ruse to convince us to spare the hostages. Did their men not make free with women while he searched out any healer that might give him power? Going clan by clan?" Diarmuid tugged on his gloves, avoiding eye contact. "Is there one called Will amongst the men?"

"Will?" Gréagóir looked to the others, but they all

shook their heads. "I do not think so."

The news gave him a slight feeling of unease.

Ignoring his circling thoughts, Diarmuid turned a stern expression on Gréagóir. "My mother sits with Aednat."

"She has awakened?"

"A miracle!"

The men murmured their awe and surprise. Diarmuid knew their relief and offered a smile of gratitude.

"I do not want her bothered overmuch by my mother."

Gréagóir nodded in understanding. "I'll relieve her myself."

"As will I," Peter added. "But yer wife does not know us."

"I will see to that anon. We will have a great celebration when our overking arrives." He smiled. "And I will introduce my wife to the clan."

If there is another ye would prefer, I will bring ye to him.

Was he still bound by his promise?

"'Tis high time she learn the benefits of being wife to a *ri túaithe*. Do not hesitate to remove Beibhinn. She could turn the ear of a saint and make him crumble into a weeping puddle on the ground. God help my mother if she causes one sweet strand of Aednat's hair to curl."

The men nodded in agreement—all of them well accustomed to Beibhinn's ability to torment by talking.

"I will need to think on the hostages now that my wife is on the mend. Prepare yer weapons. I will tolerate no disturbance from them."

He left the room with a definite sense of unease.

His men would support any decision he made regarding the hostages, but Aednat was a different matter. His gut tightened. How she could feel even one of Oengus's men deserved leniency was beyond him.

If her childhood friend lived, Diarmuid decided that he would find him. And he would indeed bring him to her so that she could see him. He would do that for her, but he would not let her go.

Aednat had dismissed the offer Diarmuid had made in an ill-conceived show of consideration for her feelings. She'd said there was no one else she'd prefer to marry. Before God and man, she was his wedded wife, and he had no desire to sever that tie.

Diarmuid did not easily give up what was his.

Chapter Seventeen

By midday next, Aednat had recovered enough to receive visitors. It was a relief when Diarmuid's men came to check on her, even more so when they said they were moving her to the roundhouse. It had been a long day alone with Beibhinn. They settled Aednat safely in a cart filled with blankets for the short journey, and one of the men, Peter, spoke to Beibhinn before they left. Aednat overheard enough to know she was being ordered to stay behind. She did not look pleased about the arrangement, but Peter listened politely as her jaw flapped in irritation.

Aednat cringed inside with guilt. There was a great relief at being separated from the unhappy woman. Beibhinn did nothing but complain. No one did anything good enough for her. And that was when she was trying to be kind. It seemed the woman was set on being miserable and making all those around her share that misery. If they saw the good in something, she would bring them around to seeing the bad.

Gréagóir came abreast of the cart. "Not a far distance, but we prefer ye save yer strength for Diarmuid's return. We expect him any time."

"D'ye know where he has gone this time?"

"He searches for the witch." The reminder of that horrible crone sent a chill down her spine.

Gréagóir was a stern-faced man who seldom smiled, a jagged scar just above his left brow.

"I am fine. My thanks, Gréagóir."

Dipping his chin, he returned to the front of the group. Men rode on either side of her, along with three at the front and the rear. The protective forces seemed a bit overdone, but she did not speak of it. Her head hurt, and her stomach burned every time she tried to eat. Though she watched for mint plants on the way to the roundhouse, she saw none. There may have been one amongst the many small jars in Diarmuid's stone house—*her* stone house—but she hadn't possessed the strength to search it out. She smiled at the memory of lying encircled in his arms last night. He hadn't once let go, as if assuring himself she would remain beside him even in sleep. But she had been unable to sleep, instead watching the strange shadows cast by the fire on the thatch roof above them.

She had thought of Diarmuid's grandfather. A Norseman. There were so many stories of their brutality and ill treatment toward the Irish whom they'd enslaved. According to Diarmuid, his powerful grandfather had been in love with one of them, enough so to stay behind and take her to wife. Had she been a slave first? Had she feared her husband and his powerful rule before they were wed?

"Aednat?"

Aednat jerked awake. Her cart was stopped and the round tower was just visible above the trees. She rubbed at her eyes.

"We have arrived."

The man who spoke to her was not one of the ones she knew.

"Where…" She looked over the men. "Where is Gréagóir?"

"He has gone to see Diarmuid. I can help ye down."

The tall, solidly built man was exceedingly delicate in his treatment of her. Scooping her into his arms, he carried her inside.

"What is yer name?" she asked.

The thick beard revealed straight white teeth. "I am from Clan Meic Murchadha. My name is Pádraig."

Aednat was surprised Diarmuid had handed over her care to a rival clan, but she did not question the man. He brought her inside and settled her on a bench before departing. No undue attention was given to him, as if his presence was of little account. She shrugged off the oddity. No doubt she simply didn't understand the clan divisions here.

Being here again brought back more memories. This was where she'd waited for Diarmuid's return, listening to Faolán's outrageous stories. It seemed so long ago now. Unlike the first time, the room was crowded with people cooking, cleaning, seeing to children, no doubt taking in her disheveled appearance. She'd had no more than a bowl of water to wash herself with before they moved her.

There were many women of marriageable age, younger than herself, who seemed a bit more interested in her. Their eyes took in every bit of her. From her bare feet, at least clean now, to the ill-fitting gown Beibhinn had brought her. One young lass with bright, curling red hair didn't hide her interest, even bringing a mug of mead to her.

"Welcome. Ye must be Diarmuid's wife?"

Aednat appreciated the kindness, smiled, and drank her fill of the sweet beverage.

"I expected ye to look… different."

"I have been through much." Aednat wished the woman would stop inspecting her, and the girls she'd been standing with were doing the same. She forced a smile. "I am called Aednat."

The redhead nodded and smiled. A tolerant smile. The type of smile you give to someone you don't really like. Then she returned to the other girls without another word. When they put their heads close together, Aednat wasn't surprised they laughed and looked her way.

A winded Gréagóir trotted through the door and draped a wool blanket around her shoulders before she could rise to greet him. "Apologies. I had some trouble with the hostages. Are ye warm enough now?"

"Hostages?"

He blanched. "Nothing for ye to be concerned about."

Abruptly he took her cup to refill it. When he returned, she asked, "Are they hostages from Black Oengus's clan?"

Gréagóir gave a slight nod, averting his gaze.

"Are there many being held here?"

When he settled beside her on the bench, he leveled his gaze on her. "I should not have mentioned them. Diarmuid did not want ye to be concerned about such things." He glanced around. "He should be here anon. Try to rest whilst ye wait. I need to get back to my duties, if ye are settled?"

She nodded, not wanting to press the matter. In her short acquaintance with Gréagóir, he had always been ready to answer her questions, giving her more information than she could even use. This turnaround made her wonder why.

Bare-chested and glistening with sweat, Diarmuid came through the front door and paused. Aednat found it hard to take a breath or look away. He was a handsome man, and though he'd shown no renewed interest in her in *that* way, she had thought he might wish to bed her again. Even this morning. But she had been disappointed.

His eyes scanned the room, but they didn't settle on her. They landed instead on the redhead, who tilted her head and smiled. Her friends silently looking on with approval as their *ri* closed the distance to her.

"Lilith, have ye spoken to Marcán?"

"I have not. But when I have"—she lowered her eyes in what Aednat assumed was a show of deference until she lifted them again with such brazen appreciation, the truth became clear in an instant—"shall I come to ye?"

Aednat's fingers curled into fists at the provocative question, and when Diarmuid smiled, she felt ready to rip both of their eyes out. Is this where he was seeing his needs met?

"That will not do." He crossed his arms about his chest, the silver band accentuating the great size of his muscles, but he did not seem overly upset by her blatant overture. "I am wed now and when my wife arrives—"

Lilith glanced toward Aednat, the regret on her face almost comical. It became even more so when Diarmuid followed her gaze, and his face lit up upon seeing her.

"Aednat! I did not know ye'd arrived." In three strides, he was pulling her up against him to receive his kiss. "I have missed ye."

His quiet voice spoke of his longing. A boon to Aednat's hurt pride, and she let go of her anger. That the lass may think it acceptable to flirt with the king was irrelevant as long as the king did not return the attention.

Glancing around as if a bit unsure of what to talk about, he finally said, "Ye look well settled here."

"'Twas Pádraig who set me here. Is he not from the nearby clan?"

"We fight amongst ourselves, but would support each other if attacked by another clan. Like brothers. My mother came from that tribe." After a slight smile, he asked, "Are ye strong enough to sit outside?"

"I believe I am."

"Then come." Putting an arm around her shoulders, he led her through the door and into the light. "Let me look at ye."

His expression softened as he searched her face. "Mayhap ye have gotten out of bed too soon."

"I cannot stay abed any longer, Diarmuid!"

His frown returned and she wondered if the change in him had anything to do with the hostages. Scanning the area behind the cone-topped dwelling, she tried to discern which building might house them.

"The hostages are in the hideaway." All pleasure was gone from his face, replaced by a rigid expression.

"How did ye know I…?"

Diarmuid's nostrils flared and his lips flattened into an angry line, but he did not respond. Instead, he began pacing. She dared say no more.

"Diarmuid?" Marcán came toward them, a pike in his fist. "They've not settled."

"What has happened?" Aednat asked. "Is it the hostages?"

Her husband gave her a withering glance. "Ye'll need to stay put. I will send Lilith out to sit with ye."

"No! Not Lilith!" The words were out before she had even thought them.

Diarmuid seemed beside himself, and his irritated tone confirmed it. "Ye do not tell me what I may do."

Marcán shifted uncomfortably, as if he wished to be anywhere but here.

"Ye wish to leave me in someone else's care?" Aednat's own irritation rose as well. So did her voice. "Does it need to be the woman who shares yer bed?"

Diarmuid stood there, an array of emotions flitting across his features—none of them pleasant. He was no doubt trying to come up with something to justify his choice of *Lilith.*

"*Ye're* the only woman who shares *my* bed. Whoever I may have sought out for release before ye became my wife is of no relevance now. *Ye* are the only one I would seek out. And she certainly never shared my bed."

Aednat nibbled at her lower lip. His explanation of her special place of honor in his bed brought her great pleasure. As did his reassurance that he would be coming to her alone for such intimacy. Why, then, did he seem so angry?

"I-I-I will stay w-with her." Faolán approached from the fields, having apparently overheard part of their exchange.

Aednat sighed her relief. "Thank ye, Faolán."

"So be it." Diarmuid stomped off, Marcán close behind.

As soon as Diarmuid and Marcán made the turn toward the stables, shouting could be heard from the men standing guard above the hideaway. They jabbed their pikes at the hostages below.

"Why does it take three men to guard the hostages?" Diarmuid asked his second.

"They have taken to climbing on each other's shoulders to try and escape."

Voices yelling from below carried to them.

"Is that yer leader?"

"My wife. D'ye have her?"

"Is my baby alive?"

Diarmuid addressed Marcán, his patience gone. "So they are concerned for their loved ones. As was I when I found my wife taken!" The bitterness in his tone increased. "Why should they receive the comfort of reassurance when they offered me none?"

"But, Diarmuid, the women did say the men tried to dissuade Oengus."

"And I believe they lie!"

"To what purpose? They do not know which of the men have survived."

"I care not! What would ye have me do? Take them into my clan? After they thought to assault my wife?"

"Have ye spoken to her about what happened? They might not all be equally guilty."

Aednat's soft voice filled his head. *I value him greatly*, she'd said about Will. *He was my friend.*

"There is no reason for us to speak of it," he blustered. "The danger has passed, and she is safe with me now. The threat has been dealt with."

"It appears the threat continues."

"BACK DOWN!" Gréagóir jabbed at the hands reaching over the edge of the hole. A corresponding scream confirmed his aim was true. "Now all of ye, settle down!"

Diarmuid approached. "What are the ages of the men within?"

"Is that yer *rí*? Let me speak with him!"

"Quiet down! He's no reason to speak to ye," Gréagóir said, looking down into the pit with a scowl.

"Two are past their prime. The rest younger," Marcán said.

Diarmuid crossed his arms and pursed his lips. The time was nigh for him to decide whether these men should be put to death. He needed to set his anger aside and find out more about them. See if they were hostages he could benefit from. Besides, he needed to ensure this Will was not amongst the hostages. He'd pledged to himself he would find the man for his wife's peace of mind.

Turning to Gréagóir, he said, "Gather more men."

"What are ye planning?" Marcán asked. His demanding tone received Diarmuid's coldest glare.

Gréagóir laid the pike aside and took off toward the cone-topped dwelling at a trot.

"Bring the hostages up."

Marcán did not hesitate to prepare the ladder, and as soon as Gréagóir returned with four other men, all well-armed, he lowered it into the hole. One by one the hostages emerged, each shielding his eyes. They were filthy, some with open sores from wounds they must have received during the battle.

While assessing each man, Diarmuid kept all emotion from his face. Two of the hostages were gray haired and hunched over. He did not envision her childhood "friend" quite so old as that. Three remained definite possibilities. They varied in age from possibly six and ten to two score. One of the younger men collapsed on the ground and the other hostages had to be held back to keep from going to him.

Gréagóir pushed the man with his foot, his sharpened spear leveled at his chest. The man still did not move, but Diarmuid could not convince himself this was not a ploy. He signaled for the others to stop moving closer and walked over to the lanky, dark-haired man. He was curled into himself and he did not respond when Diarmuid nudged him with his foot.

Diarmuid faced the hostages. "What is wrong with this man?"

"He's nigh to death! I tried to tell ye that!" It was one of the older men who spoke.

"And what is yer name?"

"I am Cairbre. I am a sword maker, the best here."

"Ye work at the fire?"

"I do. As my father did before me."

Diarmuid could feel the tension pouring off of Marcán beside him. It was best not to let the man know that he'd managed to increase his value to them. Better to let him think they cared little for what occupation any of them claimed to have.

"And this man's name?" Diarmuid pointed to the collapsed body at his feet.

"That's William."

Chapter Eighteen

The roundhouse was abuzz with activity in preparation for the arrival of the *ri túath*. Aednat kept to herself on a bench in the corner while the others worked around her. She was feeling much more herself. She hadn't seen Lilith and her group again, which was fine with Aednat. Faolán had been a preferable companion, though far less entertaining now that she was wise to his ways. She hadn't objected when he'd told her his duties would prevent him from keeping her company again today.

The pleasant aroma of roasting duck and trout started her stomach to growling. For the first time since she'd awoken, she looked forward to the meal. Additional trestles had been squeezed in wherever they could fit. Her clan—Sean's clan—was quite large, and she expected all of the clanspeople who had traveled to the meeting at Clan Meic Lochlainn would be in attendance.

Names and faces flitted through her mind as she tried to recall who'd made the trip. Truth be told, it was really Sean, Thomasina, and Lorccán she couldn't wait to see. Still, it would be nice to see the others, introduce them to her husband, and show them she was indeed worthy of being wed.

Lying in Diarmuid's arms these past few nights, she had felt at home. She'd rested so much yesterday that she had not been able to sleep through the night. When she'd awakened, well before dawn, Diarmuid's arms were still wrapped around her. But while he nestled her close against him every night, he made no other overtures. A little disappointing since she was getting her strength back. Surrounded by his scent, she'd been flooded by memories of his making love to her. His breath on her neck had set off little waves of desire, and when his hand had brushed her breast, she'd wanted more.

He'd never questioned her about her time with Oengus. Marcán had mentioned to her that they'd waited to attack, watching until just the right moment, which is why they'd been so successful. She didn't know for certain how much they'd witnessed of her ordeal.

Aednat shivered despite the bright sunshine warming her skin. Had Will fallen in that first attack? Tears filled her eyes, and she struggled to contain them. No doubt her sadness came from losing another person from her past. She knew how he'd tried to protect her, even outsmarting Oengus so she was not raped. He had looked out for her then, just as he had when she'd been young. A true friend.

The women brought in great platters of fruit, but it was a small, auburn-haired lass who caught her attention.

"Merewyn?"

The green eyes turned to her once before shifting to Astrid, whom she was following.

"Is there something ye need, Aednat?" Astrid closed the distance, Merewyn tagging behind. "Yer gown looks lovely."

"*Yer* gown does look lovely. Thank ye for letting me wear it." Aednat embraced Astrid. A bit tight in the waist and a bit large in the chest, the gown had delicate pink, purple, and red stitching along the hem and neck and was intended for a very special occasion.

"When will I ever have a chance to wear such a matronly blue?" Astrid said with a wink.

"Ah, I believe ye will. Sooner rather than later. And yer ankle?"

"Much less pain."

"Valerian root," Merewyn said, without looking directly at either woman.

"It *is* ye, Merewyn!" Aednat smiled. "And how have ye come to be here with Astrid?"

Astrid refused to make eye contact, and Aednat was left looking from one to the other, not quite understanding why no answer was forthcoming.

"Merewyn?"

Merewyn tipped her head in a defiant way before she answered. "I was brought here with the other women from Black Oengus's clan after the battle."

"She was given to me." Astrid's tone indicated her reluctance to share the information.

"Was I not to know of this?"

"No!" Astrid rolled her eyes and swung her arm about before answering. "Diarmuid wants to protect ye. None of us are to discuss the hostages or the slaves with ye. Any that upset ye will be taken away."

Aednat had spent enough time with Astrid now to know her intentions were good. Her reluctance to tell her what Diarmuid had ordered made more sense now. She turned again to Merewyn. "Have ye seen Will—William? D'ye know if he is with the hostages?"

"Please, Aednat, do not ask about them! My brother will be upset." Astrid implored her with a look.

Merewyn shrugged. "None of us know who survived the attack. Or who is being held. Or what their fate will be."

"Their *fate*?" Aednat gave Astrid a questioning glance. "They are being held here, but their punishment may still be death?"

"Aednat! It is the way of the *ri túaithe*. Diarmuid must decide these things without our interference."

"I am not interfering! I am merely curious."

"That is not the truth of it, and ye know it!"

"I wish to know who is being held. I—"

Astrid held up a hand to silence Aednat, then turned to Merewyn. "Go and help with the other platters."

Aednat smiled at the girl and waited until she was out of earshot to turn on Astrid. "What has Diarmuid told ye?"

Astrid's jaw dropped in obvious surprise, the sight of it almost enough to make Aednat laugh.

"Ye two are far closer than ye would have others believe," Aednat said.

"The hostages deserve to die! All of them. They abducted ye, Aednat."

"I do not disagree, but…"

"Ye are concerned for Will. I have heard that much." Astrid's expression closed down, leaving her even more confused.

"If he is here, I do not understand why that should be kept from me."

"It does not concern ye. What if he is here, and the punishment Diarmuid decides is death? Would ye want to know that, too?" Astrid's expression did not change. "I need to get back to work and ye need to rest."

"He is my fr—"

Astrid's hand halted her words. "I do not want to know what he is to ye. I only want my brother to be happy."

Aednat watched her retreating back and settled into her spot on the corner bench, more confused than ever. Try as she might to ignore the situation with the hostages, no one in the clan was unaffected by it. From the changing of the guard to the preparation of the food for them, everyone was involved, though no one seemed informed of the specifics. Only the warriors were allowed near the prisoners.

The announcement of Sean's arrival had Aednat breathing a sigh of relief. Tears of joy pricked at her eyes, but she took a shaky breath and wiped her cheeks dry, intent on not showing her feelings. They'd only worry for her. Thomasina's eyes lit up when she and Sean came through the door with their daughter, Brighit, right behind them. But it was Lorccán throwing himself into Aednat's arms that broke down her defenses, dampening her face again.

"Oh, Aednat, I have missed ye so much."

He wrapped tight arms around her and his sweet

words set her heart to squeezing. The loss of the lad's daily company had weighed on her. "I have missed ye as well, my sweet boy."

He pulled away, his eyes wide. "And mama is going to have another baby!"

Aednat's jaw dropped and she turned to Thomasina for confirmation.

"Lorccán!" Thomasina's scolding tone did not match the wide smile on her face.

"'Tis true?"

"'Tis." Thomasina opened her arms and Aednat fell into her warm embrace. When Sean's heavy hands wrapped around them both, she had the overwhelming feeling of being home again.

Aednat was met with the grim visage of her husband as soon as she pulled away.

"Sean. Thomasina." He came up to stand beside them, glancing at them both. "Welcome to my home."

Sean's furrowed brow matched his wife's.

"My thanks." His response sounded more like a question. "And how goes it here with ye? And our Aednat?"

"I am sure we will be discussing many things, but for now, things are well. *My* Aednat and I are still getting acquainted."

Aednat's heart sank, and the strange look on Sean's face confirmed he sensed the change in Diarmuid, too. Whatever had angered Diarmuid these last few days still pulled at him. She'd spent her time getting acquainted with the people of her new clan and had been proud to learn her husband was well loved by his people. To see him now, he did not seem pleased with his lot in life. That could only mean one thing: he was not pleased with being married to her.

"Come. Sit." Diarmuid put an arm to Sean's shoulder, directing him to a long table that had been set up at the front of the room. A place of honor for the visiting overking.

Thomasina held back, putting a hand to Aednat's brow. "Are ye not well?"

"I have been ill, but I am getting stronger every day." Aednat paused, unsure how much, if anything, they knew of her being taken. "They tracked me down."

Thomasina gasped, and Sean turned to her. "What is amiss?"

Aednat glanced at Diarmuid, but it was Thomasina who answered. "Black Oengus found her."

"And took ye?" Sean turned on Diarmuid, a fierce scowl on his face. Aednat had never seen him so beside himself with anger. "How could ye let that happen? I entrusted her to ye."

Lorccán came to stand by his father, mirroring both his stance and his expression.

"I was remiss—"

"Ye were not, brother!" Astrid spoke from across the room, where she had been speaking with their mother. She hobbled over to them, her mother following behind. "Whilst he was away, there was a problem with the Meic Murchadha. By the time Diarmuid had arrived… well, needless to say, 'tis *my* fault alone that she was taken."

The fact that Sean had rolled his eyes at the mention of the Meic Murchadha did not go unnoticed. Now that Aednat knew exactly who the Meic Murchadha was, she scanned the great room for any sign of Pádraig. There was none, though she'd seen him speaking with Astrid earlier. A heated exchange.

"As king," Diarmuid said in a level tone, "it is my responsibility alone to see to the protection of our clan, Astrid. As Aednat's husband, even more so."

"Son, ye are mistaken to take all the blame on yerself," Beibhinn said, her eyes shooting daggers at Aednat.

Aednat pulled back, mystified by the sudden hostility. There had been no ugly words between them to account for the change. When Astrid put a hand to her mother's arm in a reassuring way, Aednat was even more perplexed.

But it was the pain on Diarmuid's face that made her heart speed up. The shame he bore because of the incident and her being taken. She cringed inside that a man as great as he needed to profess to falling short. Ever. And at a duty he should never have been called upon to take. He'd only agreed to marry her because Sean had asked him to do so. Her chest tightened. Mayhap he wanted to end the marriage now that the threat had been removed. If the marriage did not please him, he had no reason now to keep her as his wife.

"My concern is for ye," Sean said, taking Aednat's hand between his own, an intense expression on his face. "Please tell me they did not mistreat my sweet cousin?"

All eyes on her, she realized that no one knew the answer for certain. She stood up straighter. "They did not touch me."

Sean reached to touch the bruise on her chin. "This was from a fall?"

"They beat me, *Datan*, but they did not rape me."

While Astrid looked relieved, her mother still seemed unhappy, her lips pressed in a tight line and her back stiff.

Aednat tried to ignore her and continued, "My friend Will, do ye remember him? He lived with Black Oengus, and he protected me until Diarmuid arrived and rescued me."

Diarmuid appreciated Aednat making him the hero of the story, but he'd prefer her expression hadn't softened so when she'd spoken of Will. Her friend. One Sean and Thomasina apparently knew of by name. A punch to the gut would surely be less painful! His wife speaking of another man who'd sought to protect her when he had fallen so miserably short?

He fought against the despair settling in his chest. When he looked up, he caught Astrid watching him, and her expression softened as if she saw his pain. Despite their dissimilarities, the great loss of their brother had brought them together, bound them closer than most siblings. But when Astrid lowered her eyes, the disapproval still hung heavy on him. His mother's eyes widened as if outraged. She'd only just learned his wife was a healer, and she was far from pleased. She believed he'd intentionally withheld the fact. Diarmuid had neither the time nor the inclination to cater to his mother's dislike of the many things she did not understand and, therefore, did not trust. Taking a deep breath, he turned to Sean.

"Despite my best efforts, Aednat was in harm's way, but there can be no question of her own ability. By the time we tracked them down and moved to rescue her, she was already well on her way to escape." He continued toward the table, avoiding eye contact with any of them. "If it pleases ye, I would prefer to speak of this as we feast. This is the first meal I will have with my"—he swallowed before continuing—"new bride, and I have not even had the opportunity to introduce her as such to my clan."

His jaw tight, Diarmuid finally leveled his gaze at Sean's face, avoiding eye contact with either Thomasina or Aednat. He'd prefer not to read his own condemnation in their eyes. He was a fool of the worst kind to believe finding a woman he desired above all else would be met with a return of that affection. Especially when his own inadequacies were so apparent.

"And ye waited for what reason?" Though not loud enough for the women to hear, Sean's question was spoken in a belligerent tone. "Was yer reluctance at wedding her so difficult to overcome?"

"She was bedridden. Oengus had nearly ended her."

"I see." Sean's nostrils flared before he spoke again. "Then 'twas no simple matter, what she was subjected to, no matter her claims to the contrary?"

"I would not have wished it upon my worst enemy. But ye spoke the truth when ye said she was strong."

"I spoke of many things to ye."

"Ye did." Diarmuid had the distinct impression he was being taken to task. A reprimand would be welcome. He knew he deserved it.

"Including that she is most special to us and an important part of our clan."

Diarmuid's jaw locked into place. He forced himself to swallow the ire. "And now she is special to *me*."

Diarmuid clenched his hands. Sean could not be speaking of taking her back with them. There was no way he could allow that to happen. Would his men willingly fight by his side against their *ri túath* if it came to that? He couldn't be certain.

But Sean merely sighed, his face relaxing, and said, "Then let us sit."

Directing Thomasina before him, Sean took Aednat's hand to pull her behind him.

Diarmuid followed, settling in his usual seat. Though it was customary for any visiting king of higher status to take that seat of honor, Sean had passed on occupying it as a show of respect to Diarmuid. Respect which was greatly appreciated after the rough start to the evening.

This was going to be a long night. Settling on the firm cushion, Diarmuid signaled for the wine. Three women approached, but it was Lilith who came directly to him. Giving him a provocative smile, she filled his horn cup to the brim.

Watching her swaying hips depart, Diarmuid wondered how satisfying himself with her had ever seemed enough. She had little feeling for anyone but herself. Having him in her bed had given her the status she wanted, nothing more. It was the only reason she sought his attention.

Aednat turned her back to him as she spoke with Thomasina and Sean. He realized how much he'd come to prefer the obstinacy of his wife. Her spark supplied something he was sorely missing. How easy it would be to rest a hand on the small of her back and remind her that he was there. Certainly she'd sit back and include him in any conversation. And yet his hand rested on the table, unmoving.

"Are ye well, brother?" Astrid settled beside him, offering him a plate of honeyed figs. "Ye do not seem yerself."

He took a bite of the sweet treat before answering. "I have much on my mind this day."

Glancing toward the others, Astrid lowered her voice. "'Tis not the best time for a visit from Sean."

"Mayhap not."

He'd witnessed Aednat's reaction upon seeing Sean and Thomasina. Pure elation. The mere sight of her happiness had made him smile. Why would she not be happy? They were her family. Did he have the right to keep her away from them? Even when she obviously preferred to be with them? If not for Oengus, she'd have gone about her life as the lone healer in Sean's clan and been satisfied with the situation. She'd said as much herself. Now that the threat was over, mayhap he should be gracious and allow her to return to them. He crushed the horn in his grasp, the remaining wine dribbling between his fingers.

Astrid stood beside him, wiping at the table with a cloth. "Diarmuid, ye do not know yer own strength."

Sean leaned forward to catch his eye. "Is there a problem with the wine?"

Diarmuid's face heated and he lifted a hand for more wine. "This wine is the best available. The Meic Murchadha gave it to us as a peace offering."

"Then mayhap we should have a tester before we partake." Sean's joking tone was evident.

Aednat turned to Diarmuid, placing her small hand on his arm. "Are ye not well?"

"I am only missing my wife's attention."

He took the silver pitcher offered him, only

realizing Lilith was the one who had brought it when she gave him a bold look and grazed him with her fingers. Disgust slithered down his back. He turned back toward Aednat, but she was again speaking with Thomasina, her back stiff.

"Mother is not pleased ye have taken a healer as yer wife," Astrid continued in a low voice beside him.

"And well I know. But Mother is never pleased."

"She says the priest will agree with her. Their healing comes from the black arts."

Diarmuid frowned. "The ability to heal a warrior and have him ready for battle again is not from the devil."

"I agree with ye." Astrid shrugged before directing him with her chin. "Ye look to have an audience, brother."

Young Lorccán stood at the table opposite them, eyeing him intently. When the lad sat on the bench, he stroked his chin in a thoughtful way. The perfect imitation of his father's habitual gesture. Diarmuid smiled, the attention from the lad giving him a pang.

"I will oversee the meal so that ye may spend time with yer wife," Astrid said, squeezing his hand.

"My thanks."

Emptying his mug yet again, Diarmuid moved to refill it. The irritating chatter beside him sounded very much like a typical welcome back celebration, and it rubbed him raw. The time had come to settle this once and for all. He stumbled a little when he stood, but righted himself before losing his footing completely, and raised his cup. The room settled down, all eyes on him.

"'Tis a great honor indeed to welcome *mo cheann cinnidh* and his family to my table this night." He faced Sean, dipping his head. Sean returned the gesture, and Diarmuid turned back to the room. "Tomorrow ye may come before us and speak of yer concerns, but tonight we celebrate. Not only for this great honor, but also because I have taken a wife." Gasps carried to his ears, but the faces were a blur. "I have the pleasure of introducing ye all to my wife, Aednat the Healer."

The cheers resounded as people stood and lifted their cups, some clapping, others banging on their tables. He was met with faces filled with joy. Even young Lorccán stood, clapping wildly. Diarmuid was not prepared for the overwhelming despair that hit him, and his mother's dark look of disapproval reflected his inner turmoil. His stomach tightened as if he'd been punched. They cheered a farce. If he offered her the choice of remaining at his side or returning to her own clan, she would surely leave with Sean and Thomasina. Mayhap she'd even hate him for not offering her the choice.

Turning to her, he was hit anew by Aednat's loveliness. Those glistening, rosy lips called to him. With the slightest of smiles, she rose to stand beside him. Such spirit. Such passion. He wanted her with all his being.

"They require a kiss." It was Thomasina who had spoken.

Diarmuid stilled, searching Aednat's lovely face for guidance. What did she want? Whatever it was, he wished to give it to her, even if it broke him. Aednat moved in close, a small hand to his chest, and reached up to offer a gentle kiss. *She* had come to *him*. He yanked her against him, capturing her lips. It took his mind but a moment to acknowledge her response. She was kissing him back just as wholeheartedly, wrapping her arms about him to hold him even closer. The room broke into wild cheers and ribald words of encouragement. The relief he felt almost made him sway.

"Mayhap the food should w-wait?" Faolán's voice carried to him.

"She's the only food he needs!" someone else shouted.

Thomasina leaned toward them. "Are ye going to take her right here, Diarmuid?"

The room burst with laughter anew.

He broke the kiss, his breath heaving, knowing Thomasina had the right of it. "Mayhap!" He lowered his voice for a private whisper to Aednat. "Forgive me."

Aednat's eyes twinkled. "Ye've done nothing wrong. I look forward to my time alone with ye."

Though her words were whispered, encouraging quips were sent their way from across the room. They both settled back on to the bench, Diarmuid praying her feelings were sincere, and he had misjudged her desire to go back to her old life.

The meal dragged, Aednat's back to him more often than not, and Diarmuid passed on the food, instead finding solace in his wine. Noticing the lad watching him again, Diarmuid motioned Lorccán closer. He directed him around the table to stand beside him. When the lad hopped onto his lap rather than stand beside him as he'd expected, Diarmuid was caught off guard.

"I think ye are a good man."

The sudden silence at the table brought awareness that Lorccán's family was paying attention to them now.

"Ye do?" Diarmuid asked.

"The stories about ye are lies."

"Uh, Lorccán!" Aednat's words sounded like some sort of warning, but the boy looked unaffected.

"And what are these stories ye've heard?" Diarmuid's curiosity was piqued.

"That ye snatch up little children and eat them!"

Diarmuid held back his reaction, instead watching as Lorccán's eyes traveled over him as if to assess just how big he was.

"Ye may be bigger than most, I'll give ye that"—his eyes finally settled on Diarmuid's face, wide in their innocence—"but I think ye are kind."

The simple declaration caused a hitch in Diarmuid's breath. Then the boy shocked him all the more by leaning in and bestowing a kiss on his cheek.

"Take care of my Aednat. I'd thought to marry her myself."

Diarmuid's throat tightened with tears, and he had to swallow hard to keep himself under control. "So ye're satisfied with me as her husband?"

"I am." Lorccán gave a sideways glance to Aednat. "And I expect babies very soon."

The table erupted with laughter, Sean reached over to tousle the boy's hair, and Lorccán's face turned red at all the attention. Diarmuid set the boy between himself and Aednat. She hugged him, a bright smile on her lovely face, but said nothing. The look she gave Diarmuid singed the whiskers on his jaw and his breath caught. Could he have been that wrong about her feelings toward him? Taking up his horn again, he exhaled very slowly.

Aednat and Sean switched seats at the man's request. Diarmuid's thoughts were running in a hundred directions, and he wished his overking had not decided to seek his counsel at such a time.

"I do not see the Meic Murchadha here," Sean said.

"Pádraig's father has taken ill," Diarmuid answered, but his thoughts continued to be on Aednat. "They will return on the morrow to show their respects."

Sean's thoughtful nod did not lessen the intensity of the look he gave Diarmuid. "That clan has always caused trouble for ye."

"Harmless and easily subdued." Diarmuid's muddled thoughts drifted to his sister. "Astrid seeks Pádraig's attention at every turn."

Sean laughed and picked up his cup. "Astrid wants a man's approval. Any man."

Diarmuid turned a sharp glance on Sean. "Ye believe she is lying with him?"

"Easy, Diarmuid. I did not say that, nor did I think it." Sean's eyes narrowed. "Why are ye in such a black mood?"

Thomasina and Aednat's laughter drifted to him, but he turned away. "I am done in this night."

Turning as if to contemplate the people enjoying their feast, Sean took a sip of his mead before facing Diarmuid again. "I do not believe I made a mistake entrusting Aednat to ye."

And there it was, laid out in front of him. Diarmuid's chin stiffened as he turned to face one of the only men whose approval he actually sought. "No?"

Sean shook his head, his eyes steady. "I do not know the whole story, but I know ye! And ye are not a man who would allow any harm to come to one of yer own."

Diarmuid appreciated the conviction with which

Sean had uttered those words. His overking and friend knew him well. Even so, Diarmuid struggled with forgiving himself.

"Pleased I am that ye have taken Aednat to wife. And apart from the fact that the other young women here show ye far too much attention, she is clearly pleased with ye as her husband." Sean pursed his lips. "Set yer black mood aside and spend time with yer wife. I will care for things here."

Diarmuid turned pleading eyes toward Aednat, wishing for just that.

Sean's shrewd eyes were watching him. "Aednat and Thomasina miss each other. 'Tis nothing more than that," he said.

Closing off his expression, Diarmuid nodded.

Sean moved in closer, lowering his voice. "Do not make me be the one to break up their reunion. Thomasina would not take kindly to that, but ye…?"

Diarmuid had trouble following Sean's words, and when he moved to take a sip of his drink, Sean clapped a hand on his arm. "Switch to water, man. Aednat will no doubt run ye dry this night."

The words sunk in and he shifted on his seat.

Sean leaned back. "Wait not on my account."

Sean's encouragement was the push he needed, and Diarmuid found his will to wait could take no more. He stood and held his hand out to Aednat, wondering for the smallest moment why she seemed to waver before his eyes even though she was sitting down, and she turned to look at him.

"Come, Aednat. I wish to be alone with my bride."

Hoots broke out, but Diarmuid's focus did not shift from her. When she moved around Sean and finally stood beside him, he dropped his head close to her. The scent of her hair drifted up to him, increasing his need, but he wanted her consent before he took her away. "If it would please ye to be alone with me now?"

Aednat's breath caught at the blatant desire in her husband's eyes, and her excitement increased. Diarmuid did not seem so inclined to send her away now. Not at all.

"It would please me greatly to be alone with ye at any time," she said.

Taking her hand in his, he led the way from the dais. The cheering that followed them halfway down the narrow path to their home would have embarrassed her had she not missed his attentions so much.

"How are ye feeling?" Diarmuid asked.

She couldn't see his face well but sighed and blew a long breath. "I am feeling much more myself. The food was quite good and I was nigh onto star—"

With three backward steps, he pressed her against a tree just off the path, shrouding them in complete darkness. Nibbling her lips, he took her mouth with exquisite tenderness before plundering its depth. Heat spread down her core to settle between her legs.

"My lovely Aednat." He pressed against her, leaving no part of her body untouched by his. Dropping his lips to her neck, he nuzzled her. "I have desired nothing but to be with ye for too long. Make me wait no longer."

With frenzied movements, Diarmuid reached down to yank up her gown, pulling at the layers of material. She looked around, afraid they would be discovered.

"Can ye not wait until we are within?"

He groaned something she didn't understand, but now his hot hands were on her flesh.

"Diarmuid," she breathed his name, need rushing through her.

When he stroked her wetness, her eyes closed in delight and his touch slowed. "Mmm, yer desire matches my own, wife."

Nearly overcome by the need he was creating in her, she shifted her feet to offer herself more fully. Waiting became insufferable, and when she opened her eyes, he was staring into her face.

"And I am well pleased to see how much ye enjoy my touch."

Her face heated.

When he slid his finger into her depths, she closed her eyes, savoring his touch. And again he was watching her when she opened her eyes.

She swallowed down her passion and forced herself to speak. "Why d'ye leave me waiting?"

Diarmuid's lips curled into a seductive smile. "When my wife asks if I cannot wait until we are within, I imagine she would prefer that I wait."

Adding another finger, he began a rhythmic motion, and her hips canted toward him in response. Moving his face closer, his voice reverberating through her, he said, "I do as my wife bids me."

When he plundered her more deeply, she groaned again and struggled to keep her eyes focused on his.

"Tell me."

"Do not wait." Her shaky breath became a moan of desire. "Take me here, Diarmuid."

He needed no further encouragement, exposing his solid length and sliding into her with a single stroke that stole her breath away. In little pants, she released her breath, wondering how this could be even more intensely enjoyable than she remembered. Lifting her off the ground, he wrapped her legs around his waist and continued to plunge into her more deeply while supporting her with his body.

"Ye are as I remembered."

She heard his words but couldn't think past the immense waves of pleasure crashing over as spasms squeezed his hard rod within her.

"I promised ye a dedicated lover." He continued his movement and the tension mounted again.

She nibbled at her lip, unable to listen to his words.

As if unaffected by fatigue, he moved more quickly within her. "No woman has ever left such a mark on me."

Aednat knew his words demanded her focus, but she was too overcome with sensation to speak. As if knowing that, he covered her mouth with his own, cupping both her breasts with greedy hands. He slowed then, impaling her so deeply, he surely reached her womb. She moaned into him, and he stilled, his own release filling her. Dropping his head against her neck, his damp hair brushed her cheek, and his labored breathing filled her ear.

Lowering her legs to the ground, he adjusted their clothing, but his hips still held her pinned against the tree.

"For now ye may rest, but I will have ye again this night."

His words struck her as a desperate plea. When she searched his face, hidden in the shadows, he added, "And every night."

She caressed his cheek, the dampness from his exertion already drying, and he shivered.

"I have missed yer attention immensely," she said.

"Attention?" Diarmuid nuzzled into her neck while his fingers again splayed across her breasts, tugging and groping. "I will surely heed ye now."

Stilling his hand, he paused before shifting to stand and pulling her away from the support of the tree. He wavered slightly, and she wondered how much he'd had to drink.

"If we do not continue now, ye may have no rest before I want ye again."

"Forgive me, Diarmuid." Her voice was barely above a whisper, and she stroked his cheek again as she spoke. "I have been remiss with ye."

"Ye have, woman."

"When I turned to include ye at table, I found ye being attended to by *Lilith*. It made me angry."

"Jealous," he corrected her.

"It was not kind of me to leave ye out of the conversation."

He swayed on his feet, looking up at the stars. "No doubt it is my lot in life."

"What d'ye speak of?"

He lowered his gaze to her. "What d'*ye* speak of?"

Aednat searched his face and realized he was quite drunk. When he slipped his hand along her shoulder to slide the material down her arm, he smiled. A wicked smile. His eyes feasted on the sight of her nearly exposed breast. She tried to pull the material back up, but he was already lowering his head to her breast, an arm to her back, arching her toward him.

He suckled her as loudly as a hungry babe, his tongue flicking her hardened nipple, and she struggled against the moan of pleasure threatening to escape.

"Diarmuid! Let us go to a private place for this."

She glanced back toward the roundhouse but still saw no one. "Come, my love."

He nuzzled between her breasts before he pulled the material back up. "Do not tease me with names ye do not really mean."

With a surprisingly strong hold, he swept her up into his arms and trotted the rest of the way down the path.

"Ye will fall! Diarmuid, cease this nonsense."

More surefooted than she would have believed him capable of in this state, he had her deposited in the middle of the bed and under him in short order. He rubbed his cheek across her bosom and sighed.

"Ye have left the door open."

He lifted a tired eye to her. "Why do women harp so?"

She gasped. "I do not harp!"

Diarmuid raised his shoulders in a shrug as he started to yank up her *léine.*

"Stop, Diarmuid. Allow me to remove it before ye rip it."

He struggled with the waist. "What are ye wearing?"

Aednat tried to get to the ties along the side of the gown to loosen them, but he was effectively blocking her. "'Tis yer sister's."

Quick as a rabbit, he jumped up to a kneeling position between her legs to glare down at her. "Ye are wearing Astrid's clothes?"

She sat up, the skirt of the gown around her hips. "I have nothing of my own."

Attending to the laces now, she was surprised by the gentle touch on her chin. He tipped her face to his, giving her an eyeful of his very serious expression.

"I will shower ye with beautiful gowns that will make all the women envious." He pressed his mouth to hers, insistent until her lips parted. Diarmuid pressed her back against the bed, his mouth still locked to hers in a passionate kiss.

Overcome with emotion, he broke the kiss and said, "I want ye here with me, healer."

Bewildered by the words, she said, "And here I am, warrior."

He picked up his head to smile at her. "Then tell me ye do not wish to be anywhere but here."

"I do not wish to be anywhere but in yer arms."

With a slight frown, he searched her face before continuing. "And ye will remain with me?"

"If that is what ye desire."

"What I desire is *ye*."

In his bed but what of his life? "And what of when ye tire of me?"

"*Never* will I tire of ye."

Aednat turned away, her heart aching. She could give him everything except the peace he sought. It seemed chaos was destined to follow her wherever she went.

Dipping to her neck, he slipped the gown off her shoulder again to free one heavy breast. With his large hand, he thumbed her nipple into a tight nub. When he looked up at her, he held her gaze as he stroked the peak with the tip of his tongue.

"D'ye wish to return with Sean and Thomasina?"

The words came out just before he took her deep inside his mouth, suckling her tight. Her eyes closed in pleasure. Distracted, she struggled for an answer.

"If that is what ye desire," she said.

Telling him what *she* desired, she pulled him

closer to her with a strong hand, moaning against him. Exhausted, her body responded as if it had not just been satiated, and she reveled in his attention.

"I desire ye here in my bed, pleasuring me." His low, seductive tone worked through her innards, giving him an added advantage.

"Then here shall I be."

He pulled away, his hand taking over for his mouth. When she opened her eyes, he fairly beamed. "Then I shall take my pleasure."

Turning to the ties himself, he worked patiently but could still not get the gown to budge.

Diarmuid turned desperate eyes on her. "I wish to have my wife naked before me, Aednat. I beg ye to assist me!"

Smiling, she scooted to the edge and stood beside the bed. He stretched out on his back to watch her, propping an arm beneath his head for a better view. The *léine* pooled at her feet and she was suddenly overwhelmed with shyness, unsure how to proceed. His hungry eyes took in every bit of her, ending at last on her face.

"I have never seen a woman as beautiful as ye." His words were clear, and his eyes were focused. "If Sean had not asked me to take ye to wife, I would certainly have chosen ye for my own."

Completely vulnerable, standing naked before him, she could not immediately form a response to his revelation. He would have chosen her. He *was* choosing her.

Coming to kneel before her, he cupped her cheek in his warm palm. "Lovely Aednat, would ye have taken me as yer husband even if ye were not being pursued?"

Aednat considered this question. She had believed herself content, but she'd also believed there was no other choice than being alone. It had seemed a waste to wish for someone to care for her the way a husband cares for a wife. The way Diarmuid cared for her. Oh yes! She would have taken Diarmuid without hesitation. If she lost him now, her life would feel empty.

"I would have chosen ye." Taking a deep shaky breath, she said with a teasing grin, "Mayhap once ye stopped threatening me with yer punishments."

"'Tis such a lovely arse to threaten." Diarmuid smiled, then lowering his eyes, he watched his fingertip as it traced her lips. "Even if there was another ye would prefer?"

Aednat hesitated, confused. "There is no one I prefer to ye."

He lifted his gaze to her eyes as if to ensure the truth of her words. A satisfied smile spread across his face, and he yanked his *léine* up, pulling it off over his head. "Let me feel yer softness against me, Aednat."

She pressed him back, lying beside him in the bed, and he pulled the blanket over them.

"I died inside when they took ye." He sounded half asleep.

She snuggled close to his side, her head on his shoulder.

"I realized how much ye meant to me, how much I wanted to have a home with ye. Children. The idea of losing ye now would kill me, *mo mhíle stór*."

Her breath stilled and she realized how much she'd longed to hear those words from him.

"Ye'll not be losing me."

"Close yer eyes and sleep until I have rested

sufficiently to awaken ye with a lover's kiss."

With a broad, unabashed smile, she did as he asked.

Chapter Nineteen

A trestle table was set up outside the roundhouse, and near twenty people waited in line before it. Sean sat beside Diarmuid, facing the people waiting to come before them with their concerns. Though he had no authority to make decisions, his presence demonstrated his support of Diarmuid in all things.

Aednat had left the table some time ago and now stood in the doorway of the roundhouse watching them, the sound of cooking carrying out to her. Astrid came alongside her, and Aednat found herself asking yet again, "How long will this go on for?"

Astrid asked, "Does Sean not have this duty?"

"I was never nearby." Aednat shrugged. "I was usually seeing to Lorccán, keeping him out of the mischief he so enjoys."

"Ah, off playing and enjoying the day?"

Aednat merely smiled at her astuteness.

"I am surprised at my brother's patience this day." Astrid shook her head. "He is usually throwing up his hands by now, at the end of his rope, as they say. Instead, he is still smiling and pleasant."

"Mayhap having Sean here is giving him more patience?"

Bright blue eyes turned to her, the hint of a smile on a pair of full lips. "I'd venture to say he is pleased with his lot in life because of ye."

Aednat blushed, unsure how to respond.

"Ye do not have to deny that ye make him very happy. I heard him speaking with Sean."

"Sean? Whatever would he say to him about me?"

"Only to say he would have taken ye to wife sooner had he met ye afore now."

The assessment pleased Aednat greatly, but when she glanced toward Thomasina, who sat obediently beside her husband, she wondered if she could ever be such a dutiful wife. The next man approached, a chicken beneath his arm, and Thomasina merely smiled as he started spouting off complaints. Could Aednat learn to listen to such nonsense with patience?

"Sounds as if Sean was planning yer match with Diarmuid even before Oengus came after ye."

"No." Aednat kept her eyes on Thomasina. Always so poised and controlled. "I was never intended to be taken to wife."

"But the legend of the healer is well known. Ye must have had dozens of suitors."

Aednat finally turned to face the petite blond. "Many men want power, Astrid, but few are willing to put up with a disfigured wife."

"Disfigured? How are ye disfigured? Ye are beautiful." She seemed honestly puzzled.

"Misshapen then. My foot?"

"Did ye truly believe that? Is that how ye were able to remain unmarried?"

"No one wanted me." Aednat's face heated. Even now, happily matched though she was, it was a subject she preferred not to bring up.

Astrid's jaw dropped. "I heard Sean. Many men sought yer hand."

"Ye are mistaken." Aednat's irritation was rising, and she did not want to be sharp with her sister-in-law. "Or ye misheard him. I need something to settle my stomach so that I can return to Diarmuid. I have yet to be restored to full health with my retching each morning."

Stepping inside, she caught sight of Lilith yelling at Merewyn. The redheaded girl towered over her, her mouth speaking cruel and belittling words. Aednat paused to listen, not wanting to form a mistaken conclusion, but Merewyn looked near to tears.

"Enough, Lilith!" Aednat rushed up to Merewyn, placing an arm about her shoulders. "Tell me what is yer complaint?"

Lilith scowled. "I was speaking to the slave! Ye need not interfere."

Aednat turned to Merewyn, and then back to Lilith. "Does she deserve to be talked to like a disobedient animal?"

"Slaves *are* animals!" Lilith fisted her hand at her hip, her eyes wide as if not quite believing Aednat's boldness in confronting her.

"Ho, ho, I do not agree!"

"And I have been here much longer than ye,

Aednat. Diarmuid does not allow slaves to disregard orders."

In the face of such insistence, Aednat's confidence wavered, and she began questioning her own decision to intervene. Lilith's place in the clan had never been explained to her. The last thing she wished to do was contradict her husband's orders. He had shown his fierce dislike for disobedience. Still… she could not believe he would allow unnecessarily cruel treatment of anyone, no matter their status. And surely as wife to the *ri túaithe,* her words carried some weight. Aednat stuffed down her uncertainty.

"*I* will be the judge. Tell me what has happened."

"No!" Lilith's mouth slammed shut.

Aednat fumed, but she turned to Merewyn and said in an even tone, "Astrid is just outside. Ye may go to her."

"Do not walk away from me." Lilith moved toward the girl, making to grab her arm, but Aednat clasped her wrist in a firm hold and Merewyn continued on her way. Wild green eyes pierced into Aednat. "How dare ye lay yer hands on me? D'ye actually believe because ye warm Diarmuid's bed, he will not soon be returning to mine?"

Lilith's audacity left Aednat speechless, and her jaw dropped. It was the girl's haughty smile that broke the spell. Moving closer, Aednat got right in Lilith's face as if she were no more than a defiant, insolent child.

"As his *wife,* that is exactly what I believe, and ye"—Aednat poked Lilith's shoulder a bit more firmly than she may have needed to—"had best keep that in mind unless ye want to experience the strike of my hand across yer face. Now leave this place, and do not return again until I request yer presence."

Lilith's expression quickly shifted to dread. That her gaze was focused on the doorway filled Aednat with trepidation. She knew without looking that Diarmuid stood behind her listening. Lilith left without another word. Turning around, Aednat was confronted with her handsome husband in all his finery.

A dark blue *léine*, delicately embroidered at the hem and neck with golden thread, his solid, bared arms graced by intricately etched silver bands where his hands were tucked beneath his arms, and his hair brushed away from his face and curling at his shoulders. She wanted nothing more than to slip her fingers through his locks and pull him in close for a kiss. His fierce expression stopped her.

"She was being cruel to the slave. I saw no rea—"

Diarmuid raised a hand, and she was silent. He approached her with slow, steady steps, his glance leaving no bit of her untouched before coming to rest on her face.

"My lovely Aednat." His expression relaxed into the seductive smile she knew quite well. "*All* that is here is yers. *I* need no explanation, nor do I question yer right to handle these women as ye see fit. I have no complaint."

Stopping just short of their bodies touching, he covered both of her shoulders with his warm, large hands.

"If I did have a complaint, I would speak of it to ye when we were alone, but I would support yer decision first." He placed a gentle kiss on her lips and lowered his voice. "And yer face flushed in anger reminds me of how ye look with yer face flushed from other more enjoyable emotions."

Diarmuid glanced around at the now-empty room before pulling her flat against him and taking her lips in a passionate kiss. "Mmm, no complaints at all."

When he relaxed his hold, she rested her head on his shoulder and sighed. "I do not like that woman."

"I can see why that would be."

Aednat looked up at him. "She keeps insinuating ye will return to her."

"She thinks much of herself. We fostered her half-brother and felt compelled to accept her, too, although her bloodline could not be proven." He shook his head. "I have no need of another woman when I have ye."

Going on tiptoe, she kissed him and smiled. "I like being the wife of the king. "

"And well ye should."

"Diarmuid?" Sean called from the door. "Clan Meic Murchadha has arrived."

Diarmuid took her hand and led them toward the door. "I do not mind that ye needed a rest. 'Tis a long day and listening to all their complaints can become tiring."

"I was going to look for the spearmint leaves I'd collected to help settle my stomach."

He paused in the doorway and put a hand to her head. "Is that all that ails ye?"

She nodded.

"Mayhap we can go on a hunt for more of yer herbs." He waggled his brows at her. "I'm certain I could locate some very fine mushrooms."

Slapping at his chest, she said, "Never mind that, Diarmuid."

The area around the trestle table was now dwarfed by a line of large, well-armed warriors. Their weapons seemed a bit overdone considering the peaceful reasons for the assembly. The idea being to work out problems before battle was necessary.

Aednat pointed to Pádraig. "I've met him before."

Diarmuid nodded, but he was distracted by the tension he could read on the warrior's faces. Something was amiss. "He is their king's son. And interested in taking Astrid to wife. A good match."

Aednat turned a frown on him. "Oh, no, Diarmuid! She should marry Marcán. *They* are a good match."

Diarmuid, shocked into silence at her shrewdness, refrained from smiling. How quickly his wife assessed all around them. She was a constant surprise.

"We can discuss who my sister may or may not marry at a later time."

They joined the group at the table and Diarmuid took his place beside Sean.

"Pádraig." Sean stood beside the table, extending his arm. "Glad I am to see ye've come."

Gripping his hand at the wrist, Pádraig dipped his head. "Mercy, please, *a thighearna*. My father has passed this night."

"My condolences on yer loss, Pádraig," Diarmuid said. The loss of his own father pained him as fresh as if it had happened just a few days ago rather than years. His father had given him much of his time, whereas Fergus had often been left with their mother.

"I did not know he was quite so sickly," Sean said.

Pádraig nodded, his eyes wide with sadness. "Nigh on three days now, but we believed he would be restored to health."

"I am sorry at yer loss. Mayhap ye should have spoken with Diarmuid's wife, Aednat. She is a healer."

Pride swelled in Diarmuid's chest, and he turned to smile at his lovely wife. But Pádraig's dark eyes dropped, and he moved closer to them. "We did not wish to offend Beibhinn."

Diarmuid's jaw tensed. His mother had spoken too freely of her distrust of healers. Covering Aednat's hand with his, he was glad to see she appeared unaffected. All the same, he would need to put a stop to Beibhinn's loose talk.

"Diarmuid's mother?" Sean's face tightened. "I do not understand what ye speak of."

"She is also Astrid's mother." Pádraig shifted his feet. "I hope to offer for Astrid's hand. Her mother believes some healers practice the dark arts."

Sean's face became suffused with anger, and Diarmuid feared what his friend would say next. He needn't have worried. Sean nodded stiffly. "Yer father was a good warrior."

Those around them nodded in agreement. Pádraig seemed overwhelmed with the loss, his face still damp with his tears. His father had kept him on a tight rein, but his son's respect for him had always been apparent.

"And who will lead yer clan now?"

"Our *tánaiste* died fall last." Pádraig swallowed. "I have gathered a warband that fights for me. I sat alongside my father whenever he dealt with disputes, so I am ready to fill that role. I am certain I can be elected by the *derb fine*."

"No doubt ye will make a fine king."

Stroking his chin, Sean put a hand out to Diarmuid, who walked into his one-armed embrace. "Now that ye are married to our Aednat, I believe another meeting of the *rig túaithe* should be called. With the warriors, land, and tribute ye have acquired from recent battles, Diarmuid, ye've demonstrated yer ability as a great leader. We will seek their agreement in making ye overking of the western clans and myself, *ri ruireach*."

"Diarmuid?" Pádraig's quick response no doubt came from the realization that he'd just offended his possible overking's wife with his insinuation. His face turning red, he said, "A fair man as well. And not one to hold ill will against another in my experience."

With a tight jaw, Diarmuid nodded.

"And tonight"—he nodded at Pádraig—"if ye are amicable with yer father having just passed, we will celebrate."

"We said our goodbyes at dawn."

Pádraig was also of Norse blood. Both Diarmuid and Sean understood the man referred to the old Norse practice of seeing a warrior's body off in a flaming boat.

Pádraig took a full breath and blew it out before facing Sean. "Moving on is best for us all," he said. "Let us celebrate this night."

Sean's glance included Aednat when he said, "Then we will celebrate."

A cheer went up and both Clan Meic Murchadha and those still waiting to address the *ri* quickly scattered, forgetting their own complaints in preparation for the upcoming feast and celebration that could very well last for days.

"A feast?" Thomasina placed an arm around Aednat and directed her inside. "Aednat and I have much to see to."

"Ye were born a leader," Sean said, once they were alone. "And yer poets are no doubt working this very moment on more stories of yer abilities." He paused, then added, "It did not seem right to raise ye above others without even a wife at yer side. A man without a wife to see to his needs can easily be distracted by any willing lass."

"So ye *were* offering Aednat to me? And was that the reason ye wanted me there?"

"It has all worked out in a pleasing manner." Sean shrugged. "And I see before me a happy man indeed."

"So do the conniving and machinations go with the new title?"

"They may indeed." Sean looked toward their wives' retreating backs. "Aednat needs no more rejection. Yer mother should be taken in hand. Ye will assure me of that?"

"Ye have my word, Sean."

"Father!" An irritated female voice preceded the emergence of a lovely lass from the roundhouse. She stomped outside, a sour look on her lovely face. "Yer son is being a nuisance."

"Brighit, calm yerself. We've asked only that ye keep Lorccán out of trouble."

"He will not listen! And I want to help with the preparations, not look after him. 'Tis high time I be given these duties."

Sean frowned. "They will not allow ye to help with the cooking?"

"No! Not the cooking! I want to oversee the planning, the seating—"

With a raised hand, he silenced his daughter. "Ye are asking to play lady of the *túath*, which ye are not."

"I soon will be! And to that overbearing man." She closed her eyes, shaking her head in an annoyed manner.

Diarmuid turned away to hide his smirk.

"Darragh is not overbearing, *grádh*. I wonder what ye would seek in a husband if not a strong protector and a good provider."

Blowing a breath, Brighit rolled her eyes. "Ugh! I cannot expect *ye* to understand."

She flounced back inside, her nose in the air. Once out of sight, Diarmuid gave in to the overwhelming desire for a hearty laugh.

"Yer daughter? Oh Sean, how could ye have such a willful lass? Thomasina is the form of nobility. A genteel lady."

Sean's ire was raised, and he turned a dark scowl on Diarmuid. "I could wish a daughter on ye myself. 'Tis the only way ye will learn how a lass turns into such a strong-minded female."

"And as spoiled as rotten meat!"

"Ye overstep yerself." Sean's growl brought a quick end to Diarmuid's humor. "Do not speak of this to Thomasina. 'Tis best if she believes Brighit is warming to the idea of marrying Darragh."

"Why does she balk? Is there another she would prefer?"

Sean snorted and shook his head. "She prefers adventure. I have indulged her since she was young, allowing her to learn the use of weapons and warhorses—I did the same with Aednat."

Much of Aednat's knowledge was falling into place.

"They are both quick to learn, and I taught them as much as they wished to know, giving no thought to the man who would eventually take them to wife."

"I have heard of Tisa and Tadhg's son. Darragh is a young warrior, but much is expected of him. Being from the line of kings, he will no doubt rise to overking as his father has."

Sean turned a worried expression to the door, though Brighit was no longer in sight. "I brought the girl to stay with Tisa and Tadhg so she could become better acquainted with Darragh." With wide eyes, he turned back to Diarmuid. "The lass got mad at him and took off to follow us! Unguarded! That is another thing ye need not mention to her mother."

"When will the joining take place?"

"I have been postponing the ceremony in the hopes of a change of heart from our dear Brighit, but it may need to be seen to sooner rather than later. Allowing him full authority over her may be what is required."

"If he can win her over," Diarmuid said.

"If he is a patient man."

Diarmuid quirked a brow. "And glad I am to not be the one saddl—" The look of warning on Sean's face was quite effective. "—married to her."

Chapter Twenty

The meats were well on their way to being finished when Marcán raced through the open room, his eyes searching, no doubt, for Diarmuid.

"Whatever can be amiss at this hour?" Thomasina asked as she measured out the precise amount of spice needed for the cook's soup before putting away the precious item.

Aednat could not help but notice he had come in by way of the hostages. There'd been no more talk about them, and she had avoided asking since it upset Diarmuid for her to show any interest. She had to face the fact that Will was gone, just as Cad and her grandmother were. They mattered no less and had been of great importance to her, but people pass on. That was the way of life.

Yelling outside roused both she and Thomasina, and they exchanged a glance and hurried through the front door. A crowd blocked their view. It was the Meic Murchadha men, and even though Aednat could not see Diarmuid, she heard him.

"Do not threaten me!" His voice shook with rage.

"Then do something for him, damn ye! He's a boy! Have ye no mercy?"

"And did ye show mercy when ye dragged my wife from her home, allowing her to be thrown to the ground, beaten, frighten and humiliated? Do not speak to me of mercy!"

Sean's low voice said something, but it did not carry as well. Aednat worked her way to the front. Lilith stood to the side, a wool cloth around her bare shoulders, her bright red hair flowing about her. She had an evil look to her, but Aednat set thoughts of the schemer aside as she took in the scene before her.

An older man held out an iron knife used for skinning the animal hides. He slid it back and forth in a threatening way.

"Stay back! I want the healer."

Maeve stood beside Pádraig, clearly within view of him, but the man showed no reaction. She must be the one he sought.

"I am here," Aednat said, making her way to the front of the crowd.

Diarmuid was immediately at her side, his face tight and nostrils flaring. "No! Ye will not do this."

"Do what? What is amiss?"

"Please, healer." The man with the blade stared at her with wild eyes. "The boy is vomiting blood now. Come. Please. See if ye can help him."

Confused, she turned to Diarmuid for an explanation.

Sean stood alongside him. "Go back inside, Aednat," he said. "We will see to this. Ye need not concern yerself."

Sean's sword was gripped tightly in his hand, and he had a determined expression that frightened her. "Are ye going to kill him?"

"Go inside." Diarmuid reached for her, but she eluded his grasp.

"Aednat!" It was the old man and she shifted her attention to him, shocked to hear her name on his lips.

"Come see William. Please. He's calling for ye."

Will? Aednat evaded both Sean and Diarmuid, closing the distance to the man with the knife. "Where is he?"

As soon as she was within reach, the man yanked her back up against him, the blade at her throat. "Now stay back! I'll kill her. I will."

She pulled at the arm around her shoulders, confronted with the horrified expressions of both Diarmuid and Sean. She was at this man's mercy, and they all knew it. "No! Bring me to Will. I can help him."

"Shhh. I need to get to the stable." The man whispered the words and started moving backward, still holding her in a tight grip, her heels dragging along the ground.

Aednat stumbled and the crowd reacted with a gasp, hands reaching toward her. The man returned the blade to her throat in response. "Stay back!"

Diarmuid's piercing gaze never left the man's face. Not when she stumbled and not when the blade was put to her throat. His attention was so intent of the man, it was as if he no longer saw her.

"Is that where Will is?" She would try to reason

with the man if it was possible. "Is he in the stable?"

The man swallowed, the perspiration dripping from his face onto her hand, which gripped his arm. "Ye'll see him."

"I'll not allow my wife to be taken again." Diarmuid's words, delivered in a low, controlled tone, were menacing and unyielding. He took a step closer.

"Stay back."

"Ye'll not live to see yer William healed if ye do not release her." Diarmuid matched their movements, a step forward for each step back. His face expressionless except for his tight jaw. "There will be no mercy if ye do not let her go now."

"I cannot. William needs help."

Another step back, and Diarmuid moved forward, imperceptibly closer, in a macabre dance. His keen focus on the man holding her never faltered.

"If she chooses to help him, I will allow it."

Dragged one more step closer to the stable behind her, and her husband closed the distance to her with another step.

"Ye will not." The man squeezed her tight, and his blade nicked her throat. She clamped her lips to keep from crying out as the warm liquid slipped down her throat. For the first time, she feared for her life. "I've been asking for days now."

For days? Aednat searched Diarmuid's handsome face, stiff with determination, for any sign the man lied. Had Will been here all along? Near death and asking for her?

And Diarmuid had not said a word?

"And *ye* will not mistreat my wife." Each word was delivered with methodical precision. The sweat from the man's body soaked the back of her gown, and his arm trembled where he held it against her.

"I want to help William." Her voice wavered with fear. "He is my friend, but ye are scaring me."

Diarmuid finally dropped his eyes to her. He took two steps closer, reaching her just as the man holding her cried out, his body going slack around her. She fell into her husband's strong arms.

The old man collapsed to the ground, a sword sticking out of his back, and Marcán behind him.

"Where is Will?" She wiped at her neck. Her relief at being released seemed irrelevant compared to the thought that Will had wanted her near him, that he was in pain and she may be able to help him.

Marcán came up behind her, gripping her shoulder, but his eyes remained on Diarmuid. He was looking to him for direction, no one else.

Before any of them could speak, Sean moved in closer to Aednat, tipping her chin up to check the injury. "A small nick."

No doubt intended to be reassuring, but the withering look Diarmuid gave him was powerful enough that Sean averted his gaze.

"It should not have happened." Diarmuid's eyes held hers. A dark, tumultuous blue. He was furious with her.

"I know—" Her voice shook.

"Ye know nothing!" His lips were tight as he spoke. "Ye are headstrong."

Aednat's legs threatened to buckle beneath her, but she was desperate to be heard. "I do not mean t—"

He halted her with his hand. "Again I must see ye at another's mercy because ye did not heed me."

She had no defense. He was correct. She was too

stubborn and not pliant, not like a wife should be.

Aednat squared her shoulders. "I was never intended to be an obedient wife. I am sorry, Diarmuid. I am a healer, and I cannot set that aside. Not ever."

Fear gripped her heart, and it became difficult to take a breath. Fear for the anger in her husband's eyes. Fear for her dear friend who cried out to her in his anguish. Fear that the man she loved would not accept her for the woman she was. "Tell me where I can find William."

Diarmuid's eyes never wavered from her. Sean seemed unsure. It was Marcán who finally answered her.

"He's in the outbuilding behind the stables." He finally turned to her, searching her face. "He's been delirious since he got here. The man lied about his asking for ye."

"Are ye certain, Marcán? I need to know!" Aednat prayed his words were true.

"I bathed him myself to try and lower his fever. I do not believe he knows ye are here."

"He is like a brother to me. Please, take me to him. If I can ease his pain, I would do so."

Sean and Marcán did not respond. Their eyes darting toward Diarmuid, awaiting his decision. As her husband, he alone had the right to answer.

"There ye are!" Gréagóir snarled the words as he came into view, wiping blood from his lip. He strode toward Lilith, a menacing expression twisting his features. "Ye good-for-nothing bitch."

Lilith's eyes rounded in fear, and Gréagóir slapped her. Hard. She fell to the ground, holding her hands over her head for protection.

It was Sean who crossed to the girl, grabbing

Gréagóir's wrist before he could strike her again. "Enough! What has she done?"

Gréagóir worked his jaw, the blood still flowing from his lips. "The little whore has been over here flirting with me every time I am guarding the hostages, making promises. Today she came over to me looking like that!" He yanked the blanket from her, exposing her nakedness to all. "A ploy! She only wanted me away from the hostages."

Sean blocked the man from getting any closer to her. One of the women helped to cover Lilith back up.

"So ye beat her for enticing ye away from yer duty?"

"*A thighearna*, I would do no such thing." He indicated the side of his head and the blood still dripping from his mouth. "When I refused to go with her, she hit me in the head with an iron pike."

Sean's face reddened, anger gripping him, and he turned on the girl. "Ye dare treat a warrior this way?"

Lilith's eyes were round. Even with two older women on either side supporting her to stand, her fear was palpable. "No, *a thighearna*. I did no such thing."

"A warrior would never lie to his king." Sean was beside himself. "All I need from ye is to tell me why."

Marcán came alongside Sean and said, "So she could drop the ladder down to the hostages. She was helping them escape."

"Lilith?" Diarmuid kept a few steps back from the woman, but her expression softened, tears welling in her eyes. "They do not deserve mercy, Lilith. They abducted my wife."

"Mercy? I offered them no mercy. They promised me they'd kill her!"

Sean and Marcán exchanged looks of surprise.

Diarmuid's eyes narrowed.

Diarmuid kept his gaze on Lilith. "Remove this slave from my presence."

A harsh sentence. Without the clan's protection, she would be at the mercy of any who found her living in the wild. The crowd that had gathered behind them murmured their surprise at the sentence.

"Do not! Diarmuid, please!" Lilith took the few steps toward Diarmuid, then dropped to her knees. "I love ye, Diarmuid," she screamed. "Do not forsake me."

Sean raised a hand to Gréagóir. "Place her in the hold with the other hostages."

"What? NO!" Lilith's eyes widened. "I have no protection from the cold. The men."

"And no shame." Diarmuid's quiet voice carried to Gréagóir, who nodded.

"I am with child!" The pronouncement filled the small space and all eyes turned to her. "'Tis Diarmuid's seed."

Aednat's jaw dropped. Her stomach roiled. She was going to be sick.

It was Sean who finally broke the silence. "A convenient ruse to see that ye not receive the punishment ye deserve."

With darting eyes, Lilith continued. "The truth."

Thomasina came to stand beside her husband, keenly watching the woman. "And if she is with child"—she shifted to face Diarmuid—"could it be yers?"

Diarmuid's nostrils flared when he tightened his jaw. "It has been many months since I have lain with her."

"And there have certainly been others." Marcán

said, before moving to stand beside Astrid. He spoke as one who knew the truth firsthand.

Thomasina said, "Then she should definitely be further along—"

"She lies!" Merewyn stepped out from behind Astrid. She had no doubt watched the hubbub unfold. "She is not with child."

"Come forth." Sean gave the order.

Astrid consented with a nod, and Merewyn, shoulders back, approached the overking. She showed no reaction to Lilith's glaring scowl. "I heard the lass speaking to her friends. She said she would have Diarmuid in her bed again any way that she could."

"And who are ye?"

"A slave! Shut yer mouth, slave!" Lilith spat at Merewyn, whose expression never changed.

"I heard her with my own ears. *I* have no reason to lie."

Emotions washed over Aednat, threatening to buckle her knees. The world began to waver around her. Her stomach gurgled, ready to heave, but Thomasina was beside her, a strong arm around her shoulders.

"Ye need to be inside," Thomasina said, her gentle voice calming.

Aednat covered her mouth and ran a few feet away. Retching into a bush, she dropped to her knees. The heaving continued even when there was nothing left to throw up. Tears pricked her eyes. A strong arm stroked her back and she allowed herself to give into the tears. It wasn't Diarmuid who had come to comfort her but Sean.

"D'ye feel better, little one?" Sean's eyes were bright with concern.

"Oh, *Datan*, this cannot be true."

"I do not believe it is."

Aednat gave a slow shake to her head. "What of Will?"

"Diarmuid has agreed to allow ye to see him. I will bring ye to him."

Thomasina reached around her husband to hand Aednat a full cup. "Drink this. Slowly. It will help with the nausea."

Aednat did as she was told. Exhausted, she just wanted to curl up and sleep. The sounds of the others dispersing carried to her, and she wondered if Diarmuid would leave her here with Sean.

"I need to see Will. Please."

"Are ye certain ye're ready?"

There was something in Sean's tone that caused a hitch in her breath. "He is truly dying?"

Sean nodded.

"Mayhap I can help him?"

"No, Aednat. He has been sick for many months now. There is nothing ye can do."

"He did not appear sick to me."

"Mayhap ye saw only what ye wanted to see."

Before Aednat could reply, they were interrupted by a fuss. Gréagóir was leading Lilith—scratching and yelling—toward the hideaway, but he stopped to turn back.

"Forgive me, please, Diarmuid. I thought she was trying to make ye jealous. I know ye are well pleased with yer bride, so I did not mind taking what she offered."

The words tore at Aednat's heart. Well pleased? In bed, yes, but Diarmuid could never find peace with a wife who would not obey him. She would not forget the way he'd looked at her just now.

"And ye remained at yer post. My thanks, Gréagóir."

Gréagóir dragged Lilith away, still protesting.

Aednat settled onto the ground, Sean squatting beside her.

"I am sorry ye have lost so many in yer short life." Sean offered her a sad smile. "Hear me, little fire, it has made ye strong! Try not to be so sad. Ye have a husband who loves ye."

"He does not! I cause him great turmoil at every turn."

"Ye are wrong. Ye give him great peace! I see it in his eyes. His time with ye restores his peace to him." He sighed. "He loves ye."

"He has never said so." The tears threatened to fall again. "And he did not trust me enough to tell me about Will."

Sean's eyes clouded. "Diarmuid struggled with whether ye should be told about Will. He did not want to cause ye more pain. Ye believed him already gone. He took me into his confidence earlier, and I said it would be best if ye did not know. I was wrong. Forgive me."

The tears slipped down her cheeks. "I cannot even stop my tears. I am not strong."

"Tears are not a show of weakness." Sean wiped at her wet cheeks. He paused, then said, "Thomasina says ye are with child."

All sound around them stopped. For an instant, it felt like her breath was the only thing moving.

Sean's eyes, flecked with gold and brown, nearly twinkled in delight, and his grin grew. "Thomasina is quite good at working out such things."

"She is never wrong! Does Diarmuid know?" She glanced over at him.

"Neither Thomasina nor I have shared that with yer husband."

"Can it be true?" Aednat could barely catch her breath. "Could I be with child even now?"

Sean struggled to control his smile, shaking his head. "I have seen the way Diarmuid looks at ye. I'd say it could definitely be a possibility."

Smiling, her cheeks heated just the same. "We are well matched."

His grin stretched all the wider. "I am quite good at that."

"Making babies?"

"No, ye and Diarmuid." His smile dropped a bit. "I knew ye two were well matched. If anyone could take his pain away, 'twas ye."

"His pain?"

"He lost his brother when the lad was small. Diarmuid believes he should have protected him better, but he was still young himself. He and Marcán were full of becoming great warriors, practicing all the time, going off to battles. And still Diarmuid always found time for the boy. Fergus went off on his own. He didn't listen to Diarmuid and got hurt."

"That is why he was so angry about Lorccán."

"And why he wants to protect ye so fiercely. Diarmuid does love children—and he is headed this way right now. Looks to be at the end of his patience and willing to wait no longer for me to be done speaking with ye."

Sean stood, his legs braced in a strong warrior's stance, and turned to face Diarmuid's unchecked anger.

"Is my wife able to speak to me yet, Sean? She seems to have little trouble speaking with ye."

Aednat stood, and though she appreciated Sean hovering near her, she closed the distance to Diarmuid, leaving Sean behind.

"I am sorry I did not heed ye, husband."

"I would protect ye with my life, Aednat. Always."

She lowered her eyes, afraid he'd see her excitement. Perhaps out of guilt, Diarmuid's expression softened, and he slipped a wayward hair behind her ear. "I am sorry ye are not well. Mayhap lamb does not agree with ye this time of year."

Aednat resisted the urge to smile at Sean. "Mayhap it does not. When ye think it is a good time, I would like to see Will."

"Are ye certain ye wish to see him? There is nothing that can be done for him."

She nodded.

"Ye do not wish me to take ye to him, little one?" Sean sounded disappointed.

"Unless my husband prefers ye take me, Sean, I should go with him to see Will. I would like for them to properly meet."

Diarmuid studied her before responding in a quiet voice, "I will take ye to him now if ye are ready."

Her hand on his arm, he led the way to the small shed where Marcán had moved Will. They paused outside and he turned her to him. "Maeve has been doing what she can to ease Will's pain, but he has been getting worse each day."

"Maeve knows little of healing, but seeing how yer mother feels about healers, I can understand why she was all ye had."

She turned toward the open door and braced

herself before entering. Diarmuid stopped her.

"I do not know if this is of any importance to Will's condition, but his fingers are not all that has been removed from his body."

Aednat searched his face. When they were young, Will's missing fingertips seemed such a great loss, but he had learned to use his hands just fine, even using a bow and arrow. She could not remember seeing anything else missing.

"When Marcán removed his clothing, he discovered… he had been castrated." Diarmuid searched her face. "'Tis the sentence for fornication."

"Was it recent?"

"No. It was well healed."

"Then I do not believe it could be the cause of his illness." She put a hand to his cheek. "My thanks for sharing that with me."

Taking a breath, she pushed the door open. Will's labored breathing only added to the oppression of the small area, and she went to remove the covering from the window.

"Is that wise?" Diarmuid asked.

Aednat nodded. "Grandmother insisted fresh air was not harmful but helpful. She believed it helped the lungs to fill and clean themselves."

In the brightened room, Will's pallor was shocking. He was even thinner than the last time she'd seen him. She knelt beside the little pallet, picking up his limp hand, assessing his color, his gums and eyes, and the touch of his skin. "His humors are dismal. He did not seem so poorly afore. Only thin."

Tapping on his chest, her ear close, the weak sound was far different than when she had ridden with him.

"Will? 'Tis Aednat."

There was no change in his breathing.

"I am not sure what to do for him. He is so weak." Tears rushed down her cheeks at her own inability to help him. She had hoped, at least, to speak with him. She brought his hand to her lips and kissed it. "Will? I've brought my husband, Diarmuid, to meet ye."

Diarmuid squatted down beside her, his eyes darting between them, hesitating but a moment. "Glad I am to meet ye, Will. Aednat has told me of ye."

She turned a thankful smile on him. It was difficult to swallow.

"And ye have my thanks for protecting her from Black Oengus."

Will's eyelids twitched right before they opened. He looked at her. "Aednat."

His words were barely discernible, they were spoken so softly.

"Sweet Will. I am here."

Will's eyes shifted to Diarmuid. "And the husband ye'd always hoped for."

"Will," Diarmuid said.

"Ye are a blessed man. She loves ye."

Diarmuid turned his face, lined with confusion, to Aednat.

She shrugged. "I have always told Will everything."

"And ye told him ye loved me?"

Her face heated.

"She did not need to say those words." Will's voice was barely a whisper.

Diarmuid kissed her, the slightest touch on her cheek. "I know how she feels."

Will's lips turned into a smile and his eyes drifted closed. His breathing seemed quieter, or mayhap she was simply getting used to the sound, but the air still rattled in his chest.

"Aednat could not have had a better brother than ye, Will."

Will's shoulders lifted with a deep breath. Aednat stilled, waiting for him to open his eyes again.

The breath came out in a quiet hiss.

Aednat stared at his chest, willing it to move again. The silence in the room became unbearable. Diarmuid wrapped an arm about her shoulders. She dropped her head to his chest and gave in to her sadness, unable to hide the depth of her emotions with a show of strength.

<h1 style="text-align:center">Chapter Twenty-One</h1>

"William?"

A call outside startled Aednat and she lifted her head.

"William? Are ye in there?"

It was Merewyn's voice!

Diarmuid opened the door to her. Her gasp at the sight of William's body seemed to push her into action and she settled down beside him, holding a cup to his mouth.

"He is gone, Merewyn." Aednat knew the other woman's loss was as deep as her own, even more so. "I could do nothing for him."

Merewyn continued to drip the liquid into his mouth.

Aednat touched her arm. "'Tis a waste of time."

"*No!*"

The familiar hiss filled the room.

Aednat backed away from the scene, standing beside Diarmuid.

"I do not know what she is about."

"I am saving him!" Merewyn shot the angry words over her shoulder.

"Ye are too late to save him." Diarmuid's calm words held the edge of watchfulness.

Aednat knew he worried that the woman was mad, but then Will's lungs filled again, his chest rising. She did not believe her ears or her eyes.

"What have ye done?" The awe in Diarmuid's words was undeniable.

When he began to say more, Aednat turned and put a finger to his lips. "Do not say the words. She did not do that! He was not dead."

Diarmuid gripped her fingers, his eyes wide with disbelief. "He had taken his last breath."

Aednat glanced at the proud woman. She was indeed a healer. A great healer, but she must have feared what Black Oengus would do to her if he knew the truth. Mayhap she had been treating his condition in secret. That would explain his quick decline.

"Hear me, Diarmuid! Will was not this sickly when I saw him last." Memories cascaded through her. He'd helped her from the horse, shifted her away from Black Oengus's sight, and even when he had tugged against the material of her gown. "He was strong. Vital."

"I had him moved when I saw how sick he was. I swear it, Aednat! He was near death and they said he had been ill for many months."

"They lied!" Merewyn continued her ministrations.

"I have seen these signs before. His lungs are not strong, but he was made stronger. I knew what he needed. When we were separated, he no longer received the tincture."

William coughed and she wiped the phlegm from his mouth, studying it before returning to her sack. Pulling a satchel out, she measured some of the crushed herbs inside. An odd odor, not anything Aednat recognized, but she refilled the mug with water and handed it back.

Merewyn gave a curt nod. "My thanks."

Diarmuid's frown remained, but Aednat put a hand to Will's forehead. "He is warmer now."

"That is necessary to balance his fluids." Crushing more herbs, Merewyn added them to the cup. "We need him to drink this as well."

Aednat smelled it. "That will cause movement in his bowels."

"No, it will tighten his air and strengthen his breath."

Nodding, Aednat sat him up so she could bring the cup to his lips. When his eyes fluttered opened, tears slid down her already wet cheeks. She had thought him lost forever. He drank down the liquid while Merewyn tapped on his stomach and moved up to his chest. When his eyes closed again, Aednat settled him on the bed. Sitting back on her heels, Merewyn sighed at last, and a slow smile covered her face.

"He will be restored!"

Diarmuid backed to the door, barring anyone from leaving. "Ye must tell me how what ye know is not from the dark arts, Merewyn, or I cannot allow ye to return to the clan."

"Diarmuid!"

"To see a man"—Diarmuid glanced at her before continuing—"to see his breath restored in such a way goes beyond what we know. 'Tis frightful to witness."

Though shocked by the fear she witnessed on his face, Aednat understood and couldn't blame him. She turned to Merewyn. "Where *did* ye learn these things?"

Merewyn tucked the covers around William and kissed his forehead before settling on the ground before them. "I was born in the islands to the north of Alba, but I've traveled from there, learning many things, *seeing* many things that no longer frighten me. I do not know why the herbs mixed in this way make his breathing easier, but he needs them to live."

The endearing look she turned on William caused a catch in Aednat's throat. "Ye are in love with William?"

"Ours is not love as ye know it."

Aednat studied her face, the freckles covering the bridge of her nose and the dark green of her eyes. Finally, she said, "Ye are the Great Healer!"

Diarmuid bent down, his frown replaced by awe. "Is it true?"

Merewyn shrugged. "Legends are told, many are made-up stories that have little truth to them."

Aednat glanced at Will, his chest gently rising and falling. "He took ye to his bed to protect ye, but ye remained chaste."

Unprepared for deception, Merewyn's open expression confirmed the truth.

"Ye do not need to say so." Aednat held up her hand. "'Tis better if I do not hear the words from ye."

Diarmuid seemed satisfied. "No one else needs to know what happened here."

"My thanks," Merewyn said. "William and I were

planning to return to the islands when Black Oengus came after ye, still searching out the Great Healer."

All while she was right under his nose.

"And ye wish to return still? Ye could remain here, living free as a member of our clan," Diarmuid said.

"My thanks." Merewyn smiled. "We should leave when William is returned to good health."

"So be it. But Merewyn?" Diarmuid's eyes rounded in kindness toward the one he had feared. "Ye will be safe here for as long as ye choose to stay."

"What of yer mother?" Aednat had experienced firsthand the woman's intense dislike for healers. "If she finds out Merewyn is also a healer, her mouth will never be still."

Diarmuid said, "If I must, I will remove her to the Meic Murchadha clan. I wish to have peace, and my mother thrives on stirring up trouble."

"That may be the only way to find the peace ye seek." Merewyn's words of wisdom were met with a thoughtful nod by Diarmuid.

"That and an obedient wife," Aednat said.

Merewyn smiled. "Methinks what ye call disobedience is what Diarmuid would call passion and that 'tis something he would ever change about ye. Do I have it aright, Diarmuid?"

Diarmuid's deep sigh expanded his chest and a quiet smile curled his lips. "There is nothing I would change about my Aednat. 'Tis the rest of the world I have complaints against."

Beibhinn's dirty looks and snide comments were getting to be too much. Apparently, her son marrying a healer was more than she could stomach. Aednat did not know how to respond to her. Diarmuid had been away nigh on two weeks now. He'd met with Sean and Tadhg to finalize the *Declaration of the Rig Túath* and put their seals to the document. A meeting was planned for summer next to include the northern clans in the signing, uniting the overkings.

They had waited until William's full recovery so that he and Merewyn could travel as far as Lough Bofin with them. Then they'd head to Achill Island and Croaghaun. The eggs along the cliffs there were believed to contain a strong aphrodisiac, strong enough to overcome any malady, natural or otherwise, of a man. Though Aednat had never heard of such a remedy, she had learned not to question.

Although Astrid was directly under her mother's thumb, she managed to shift the running of the kitchen and keeping of the supplies to Aednat with no questions asked. The others were more than happy to follow her instructions. And in appreciation, she worked alongside them on occasion.

For Aednat, these new tasks were tiring, and with the pregnancy moving along, she slept like the dead every night. But each morning she awakened to memories of being in Diarmuid's arms while she slept.

She said as much to Astrid one afternoon while they were out doing laundry.

"No doubt that is from the time after ye were rescued." Astrid heaved the clothes back onto the large rock so the material could catch the sun's bright rays. The other women were spread out along the banks talking amongst themselves. "Marcán told me he'd feared ye would not be right in the head if ye were healed."

Aednat scrubbed the coarse material of the hose against a smaller rock. "I remember little from that time. Only waking in Diarmuid's arms."

The bubbling in her gut was increasing. A good sign that the pregnancy would hold. She had been waiting for just such a sign to finally tell him she carried his child.

"See?" Astrid smiled, her eyes bright with mischief. "D'ye know when ye will tell him ye are carrying his son?"

Astrid's words had her jaw dropped. "Son? How can ye know it is a boy I carry?"

Astrid shrugged, shoving the loose hair from her face, a smile on her lips. "'Tis just something I know."

"Do not let yer mother hear ye say that." Aednat realized she was not jesting. Beibhinn was relentless in her search for any wrongdoers. And she spoke her mind all the time, shaming anyone she decided to reprimand.

Poor Astrid had been the recipient of a tongue-lashing twice in just the week since Sabbath. This time finding fault with how Astrid and Marcán were spending their time. Aednat doubted Marcán was having his way with Astrid. He respected both her and her brother too much for that. Certainly it was just a kiss, as Astrid had claimed after they were caught. Passionate, certainly, but no more than that.

"My mother thinks much of her own opinions. She has even sent for the priest to stand beside her when next she makes her declarations against one of us."

Fear dropped like a stone into the pit of Aednat's

stomach. She prayed it would not be her the woman was after. Why did Beibhinn find it necessary to be so cruel to others? Even her son's wife? Aednat knew as wife of the *ri túath,* she had every right to call a cease to the woman's meddling. Diarmuid had said he would support her, but to act against his own mother seemed wrong. She preferred to have him handle her.

"I hope Diarmuid returns soon."

"And here I am." Diarmuid, still covered with dust from his travels, was unbelievably handsome in his mail. More so for the way he was looking at her.

When he came to offer Aednat a kiss, Astrid excused herself, saying. "Do not be overlong. The preparations for the evening meal still await yer wife's oversight."

Once she'd disappeared through the trees, he turned to Aednat with a frown. "Is this true? Ye have taken over the kitchens whilst I was away?"

"What else was there for me to do? I am a very diligent worker. Idle time does not settle well with me."

He kissed her lightly. "I care to see this diligence in our bed."

"Diarmuid!" She slapped at his chest, the mail painful against her hand.

"Are ye hurt?" He bestowed a kiss on the end of each finger. "I have missed my lovely Aednat."

"I have missed ye as well, but for this unwieldy cloth of mail, I would press against ye and show ye how much."

He quirked a brow. "Then I would have yer lips alone convey to me yer depth of feeling."

Aednat paused before meeting his lips in a passionate kiss, showing her pleasure at his return, while the rest of her remained apart. His tongue was soon sparring with hers, demanding more.

Winded and completely aroused, Diarmuid broke the kiss. "The meal will be late this night." He lifted her into his arms. "I have a more pressing need that food will not satisfy."

Aednat laughed. "Are ye destined to always carry me from place to place?"

"And with great pleasure."

As they traveled the wooded trail to the small stone house, the birds called in the distance, and Diarmuid found the peace in his heart could not be contained. When they arrived home, he closed the door with his foot and lowered her to the center of their bed. Adding peat to the amber glow in the hearth, he removed his sword and belt. Then he held up a small leather sack. "I have brought ye a present."

She stood on the bed, helping him to remove his heavy mail before taking the sack from him.

"For me?"

He nodded, her excitement bringing a pink hue to her cheeks. He would need to remember how much she enjoyed presents.

"We will exchange surprises," she said.

He glanced again at the slight bulge at her belly. His child within.

Aednat gave him a petulant expression. "Ye know!"

His chest swelling with joy, he leaned in to kiss her on her nose. "My greatest pleasure is to know *everything* about ye." He cupped a breast, heavier in his hand now. "And naturally I would notice any changes."

"So ye've known longer than me?"

"I have known since before I left."

The bag forgotten, she lay flat on her back to move his hand to the small rise. "Close yer eyes and ye can see his little body within me."

Diarmuid obeyed. "So Astrid has told ye 'tis a boy?"

He opened his eyes to Aednat's mouth gaping open. "Is there nothing I can do to surprise ye?"

Hard pressed not to slide his hands up to the swell of her heavy breasts as was his wont, he instead said, "Is not pleasing me more important than surprising me?"

"Ye are pleased?" Her sincere question brought home to him yet again that she sought his approval in all things, and he vowed to never leave her wondering again.

He smoothed his hand over the bulge, and his smile widened. "Very pleased, *mo mhíle stór.* Have ye given any thought to a name?

"I have."

He watched her, surprised to see her now averting her eyes. "And what would that be?"

She glanced at him, taking her bottom lip between her teeth, before again looking away.

Diarmuid put a hand to her chin, turning her face to him.

"Is the name so horrible ye are afraid to share it with me? 'Twould make it difficult for me if I do not know what to call the babe."

Aednat smiled. "Fergus?"

The timid way she spoke his brother's name told Diarmuid she had heard the story of his death. He searched her face for any sign of condemnation. There was none. He cupped her cheek.

"Who told ye about my brother?"

"Sean?" She said it like a question. Like she needed reassurance that her knowing about Fergus did not displease him.

He nodded. "I think of him often. I miss him." The words seemed inadequate, and the need to share his pain with her became overwhelming. "Marcán and I had been called away unexpectedly. I had promised to take Fergus to the caves where Brian Boru had stayed. After the long winter, the lad needed to be outside with the sun on his face, a cool breeze in his hair."

"I promised him we would go upon my return. Instead of waiting, he went off on his own." Tears filled his eyes. "My mother treated him like a trained dog, not an inquisitive lad who needed watching over. She never sent anyone after him, believing he was merely hiding somewhere within the village."

"We found his body the next day. He must have gotten lost. The wolves had made a meal of him."

"I am so sorry for the loss of yer brother, Diarmuid. What a terrible thing to have happen." She squeezed his hand. "Ye were a warrior and did what ye needed to. 'Twas not yer fault. An accident. A terrible accident."

He glanced at her, wiping at the tear sliding down his cheek. "My father had agreed to leave Fergus behind with my mother whilst he saw to my training. She was a terrible *báirseach* and made him miserable with her mouth. He believed he had bargained for a greater peace, but the loss devastated him, and soon he stopped coming home."

"We will name our son Fergus and we will see that he is well trained. Strong. Nothing bad will befall him," Aednat said.

"That would please me greatly."

Her face relaxed into a wide grin. "Then Fergus it shall be."

Diarmuid took a deep breath, feeling the weight of his guilt lessen. Aednat spoke the truth. There was little he could have done to protect his brother. It was an accident that might have been avoided if his mother had been more attentive, but there was no changing the past.

"And I am pleased ye are back." She kissed him, then propped herself up on an elbow, feeling the sack before opening it. Her eyes narrowed. "Have ye brought me mushrooms?"

Diarmuid laughed, surprised at her astuteness. "Ye do know how much I enjoy yer boldness in bed."

"But 'tis yer love alone that I require to lessen my shyness."

"Ah, healer." He took the sack, dropping it forgotten on the floor, and yanked off his *léine* to climb in naked alongside her. "Show me yer boldness."

Pressing her small hand to his chest, she urged him to lie flat on his back. Her coy smile and twinkling eyes promised she would do just that.

THE END

GLOSSARY

Kingship in Ireland:

ri means "king" (plural is *rig)* and the second word below refers to the number of people and the amount of land that each *ri* is king of:

ri túaithe – The king of a *túath* (small territory)
ri túath – The overking of several *túatha* (several small territories)
ri rúirech – The king of a *rúirech* (lordship, a huge territory)
ri cóiced – The king of a *cóiced* (province)
árd rí – The high king

Definitions:

a ghráidh – sweetling
a thighearna – oh lord
báirseach – termagant
derb fine – council that advises the king
grádh – darling
lough – lake
mamaídh – mama
miodóg – dagger
mo mhíle stór – my love
tánaiste – selected as successor at the king's inauguration

Pronunciation of Names:

Diarmuid – Deer-mid
Aednat – Ain-it
Lorcánn – Lurk-an
Marcán – Mork-an

To hear many of the names pronounced by the late, great Frank McCourt, please visit this website: http://www.babynamesofireland.com

ABOUT THE AUTHOR

Aside from two years spent in the wilds of the Colorado mountains, Ashley York is a proud life-long New Englander and a hardcore romantic. She has an MA in History which brings with it, through many years of research, a love for primary documents and the smell of musty old libraries. With her author's imagination, she likes to write about people who could have lived alongside those well-known giants from the past.

Connect with her online at:

Website: www.ashleyyorkauthor.com
Email: ashleyyork1066@gmail.com
Twitter: @ashleyyork1066